CW01499163

THE STALKER

TERI TERRY

Boldwood

First published in Great Britain in 2025 by Boldwood Books Ltd.

Copyright © Teri Terry, 2025

Cover Design by Lisa Horton

Cover Images: Shutterstock and Magdalena Russocka / Trevillion Images

The moral right of Teri Terry to be identified as the author of this work has been asserted in accordance with the Copyright, Designs and Patents Act 1988.

Every effort has been made to obtain the necessary permissions with reference to copyright material, both illustrative and quoted. We apologise for any omissions in this respect and will be pleased to make the appropriate acknowledgements in any future edition.

A CIP catalogue record for this book is available from the British Library.

Paperback ISBN 978-1-80600-834-6

Large Print ISBN 978-1-80600-833-9

Hardback ISBN 978-1-80600-832-2

Trade Paperback ISBN 978-1-80656-016-5

Ebook ISBN 978-1-80600-835-3

Kindle ISBN 978-1-80600-836-0

Audio CD ISBN 978-1-80600-827-8

MP3 CD ISBN 978-1-80600-828-5

Digital audio download ISBN 978-1-80600-831-5

This book is printed on certified sustainable paper. Boldwood Books is dedicated to putting sustainability at the heart of our business. For more information please visit https://www.boldwoodbooks.com/about-us/sustainability/

Boldwood Books Ltd, 23 Bowerdean Street, London, SW6 3TN

www.boldwoodbooks.com

To Halton Tennis Club
for both inspiration & always making un-sporty me feel welcome

1

LOU

IF I WERE YOU, I'D GO HOME. NOW.

Each letter has been formed with so much pressure that the pen has almost ripped through the paper, as if they were in a rage when they wrote it. An anonymous note in red ink – the colour of warning lights. Stop signs. *Danger.* The words swim in my vision and take me *back, back,* to another time and place – to another note left on a car, and what that led to. Fear floods my body with adrenalin.

But that was a long time ago. This is a time and place so far removed, there can be no connection between them. I should ignore it. It was probably left by some random prankster, watching and laughing when I found it under my windscreen wiper. I look around at the familiar street of Beaconsfield Old Town – my car and others parked between the crumbling grave-yard of the church opposite and the café I just left, my Americano to-go warming my hand. Patrons there at tables, alone or with a friend. A few more queuing at the counter. Two elderly gentlemen stroll past with papers tucked under their arms. Over the road is a dog walker with three spaniels, tails wagging madly as they pull her past the church and towards the park. All is completely usual and normal, and no one is paying any attention to me whatsoever.

One note, eight words. All in capitals. Uneven and deliberate, like a child's, or someone trying to disguise their handwriting. I don't know what to do. If I don't leave for London now, I'll be late.

I can't ignore it. Dread churns in my stomach as I get into my car and pull out, then turn left instead of right at the nearby intersection. I drive the few miles to our street on autopilot. The closer I get, the more I'm afraid of what I might find.

I reach our house. Everything looks the same as always – expansive front garden covered in spring blossom just now, gleaming windows. The garage doors are closed and the long drive empty, as I left it. No cars are parked on the road out front, either. I pull onto the drive, get out of the car and go towards the front door, each step more hesitant than the last.

Something's wrong. I can feel it, in my dry mouth, the pressure in my chest that makes it hard to breathe. The band of pain across my temples.

When the twins were little, I had a kind of sixth sense – a mother superpower – so closely tuned in to their well-being that any tiny little sound out of the ordinary would have me flying across the room, fishing a coin out of one mouth or catching another as they fell. They are eighteen and at university now, well past putting things in their mouths that might choke them, but it's that kind of feeling I'm having as I turn the key to open our front door.

I hesitate. Step in and close the door quietly behind me. Stand there, barely breathing, listening with every ounce of attention—

There. A slight sound – footsteps, maybe – upstairs?

Philip is at work. Flick never visits without calling and usually asking me to collect her and our grandson. The twins are hours away in Brighton. The cleaner only comes once a week, and she was here yesterday. Now I've run out of people with keys. The sensible thing to do would be to leave, go next door, call the police – or at least have a neighbour on standby to do so. But it's like I'm trapped in a horror movie, the scene where everyone is shouting at the screen – *no, go back* – while the next victim walks to their fate.

I slip off my shoes. Extract my phone from my bag to have it to hand for emergency calls. I creep in and look all around the entranceway, the hall. On to the open-plan downstairs – lounge, snug, kitchen, dining room. No one is here and nothing is out of place. There are no broken windows or any way someone could have got in. I must have imagined—

Then I see the back door, the dead bolt. It's not locked. I always check it is locked before I go out. Did I definitely do so today? It's an automatic habit, something I do without notice. I can't be completely certain.

I stand at the bottom of the stairs, stock-still, listening. There are faint voices, somewhere above, then low laughter – it sounds like a woman. Could I have left the bedroom radio on? It's not impossible, but although I can't make out the words, the cadence doesn't sound like a DJ.

Then there is a soft thud. I'm not sure what that was, but what it most definitely was *not* is the radio.

Someone is upstairs, in our home. Whoever gouged their words onto the note that brought me here must have known, which means it wasn't a random prankster at all. Instead, it was someone who wanted me to be here and find whatever is happening upstairs, and I can't think of any reason that isn't a threat to me, my safety. I'm caught between wanting to flee and needing to carry this through. To know who has violated our home.

I can't stop myself. I slip up the stairs silently, questioning my sanity with each step. I put my phone in my pocket and take a heavy vase from a window ledge on the way up, hold it in my hands like a weapon.

I reach the top of the stairs.

The dread in my gut is almost choking me. I want to turn around, run. Never come back.

I take one step forward and another, down the hall. Past the kids' rooms, bathroom, guest rooms. The sound is coming from the end – our bedroom.

The door is ajar. I edge it open a little more so I can see into the room.

My eyes can't take it in, or my brain refuses to unscramble the messages they're sending. This isn't real; it can't be. I'm frozen and can't look away.

It's not an intruder or burglar or anything else my imagination could come up with. It's Philip, my husband. And a woman, underneath him, on our bed. She has blonde hair, so fair it is almost white. I can't see her face. I can hear her moaning. She moves a little, turns her head to the side so she is looking towards me, as if she sensed I was there. Blue eyes widen but then she stares back, an odd lack of reaction, almost like she's studying me as I do her. Then she cries out, taps on Philip's shoulder and he turns. Sees me, too. The horror in his eyes – at what he has done, or that I've caught him?

The vase slips from my hands, smashes on the floor. I back away. To the stairs. Stumble down them, almost fall. Reach the door. Nauseous, I'm close to being sick on the step, but I breathe through it and get in my car. I'm reversing when Philip appears in the doorway, trousers on but chest bare. He steps out as if he's going to try to stop me and there is a moment, my eyes on his, when I think, I could – couldn't I? – just throw the car back in drive. Put all my weight on the pedal and slam him into the side of the house.

He steps back as if he sees murder in my eyes. I reverse down the driveway, squeal up the road. I see what I didn't notice earlier – his car. It's around the corner. They probably went the back way down the lane and through our garden to avoid being seen by any of our neighbours. I swerve into it, take out the mirror, scratch all along the side. His Porsche is no match for my 4WD Jeep.

I'm shocked at what I did – the thrill of violence throbbing through me.

He *loves* that car. Doesn't he? I reverse and sideswipe it again.

2

FREJA

I stare at the ceiling.

I *can't* let this be the end. Even thinking that it might be fills me with fear, panic. I need Philip. How do I keep him? It's too soon to push him to decide; I'm not sure enough of what he might do. This could ruin everything. I sit up, glance at our clothes, strewn on the floor. I could get dressed and disappear out the back door—

No. Not that. Never that. I will find a way – *we* will find a way. But it isn't just the two of us any more. It never was, not really. But before today, Philip could pretend. How can he do that now?

Footsteps come back up the stairs, down the hall. Philip stands in the doorway. No sign of his wife. I sit up, holding the sheet to cover my chest.

'Whoops,' I say.

'Rather.'

'I thought she was out for the day?'

'So did I.'

'Is she gone?'

He nods, but what does that mean? Is she gone for good, or just for now?

He walks across, sits next to me on the bed. Takes my hand. 'Are you OK?' he says.

'I don't know.' I look down. We've never been about this – saying how we feel. It's been easy and light, for him, at least. Change brings risk, but without it, we can never move on from what we have now. I meet his eyes. There are tears in mine. I blink and one slides down my cheek. 'Are we OK? Because if we are, I will be, too.'

He doesn't answer. Gently kisses away my tears and pushes me back down on the bed.

Not over, then. At least, not yet.

An hour or so later we get dressed. I follow Philip down the stairs, past framed photos of his children. It took me ages to persuade Philip to bring me here, and I want to catch this glimpse of his family now, in case he won't bring me back again. I slow and study their smiling faces. At home and on ski holidays; on tropical beaches and yachts. A life so different to mine that it looks staged, unreal. There is a framed wedding photo, too, of a much younger Philip and Lou. The happy couple, but not so happy now.

Philip waits at the bottom of the stairs. I join him and we go to the back door.

He holds it open, and I hesitate. 'Should we talk about what happened?'

'We most definitely shouldn't,' he says. 'Though we might need to cool it for a while.'

'I understand,' I say, but I don't. Or, rather, I *won't* – do as he says.

The swearing starts when we get to his car. The side facing the road has been sideswiped, maybe more than once. I check it out, impressed at the level of damage. There are fragments of red paint embedded in the black.

'Does your wife drive a red car by any chance?'

'How did you guess?' He looks far more upset now than he did when she walked in on us in bed.

'It's a hit-and-run. Call the police.'

'Don't be ridiculous.' He's shocked, angry, but if that is the worst she does, he should count himself lucky.

'Hell hath no fury.' With my eyes I'm telling him that doesn't just apply to his wife. I call an Uber, and he calls RAC.

3

LOU

I drive for hours, no destination in mind. Options occasionally suggest themselves, like to go to Mum's, but I know her mindset. She couldn't believe it when Philip married me. That someone like him – with connections, a moneyed family, good-looking and charming to boot – would take up with ordinary working-class me, who failed at the only thing I was ever any good at when I dropped out of tennis. Despite the facts, assuming she believed them, it'd be my fault. Everything always was. She'd have me doubting anything I feel or should feel. Or maybe I should go to Flick's. Holding my little grandson and breathing in that precious baby smell – a mix of powdery notes and chamomile from the same baby soap I used, so many years ago – might be just the antidote to the mixed-up thoughts and emotions surging through me now. But I can't inflict the shock of what her father has done on Flick, not yet. Not when I haven't figured it all out. And I wouldn't be able to hide how upset I am from her, either.

Figured it all out? What does that even *mean*? What is there to figure out?

It takes a few flashes in my mirror for me to register that a police car wants me to pull over. Philip hasn't, has he? Called them about the damage to his car?

I pull over to the shoulder and open the window. An officer is approaching the car – a woman – while a man, on a radio, hangs back.

'Good evening,' she says. 'Could I see your licence, please?'

I turn to the passenger seat where my handbag would normally be, but it isn't there. I'd put it by the front door when I got home and didn't think to grab it when I left.

'I'm sorry. I haven't got it with me.'

'Step out of the vehicle, ma'am.'

I do so, forgetting I'm not wearing shoes until I step out into a cold puddle – something else I forgot in my flight. She's looking at my feet, an eyebrow raised.

'We've pulled you over because there appears to be some damage to your vehicle, and the left brake light isn't working.'

'I'm sorry. I'll get it seen to.'

'Have you been involved in an accident?'

'Not exactly. I accidentally bumped into my husband's car. It was parked at the time.'

'Must have been quite the bump. And do you often drive without shoes?' she asks. The other one joins her now and they're exchanging a glance.

'No. I just… I had to leave in a hurry, that's all.'

They're getting more and more suspicious and the only lawyer I have on speed dial is Philip. They take my details. Check the car is insured in my name. Have me do a breathalyser test and are so surprised when I pass that they ask me to walk a straight line on the muddy shoulder in socks, just to make sure.

They give me a verbal warning about the brake light and say I may go. I'm relieved. I'm sure Philip knew it was me who damaged his car, but it looks like he hasn't reported it. Of course not. No matter how much he loves his car, he wouldn't want this story getting out.

I head for the M25 and then stop for petrol at a service station. There are few shops and the only footwear I can find are novelty slippers. I go to the ladies, throw away my filthy socks. Wipe the mud off my feet and slip them into giant bear claws. They look so ridiculous that I'm laughing. It sounds off key, edged with hysteria. The only thing I do have with me is my phone – thankfully in my pocket with my car keys when I ran, as I used it to pay for petrol and these ridiculous slippers. I hesitate, then take a photo of my feet and send it to Iona. Suddenly I'm sure where I need to go.

She answers almost instantly.

> Are those your feet?

> Yes.

> Interesting fashion choice.

> Long story. Can I come over?

There's a pause. I can't just expect her to be free. She might be on a date or away for work – she is a high-end London real estate agent and flies all over the place to meet with buyers. We were very close once – she is Flick's godmother – but we've barely been in touch in recent years.

Then she answers:

> I can be home in half an hour.

> Thank you xx

There is an M&S across from where I bought the slippers. I

buy crisps, wine, chocolate, then head back to my car. The slippers are an odd contrast to my black jumpsuit from Net-a-Porter, and the sidelong glances on the way tell me I've become one of the strange people at a service station that people avoid, lost in my own misery. But at least I know where I'm going now.

4

LOU

I'm about to ring the doorbell of Iona's Islington flat when the door opens; she must have been watching for me. She looks down at my feet.

'I didn't really believe they were yours,' she says. 'I thought it was an early April Fool's.'

'It's a new trend. Haven't you heard?' I look at her properly – the careful make-up, a simple blue dress that hangs so perfectly it could have been made for her. She looks amazing, as always. 'You were out, weren't you?'

'It doesn't matter. My date was as boring as death. I can only thank you for giving me an excuse to escape. Come in.' She gives me a hug and I follow her into her flat. It's the ground floor of a divided terrace, that she bought when we were still teenagers. I loved it so much – a place I could come and stay to get away from my parents for a few days. It was all IKEA then; she's renovated and upgraded with stylish pieces over the years, but coming through her door still gives me that same feeling, even now – a rush of freedom and sanctuary.

I hand her the jute bag I bought at M&S along with its

contents. She looks in and whistles. 'It's a three-treats emergency? Have you finally left that idiot?'

Usually this is when I defend Philip and we end up agreeing to disagree, but mostly disagreeing, in a way that has made it difficult to maintain our friendship. But today, without the usual script, I don't know what to say. I'm just looking back at Iona, not trying to hide what I feel, though I don't even know what that is. A mixture of anger, pain, confusion. A feeling like my world has gone the wrong way up and without gravity to orientate myself I'm not sure how to hang on – or if I even want to.

She gasps. 'Oh my God. Have you? Actually left Philip?'

'I... I don't know.'

She puts the wine I brought in the fridge and takes out another cold one, gets two wine glasses from a cupboard. Her cat, Ginger Biscuit, appears, yawning and stretching. But then he sees my feet and all signs of sleepiness are gone. He circles around, eyes intent, as if trying to decide if my feet are being eaten by some new and unknown creature.

Iona pours two glasses of wine. 'You better pay the slipper tax, or your feet might need recovery time.' I slip them off just before he pounces, then carries them triumphantly, one at a time, to a crawl space under the stairs.

'Tell me,' she says. 'What's happened with Philip?'

'I stopped for coffee before heading to London, for a cookery course I'd booked. When I got back to my car, I found this, under the wiper.' I fish the note out of my pocket, hand it to her.

She reads out the eight words imprinted on my consciousness. *IF I WERE YOU, I'D GO HOME. NOW.*

Her eyes are wide, her hand on mine in an instant. She doesn't just know my history – she was there and suffered the consequences more than I did – but her concern is still for me. 'Are you OK?'

'More or less. But it felt very déjà vu. And I just couldn't ignore it.'

'Any idea who wrote it?' I shake my head. Along with everything else there is to think about, the note has been a red flag going around and around in my head. I can't begin to think who it could have been from. 'Do you recognise the handwriting?'

'No. But would I recognise anyone's handwriting when it is printed in capitals like this?'

'What did you do?' she says, as she hands me a glass.

'Just what it said. I turned around and went home. The whole time, I kept thinking, why am I doing this? What if it is one of Philip's clients, opposing counsel or claimants after revenge for something I know nothing about? Or even...' I swallow, mouth dry to even think of it '...the one from so long ago,' I finally manage to say. He did so much damage to both my life and Iona's, but I never even knew what he looked like, let alone his name. To call him *my stalker* gives him a power, a connection to me, that I don't want him to have. I take a long sip of wine. It's ice cold, soothing, and I have another.

'You know that is very unlikely,' she says, gently. 'It was more than twenty years ago.'

'Twenty-five. I know.' And I do, she's right. Why would he reappear after so long? But the note on my car triggered a fear reaction that I couldn't suppress.

'When I got home, there were no cars in the drive or on the street out front. I went in and the lock on the back door wasn't on dead bolt. And I just *knew* something was wrong.' I swallow, not wanting to say it out loud, as if hearing the words will make it more real. 'Anyhow. It's the oldest story in the world. I went upstairs. And Philip was there – he was with a woman. In bed. Our bed.'

She reaches out, holds my hand tight. 'Did you scream and throw furniture at them? Tell me that you did.'

'No. I did something better. I left.'

'Like, really left? As in, not going back, left? Did you tell him so?'

I shake my head. 'I didn't say anything to him. But that's not all. He followed me down, half dressed, to the door. I was starting to reverse when he came out. And I thought, I could change gears, hit the accelerator and slam him between the car and the house.'

'But you didn't.'

'No. Instead, I did it to his car.' I have another long sip of wine and tell her about finding it around the corner, and the satisfying crunch of my four-wheel drive into expensive bodywork. That I backed up and did it again.

'I can't believe you did that, but I love it!' she says, eyes wide, and then we're both laughing. Then I'm crying, tears of pain and rage, and I'm not sure which is the stronger emotion. She hugs me, finds tissues. I finally get myself back together and tell her about the police pulling me over and having to do a sobriety test in my socks. Now we're laughing again.

Too much wine and not enough food give the expected result. A few hours later, she's helping me into her guest room.

'My head is going to hurt in the morning,' I say.

'All in a good cause.'

'Thank you, Iona.'

'You're welcome. And you can stay as long as you want, though I won't be around much the next few weeks. Sorry. It's the final push to win agent of the year before financial year end.'

'Impressive. Is it for the glory or is there a prize?'

'Both. That's where I got my BMW last year. This year, it's a

Mercedes. But getting back to you staying as long as you want: this isn't a free ride.'

'No?'

'No. If you even *think* of going back to Philip, you're out on your ear.'

'I don't think he wants me back.'

'If that's so, he's an idiot, though it'll make holding your resolve easier. But why do you say that?'

I waggle my phone at her. 'No calls, not even a message. Nothing.' I hadn't been able to stop myself from checking it whenever she wasn't looking.

'Maybe he's too embarrassed and ashamed. Or afraid you'll scream at him.'

'Maybe I should call him—'

'No. Promise you won't, or I'll take your phone away.'

'You wouldn't.'

'OK, I wouldn't. But seriously – if you want to talk to him, do it when you're sure of what you want to say. And preferably sober.'

Her eyes are steady on mine, and I know she's right.

I sigh. 'I promise I won't call him.'

She says goodnight. Closes the door softly.

My head is spinning with the wine, but without Iona to focus on, there is nothing to hold back what I saw – the image of Philip, that woman, in bed. *Our* bed. And what I didn't tell Iona.

I recognised her – the woman with Philip. I couldn't see much of her, just her blonde hair, the side of her face briefly when she'd turned to look at me. She was beautiful, but in a different kind of way: skin so pale, her shiny hair almost white-blonde – other-worldly, like a grown-up Luna Lovegood from the Harry Potter films that the twins loved so much. But I didn't see enough of her to know this. It's like I'm filling in detail from a memory without being able to connect it with who she is or when it was. She was younger than me, definitely; maybe mid-twenties to my forty-four. What a midlife crisis cliché. A younger version, but not of me: with my dark hair and eyes, it's almost like he set out to find my opposite.

It was odd how she'd just stared back at me for a moment before she reacted, alerted Philip that I was there. There was a calculating look, as if she was assessing me in an instant and finding me wanting. Or maybe she recognised me, too. Is she someone Philip works with? Or she might be from our social circle – someone's daughter, perhaps. It'll probably come to me eventually. I'm not sure why it's bothering me so much; it's not like knowing who she is will change anything.

There is a scratch at my door. I get up, open it. Ginger Biscuit follows me across to the bed, jumps up and settles himself next to me, purring when I give him head scritches. His solid warmth is soothing, and I'm remembering our family cat, how much I'd loved him. How devastated I'd been when he died. I'd wanted another when we married but Philip was allergic.

There's a plus. If I get my own place, I can get a cat. Or two, maybe three. Everything I owned would be permanently covered in fur and I wouldn't care. It'd be the perfect Philip-repellent.

My own place? I can't take this in. Is that what will happen? I'm not sure I could live alone. Just thinking of it makes me feel panicky, and then I realise something else, too. Maybe I got things wrong today. I shouldn't have fled – I should have pushed the pair of them out the front door and then changed the locks. It's *my* home. I've spent so many years making it perfect, and I haven't done anything wrong – why should I be the one to leave?

Then I think about it, and realise – there's no way I could live there again, not with the memory of what I saw in our bedroom this morning. But what if he moves her in to take my place? Everything we own is half mine. I'm not walking away from that.

Ginger Biscuit is soon asleep. I try and join him but can't stop myself checking my phone as the minutes of the long, dark night slowly tick by.

Somewhere near dawn I finally drift away. Troubled dreams play like a video clip on a loop. Finding the note. Walking up the stairs, down the hall. Into our bedroom. Philip and a woman in our bed, but in my nightmare it is a different one each time. They know I'm there but ignore me. I'm invisible.

5

FREJA

Usually after being with Philip, I'd be, if not happy exactly, content. Content that something was going the way I wanted it to at last. But I'm not sure where I stand with him now. After seeing his wife off this morning, he still wanted me, but what does that even mean?

I reapply lipstick in the staffroom mirror – a precise application of a deep rosy pink, one of my favourite shades, remembering as I do so that it is called *Next Romance*. Huh. My supervisor, Yasmin, is here.

'Smiles sell, Freja!' she says.

My lips turn up, but the smile doesn't reach my eyes. A clear message to back off, but she doesn't.

'Something is wrong. What is it? Tell me.'

I sigh. Maybe talking it all through – even with someone as annoying as Yasmin – will help. 'OK, but not here. We could go for a drink after work?'

She agrees and we head back to the shop floor together – selling high-end make-up, perfume, to women who hope that the right potion or lotion will make them look more like me and less like themselves; men, who hope I can do the same for their wives or girlfriends, or maybe be their bit on the side, instead. We are in the midst of designer's row, The Village at Westfield. Tucked between Notting Hill and Kensington as we are, there's no sign of financial hard times tonight – so many are spending money without thought, in a way I've never been able to. In a way I've been dreaming of lately, but is that all over?

Time ticks slowly by. When it's finally closing time, I'm having second thoughts about having a drink when maybe I'd rather just go to bed early with a book. But Yasmin won't hear of it and until I'm able to quit this job – let it be soon – best to keep her onside.

We head to a favourite pub nearby, find a table in a quiet corner. It'll be noisy later, a mix of city types heading home and those stopping on their way for a night out. And a few mall refugees like us.

'I'll get these,' she says, and goes to the bar. Soon there is a glass of white in front of me, chilled so well there is condensation on the glass.

'Thank you.'

'You haven't been yourself at all today,' she says.

'I know. I'm sorry.' I sigh and have a sip. Nice. 'I met Philip this morning – he said his wife was at some course all day, so we went to his. Anyhow, just when things were getting... interesting, she walked in on us.'

'What? Oh my God. So, she wasn't out for the day after all.'

'No. Either he got the story wrong, or she changed her mind, I don't know.'

'That's quite a coincidence. Maybe she was onto him somehow?'

I shrug. 'Maybe,' I say, but she could be right. I didn't think of it that way before, but for his wife to happen to change her plans on the one day we were at their house seems like a huge coincidence. Now I'm wondering if Philip will think the same, and what that might mean.

'What happened next? What did she do?'

'She didn't say anything, just ran out of the house. He pulled on his trousers and went after her.'

'And then?'

'She drove off, tyres squealing. Philip was parked around the corner; she must have spotted his car – a Porsche – when she left. And she *destroyed* it. Must have sideswiped it at least a few times to cause so much damage.'

'Woah. You better watch out for her.' No. She better watch out for *me*. 'And what next? Is she going to leave him? Is he going to end things with you to keep her?'

'That's just it. I don't know.' I don't tell her that we took up where we left off soon after his wife left – she'd be shocked. 'He did say we might have to cool it for a while.'

'Sounds to me like he's hoping for the status quo – keep the wife, you on the side.'

I wince, but she's probably right.

'I've told you before – you need to find one who isn't married.'

'I know. But I want this one.' She doesn't understand. He's got to be twenty years older than me; even if he leaves his wife and family, he'd likely have to support them. But I'm playing a long game.

'And since then? Have you heard from Philip?'

'Not yet.'

'He's probably busy trying to save his marriage.'

I narrow my eyes, annoyed. 'If you say so.'

'Are you going to contact him?'

I shake my head. 'Knowing Philip, the best thing to do now is ignore him. Let him come back to me when he's ready.'

'He might not.'

'I know.'

'Are you OK?'

'I'm always OK. Let's have another glass of wine.'

The place is livening up. Soon I'm flirting with one man, then another, but all along I'm thinking of Philip, where he is, what he is doing – who with.

If Philip wants to cool things, let him do that – for a while. If he takes too long about it, though, he *will* regret it.

6

LOU

In the morning, I find a note from Iona with a key on it next to the kettle:

Spare key if you need one. No matter what he tells you, GB has already had breakfast. xx

Being the mind-reader that Iona is, she's also left a box of paracetamol next to the note. I take two, then fill the kettle, make tea. There is a thump at the kitchen door and Ginger Biscuit appears through the cat flap. He jumps up on the counter, meowing piteously, and I can't resist. I find some cooked chicken in the fridge, give him a few pieces.

I settle myself in an armchair with my tea and he curls up on my lap. I stroke him, soothed by his presence, but my head is still reeling from yesterday. I know what happened, but at the same time, I can't take it in. Being here, looking around at Iona's things, it's a lovely flat, but despite the happy memories it invokes, that's still what it is: a flat. It may be spacious for London but the total floor space including bedrooms is probably less than our open-plan kitchen-diner. The one I planned and designed, all the details just as I wanted them. Is this what being on my own will be like – a flat, where, assuming GB would let me, I could barely swing the proverbial cat?

I shouldn't have left. I should have pushed the two of them out the door, thrown the bed out on the lawn and set it on fire. Now, *that* would have got the neighbours' attention.

Then I cringe inside. It isn't just Philip who'd rather this story didn't get out. If it does, everyone will know that my husband cheated on me. I'd be pitied. Laughed at probably, too.

Ginger Biscuit jumps down and goes to the back of the sofa to look out the front window. Then my phone starts to ring.

After checking it again and again last night, now that it's actually ringing, I'm not sure I want to know who it is. If it is Philip, I won't know what to say. If it isn't, why hasn't he called? Do I mean that little to him? But I can't stop myself from looking at the screen.

It's him. I reach to answer then pull my hand back, unsure. Just when I decide I will answer, it cuts off.

A message follows.

I'm out front. I'll take you home.

I get up, peer through the curtains, and there he is: standing on the pavement, leaning against a car I don't recognise. A rental, maybe. I must have done enough damage to take his off the road. I'm glad.

He wasn't who I thought he was. Were the signs there? He's always drawn eyes, still does – he's the whole tall, dark and handsome cliché. The slight silvering at the temples now doesn't diminish his appeal. He dresses well, his suits tailor-made, and the way he holds himself – confident, assured. Even now. He's looking straight at the window where I stand, and I let the curtains fall back and step away from the window.

How did he know I'd be here? I had no idea where I was going when I left. Am I that easy for him to figure out?

The last four words of his message: *I'll take you home.*

Does he actually assume that is all there is to this, as if I've had my night out after he had his, whatever she was, and he thinks I'll just go home with him now? I'm angry, but when I think about it, not completely surprised. I've been with Philip long enough to know he assumes everyone in the world will bend to his will, and they usually do.

Not this time.

I want to ignore him; pretend he doesn't exist. Leave him out there long enough that he finally gets the message and goes. But somehow, I can't.

I send a message of my own:

> No. I'm not going home with you. Go away.

After I send it, I stare at the words. Is it *home* any more? Can it ever be again? I sit on Iona's sofa under the window. Rigid. Hot tears on my cheeks but they are angry tears. I can't stop myself from looking a few minutes later – carefully, without disturbing the curtains this time. He's still there.

My phone vibrates.

> I'm sorry, Lulu. I love you. You know that.

A nickname he's not used in years. And now I'm trying to remember the last time he's said those three words: *I love you.* I can't remember. After being together so long is it not said because it is assumed, something – like he said – that you just know? Or maybe it is because it isn't true any more. I don't know. Does he still love me? I'm not sure how you can love someone and do what he did. And I don't even know how I feel about him now. If I'd never received that note – not gone home, seen what I did – would we just have continued on and on? Not saying I love you, assuming there was still something that bound us together.

My phone vibrates again. This time it's Iona.

> I see on my video doorbell that you have a visitor.

I send:

> What should I do?

And then hate myself for asking, for being so weak.
There is a pause. Then:

> You know what I think. But it's your life, hon.
> Either way, you've got me in your corner.

In your corner: a general expression but one with more meaning for us. We were doubles champions so many years ago at Wimbledon. I'd always struggled with confidence but with Iona in my corner we found a way to win. Is it really over twenty-five years ago now? Iona had injuries from a car accident a year later that took her out of tennis forever. And me – I guess I had another sort of injury.

I look again. He's still there. He sends another message.

> We need to talk.

He's right. We do. But not yet.

> We will. But not here and not now.

When then?

> I need some time. Please – just go.

I watch as he gets back into the car. He slams the door – in anger? Or perhaps it was more disbelief that I didn't scurry out and instantly forgive him. Maybe he even expected me to apologise for what I did to his Porsche, as if that made us even.

Another message alert. This time, it's Iona.

Well done, hon.

I'm crying again. And it isn't because of how I caught him yesterday. It isn't even because this might be the beginning of the end for Philip and me. It's something else.

It's feels like it is the first time Philip has asked something of me – something serious, not all the trivial ins and outs of living together – and I've said no. After over twenty-three years of marriage. It's like it draws a line between before and after. Changes who I am and our relationship – or its ending – in an irretrievable way, one that can never be taken back.

The walls around me are too close. I need air; I need to get out. I long to go for a run, to push myself physically until my mind is quiet. To do that, I need to go out and get some running kit, and I need other clothes, too. But not in whatever is left of my bear claw slippers, assuming Ginger Biscuit lets me extract them from his lair.

I message Iona. She directs me to her wardrobe, and I find some ankle boots that almost fit when I borrow extra socks. I splash cold water on my face. My eyes are still red but that will have to do. I put on her boots and head out.

It's sunny, mid-March. A bright day this time of year brings everyone outside, blinking, with more of a smile on their lips, a spring in their step. Even in London. But it's lost on me. I'm both more inward-focused than I'd usually be and more aware of others around me. So many people, rushing in all directions with somewhere to go: to work, to visit a friend, a lover. And then there is me.

I head for Angel shopping centre and find trainers, shoes, a few things to wear, not really caring what I buy or how much it costs, not sure how many changes of clothes I need. How long will it be before I go home?

If I go home, that is.

Even if I'm not going back, I need to get some of my things. But thinking of going there, even just to pack a few bags – it makes me feel panicky, sick.

My phone is ringing. I glance at the screen, ready to decline the call if it is Philip, but it's Flick. I almost don't want to answer, not sure what to say, but then worry something is wrong with Lachlan and answer before it goes to message.

'Hiya.'

'Hi, Mum. Uh… where are you?'

I'm panicking – does she somehow know? What should I say? But then a memory slips into place. Babysitting – I'm supposed to be babysitting for her today and overnight.

'Oh no. I'm so sorry, Flick. I forgot.'

'Well, OK. Come over now and I'll get a later train.'

'I can't. I'm not at home. I'm in London – at Iona's.'

Silence. I don't want to tell her about her dad, at least not yet, but it'd have to be a good reason to explain how I forgot and why I'm not there.

I turn things around. 'I'm really sorry. She's having a difficult time – relationship stuff. I had to come. I'll make it up to you – another time?'

She says it's OK, but she's subdued, and I know she's really upset. It was a night out with her school friends, friends she rarely sees since she had Lachlan six months ago. I know exactly what it is like to be twenty-two and home alone with a baby, though to be fair, despite all the hours Philip worked he was still there part of the time. I wasn't completely on my own, not like Flick.

I'm appalled that I didn't remember. I'm even more appalled that I lied to her. But what was I going to say? And I'm realising now if Philip and I separate, there are decisions to be made – what we tell Flick, the twins. Jessie and James are only eighteen. My babies. I don't want to hurt them.

* * *

Philip's calls and messages start when I get back to Iona's, almost the moment when I step through the door. It's hard to shake off the uneasy feeling that he has somehow been following me and knows where I am. I'm still stricken by guilt for having let Flick down, and now more guilt, for how I've treated Philip, both this morning and now, ignoring his calls. And why should I be the one who feels guilty, after what he's done? It's ridiculous.

Another message from Philip appears:

I'm worried about you.

I put my phone on silent and change into my new running kit. Within minutes I'm out the door.

I head for Finsbury Park, then the loop from Alexandra

Palace to Highgate Wood. A long run and I go as fast as I can while dodging pedestrians and other runners, feeling a sense of satisfaction to leave them in my wake.

I've always thrown trainers on and headed out whenever I've been upset or worried. It helps me put things into perspective, to cope.

Today, some of the tension goes with the relentless pace I set. But no matter how fast or far I run, my problems won't go away.

7

LOU

A much-needed shower later, I still can't sit still. I need to fill the time and busy my hands. I find the hoover, then clean the kitchen. Ginger Biscuit watches from various perches, a bemused look on his face.

I've moved on to dusting when Iona finally gets home, a bottle of champagne in hand. She looks around. 'You can definitely stay forever if you keep doing the housework, but it wasn't necessary. Cleaner comes in a few days.'

'I needed something to do. Why the bubbles?'

'Two reasons. A huge deal closed today and I'm only one sale away from world domination, and a new car!' She's grinning, holding up her hand for a high five, just like she used to do when we won a match. The need to compete, to win, whether a grand slam, the best parking spot or top agent – Iona *always* plays to win.

'Congratulations! And the second reason?'

'I'm proud of you. For not opening the door. Come here.' She gives me a hug and as she does so, my phone vibrates again on the table. I try to pretend it doesn't exist.

'Aren't you going to check that?' Iona says.

I sigh, turn it over. It's yet another message from Philip:

> Just let me know you're OK.

I show it to her and the last few before it.

'You haven't answered him so far?'

'No. But I probably should.'

'Give him a call if you want to; tell him you're OK. Just don't let him muddle you up. Do you want privacy?'

'I don't know. I guess so.'

She goes through to the kitchen.

I stare at my phone. *Be the adult*, I tell myself. He's the father of my children. I can't just ignore him forever. *Have a calm conversation. You can do this.*

I hit return call, and he answers first ring. 'I'm glad you called. Are you all right?'

'I'm not sure *all right* fits, not after what I saw in our bedroom.'

'I get that you're angry. But we need to get past this. Come home and we'll talk it through.'

'No, Philip.'

A silent pause. 'No, now, or no, forever?'

I know what I'm supposed to say. We'll work on our marriage, come to the other side of this wiser and stronger. It's in the manual – isn't it? *Stand by your man.* To not at least *try* to fix things feels inherently wrong. I'm a wimp – I never had the killer instinct I needed all those years ago – maybe that was the real reason I dropped out of tennis. Philip and being pregnant with Flick were just my excuses. Somehow, I've become what I rebelled against as a teenager. Be nice. Smile. Take up less space. Be quiet. And most definitely don't stand up for yourself.

But I'm done with being that person, that wife.

'Lou?' he prompts.

I can't bring myself to say that no means forever. Because I'm such a wuss or I'm not sure? I don't know.

'Honestly, I can't answer that question just now.'

'Look. Why don't you come home, use a guest room for a while if you want to. We need to talk.'

A reasonable suggestion, maybe? Despite what Iona has said, I can't stay in her spare room forever. But I don't know what to do. I don't want him in proximity, pressuring me when nothing is clear in my mind.

'I'm not coming home, not even to a guest room. Not yet.' Two words that snuck in without thought and he'll seize on them – I know he will, but it's too late to call them back.

'All right, then. Let's go out for dinner. Tomorrow.'

I find myself agreeing, though stipulate not in the usual places where we are known, where I'll be Mrs Kingsley. But I'm not sure it's a good idea. When he's there, in front of me, will I be able to hold my resolve, to... to what? I don't even know.

I go into the kitchen. Iona has opened the bottle, is looking in a cupboard for glasses.

'How'd it go?' she asks.

'OK. He asked me to come home, to stay in a guest room if I want to. So we can work things out.'

'And?'

'I said no. But we're having dinner tomorrow, to talk things through.'

She nods, pours into two champagne flutes at just the right angle for the right amount of bubbles.

'Apart from your deal, I'm not sure if this is a day to celebrate in any way,' I say.

She looks at me closely. 'Has something else happened?'

'Stop reading my mind.' I sigh, tell her about Flick. 'I can't believe I forgot. And then lied to her?'

'Tell her the truth. She'll understand.'

Iona is probably right. But I can't face it, not yet. And until I work out how much of the truth Flick needs to know, how can I?

She holds out a glass, and I hesitate. 'Go on, take it. Look at it this way: you can laugh, or you can cry. Which would you rather?'

'Is there an in-between state? I'll go for that.'

'Fair enough. But you have to stop me from drinking all of this myself. I'd have a terrible headache in the morning, and I've got a busy day.'

'OK. One glass.'

'Change of subject. Tell me about that gorgeous grandson of yours. And is his dad still out of the picture?'

The photos come out – the baby no one knew we needed has brought such joy. Flick's had such a hard time but she's so good with Lachlan. Andy left before he was born; we bought out his share of their terrace house and paid off the mortgage for Flick. Tring is only half an hour away, but we'd have loved her to be closer – even move back home if she wanted to – but she needed some independence, wanted to stay where she was. Near her friends.

One glass becomes two and, like Iona gets that I need a timeout from all the heavy stuff, she soon has me laughing at stories from her day while we prepare and eat a simple dinner. Some of the things people ask for in a new property are unbelievable. And she tells me she'll be away for work for a few nights, leaving the day after tomorrow – meeting with wavering buyers she's hoping will close before the end of the financial year, and clinch her top spot. She asks if I'll be OK on my own.

What can I say? I'm an adult. 'I'll be fine.'

She knows. She has known me so well for so long, despite it being less often in recent years.

'Are you sure? Because I'll cancel the cat sitter if you're sure you're definitely going to be here. But if you're not sure, then I won't.'

'I promise. And I won't be alone – not really. Ginger Biscuit is good company.'

We're heading for bed a few hours later when Philip messages a pub address and booking time for dinner tomorrow. It's in Greenford, more or less halfway between Iona's and our home in Beaconsfield – a gesture, maybe. But I'm not sure this is a good idea.

I get settled in bed. I've left the door ajar, hoping Ginger Biscuit will join me again. I'm unsettled and not just by the situation with Philip. Thinking about the past, even obliquely, is something I've almost managed to eliminate. A busy family life filled my thoughts and time, but now there is too much space to keep the darkness away. It isn't just my faltering marriage that I'm worried about. That note left on my car means someone else is involved. A stalker derailed my life so many years ago. One of the things he did to terrorise me was leave notes, somehow knowing where I would be before I even knew where I was going. The note left a few days ago was similar in that respect – I hadn't planned to stop for coffee, it was a spur-of-the-moment decision. And my stalker was never identified. What if he's back?

When sleep finally finds me, it takes me from one uneasy dream to another. A white square of paper, red letters. I watch myself find it on my car, read it, an out-of-body experience, one where I can both see and feel my fear.

But then everything changes. Another country. A different car. I'm not alone this time; Iona is with me when I find a note. I'm shouting, screaming, at my past self to not read it, to crumple it up and throw it away. To change the past in my dream if not reality. But past-me can't hear a word I say.

I try to force myself awake. When that doesn't work, I try to change what happens next. It's my dream – I should be able to control it – but I can't.

I retreat, make myself small and hide. Try to pretend none of it is real. But the truth of what I did is rushing towards me.

8

LOU

After another long run the next morning, I take my car to a garage Iona has recommended to get the brake light fixed. The mechanic also inspects the scrapes and damage on the side of the Jeep.

'What happened?' he asks.

I can't stop myself. 'You should see the other car,' I say.

'What was it?'

'A Porsche.'

He whistles and runs through what needs doing beyond the brake light. The passenger door won't easily open, mirror on that side needs to be replaced. The car needs bodywork, paint. When I press him, he admits none of it is urgent. I promise to get the work looked into – not sure if I should book it here because I don't know where I'll be.

Where I will be – another thing I can't think about just now, along with all the rest.

After the brake light is fixed, I make a stop to buy Iona some flowers, then head back to hers. I arrange them in a vase, put a thank-you note next to them.

It's time to get ready for dinner with Philip, and I have no idea what to wear. There are limited options, just the few things I bought yesterday. I wonder if I have enough time to go out and get something else to wear, something lovely, to look good and feel stronger in myself. But I don't want Philip to think I'm doing that for him. No. Stay with nondescript jeans, a shirt. It'll do.

I brush my hair, stare at myself in the bathroom mirror, almost like I'm looking at myself in a way I haven't before – objectively. From the outside. Can I be single? Be on my own? My dark hair has a few silvering strands. I ignored them when they started sneaking in, not long ago now. I'm slender, fit. I've always run, gone to the gym at least a few times a week, even when I wasn't officially training any more. Pushing myself physically was too much of a habit to break even when I was pregnant. My face looks unlined until I smile, and then, there they are, slender spider webs crinkling around my eyes. Friends have been dyeing their hair, getting Botox. Fillers. I've never felt the need. Have I let myself go? Is that why Philip has looked elsewhere?

I give myself a mental slap. Even if there is any truth to that, it's a pathetic excuse, one I shouldn't accept. But it's hard not to see the signs of age – to compare my body to what it was an entire quarter of a century ago, when we met. We've spent more than half of our lives together. As I am now, could I be single – go to bars, clubs – like Iona? Though from what I've heard it is more about dating apps these days. What a concept.

I check my map app. It's time to go if I want to be on time, but I wait ten minutes, twenty, before I get in my car. Let him wait for a change.

Throughout the drive, my mind is wandering so much that I have to remind myself to check the satnav so I don't go wrong. Everything has changed in so few days. There is hurt and anger there, but at the moment I feel more... numb, as if I've gone beyond feeling. Or maybe I'm walling it off inside me, afraid that if I give in to it, I might fall apart.

I take the final turn for the pub, pull in and park.

OK. I can't put this off any longer. *Don't be hysterical, don't cry; he'd just manipulate that. Be calm.*

I go in. Philip is at our table, an open bottle of wine and half a glass of red in front of him. He watches me as I walk across the room. His eyes, when he focuses on me that way – I feel *seen* in a way I've rarely felt with anyone else. But is his gaze different tonight? More like I'm being examined, assessed. Caught in a spotlight. About to be cross-examined by a famed King's Counsel, one used to twisting words, making them take the shape of his argument and always sound more reasonable than anyone else's. Maybe I shouldn't have agreed to meet him on my own. It feels too soon.

But it's too late to run away now.

He stands when I near the table.

'You're looking lovely tonight.' He holds out his hands as if to draw me in for a kiss on the cheek, maybe more, but I can't risk his touch, unsure whether it would make me angry enough to slap him or sad enough to fall apart. I don't move closer, and his hands drop down.

We sit, opposite each other. He's looking well, as always. He can smile with just his eyes, frown with them as easily. I will myself to look away, but I can't.

He has something – a kind of presence that has always turned heads, the way he turned mine all those years ago. And it's hard to be sitting here, across from him, seeing the eyes I always sought, the hand that held mine. The years we shared, our children, all the things that should have held us together, forever. It's not right, how he seems just the same. He should look different – changed. Anguished, at the very least.

'I've missed you,' he says, low voice, a half-smile that could always win me around in the past. 'Come home with me tonight.' He fills and pushes a wine glass across the table towards me.

I shake my head, words too difficult.

He smiles, so sure of me, the one who could never say no to him about anything, and certainly not about going to bed with him. And then there'd be nothing to talk about, would there? He thinks that if we make love, it'll somehow make it all go away, like other arguments in the past. It's that thought – the surge of anger that comes with it – that makes me find my tongue.

'Are you seriously thinking we can just go back to how things were before?'

'I made a terrible mistake. Come back and I promise it'll never happen again.'

I've lived with a barrister long enough to know to examine words, see what is said and not said.

'So, you admit a mistake, but don't apologise. You promise it'll never happen again, but only if I come back. Is she waiting in the wings, just in case?'

'That's not what I said.' But he doesn't deny it.

'Was that the first time with her? Who is she?'

'Just a girl,' he says, and shrugs, dismissive. As if she isn't human, just a doll he played with for a while. And he didn't answer the first question, so no way to know if it was a one-off or something that has been going on for a while. Am I *just a wife* when he talks to her?

'Don't be jealous,' he says. 'You're the only one I love.'

'If you really felt that way – how could you? And in *our* bed. No. Forgive me if I struggle to believe you.'

Before he can reply, a waiter approaches our table. He's bringing starters – scallops for Philip, a salad for me.

I raise an eyebrow.

'You were late, so I ordered.'

How many times has Philip done things like this? Just assumed he knew what I would want, and ordered food – and our lives – accordingly?

And I'm angry with myself for not protesting, like so many times before.

'Lou, I know you better than anyone – better than you know yourself. Don't throw away what we have because of hurt feelings. It was nothing.'

Now I'm furious, so angry I'm shaking. '*Don't* trivialise my feelings.' Fury pushes me to say the words that will hurt him the most. 'But this is beyond that, Philip. You and me – it's over.'

'You'll change your mind. Once you think things through.' Said with complete conviction, confidence. He can't accept I mean what I say. He could always see through me – is that why? Maybe he can see the doubt behind my words. Even thinking that makes me more unsure.

For now, he'll be reasonable, trying to show what I'll be missing. If he accepts me at my words, though, things will change. I know what he is like to anyone he feels has crossed him.

'I won't change my mind,' I say, but do I mean that or am I just trying the words out loud, to see how they sound? I repeat them silently now, to try to convince myself. Can I actually do this – leave Philip – for good? Do I even *want* to? If I take him at his word – that he loves only me – maybe not. I don't know. But I'm not sure I believe him.

'You'll never last alone, Lou. I know you through and through. You'll never cope on your own. You haven't stayed anywhere by yourself since Paris.'

I'm shocked, hurt. That last trip to Paris was the worst time of my life, at least until a few days ago came close to rivalling it. And he wants to use it against me now?

I pick at my salad, think through what he has and hasn't said.

'There is something I want to ask you,' I say.

'Go ahead.'

'Why do you want me back?'

'I've already told you.'

'You've told me about feelings, whether or not they are genuine. But I know you too, Philip. Inside and out like you say you know me. You never decide based on feelings alone. There are always other considerations.'

He's deliberately taking a bite of a scallop. Chew, swallow. A sip of wine.

'We just work together,' he finally says. 'Don't we? We're a good partnership. Our lives make sense the way they are. It's been chaos these last few days without you.' Then, like he realises what he said doesn't cut it, he adds, 'I miss you, Lulu.'

A good partnership sounds like a workplace, not a marriage. For so many years, what Philip wants and needs have taken precedence. All the hours I worked to support us when he left the police and went to law school, juggling that and baby Flick. If we were a partnership, one of us was steering the ship; I was more the deckhand. Even after his practice was well established and I didn't need to work any more, there was always so much more that needed doing, organising, and not just for the children – dinner parties and socialising with the right people, all in furtherance of Philip's ambition, his eye not just on courtrooms but parliament.

'You don't need a wife for that, Philip. You need a PA. Probably two of them, because most employees won't be on call twenty-four hours a day.'

'Please, Lou. I love you; you know I do. I need you. Nothing is right without you there.'

'You should have thought of that before.'

'I know I've messed up. I'm sorry I've hurt you. It will never happen again.'

Even if that is all true, does it even matter any more? I don't know. He must read it on my face.

'Take a break and think about things – a trial separation,' he says. 'Then come home and we'll make things work.'

'A separation, yes. But no trial about it. I mean it, Philip. I'm not coming back. And it isn't just about... recent events. This has been building up for a long time.'

I've had enough and stand up, leave. Philip was looking at me differently as I did so. Almost appraisingly. He thinks this is round one; I've done better on the stand than he thought I would, but never mind that because round two is coming. He doesn't believe I'll stay away, that I can go through with this.

He's wrong.

I go to my car, press the button on the key fob to unlock it and I'm about to get in when I notice something white tucked under my windscreen wipers. Maybe it's just advertising or someone complaining about my parking – I'm a bit close to the line on the driver's side – but as I stand there, staring at it, shaking again but with fear, not anger, I know what it must be. It looks just like the other note, the one that led me home and shattered my world a few days ago. And made me remember so many things that I never want to think about.

Who knew I would be here? It was Philip's choice of venue, but he only arranged it last night. I can't see any reason he'd have told anyone else where we'd be. I told Iona we were meeting, but not where. Philip has been inside the restaurant the whole time I've been here, so it can't be him.

My hands are trembling as I unfold it. Red ink, as before. Capital letters that gouge into the paper, almost ripping through.

*DON'T EVEN THINK ABOUT GOING BACK TO PHILIP. YOU
WILL REGRET IT.*

Is the person who wrote this note still here, watching
me, now?

I get into my car and lock the doors. My breathing is too
shallow and my heart is racing. I'm safe, I tell myself. No one can
get into my car. I'm safe. I study the car park and cars around me.
No one is in sight and the cars are all empty, unless someone has
ducked right down.

I start my car, pull out of the car park, watching and making
sure that no one follows. I set out for Iona's, checking in the
mirror the whole time. I take odd turns now and then to see if
anyone follows along, but no one does.

When I finally get to Iona's street, there aren't any spaces out
front and I'm on the next street along before I find one. I park. Sit
in my darkened car, watching. Waiting. Making sure no one is
around before I get out of the car and then walk briskly to her
door with keys ready between my fingers, a weapon. It's hard to
unlock the door with shaking hands and it takes a few goes to
insert the key into the lock, all the while thinking someone might
be rushing towards me.

Inside, at last. Locked and deadlocked. Looking out through
the peephole – no one is there.

I hope Iona is home. She doesn't answer when I call her
name but then I hear that the shower is running down the hall.
Ginger Biscuit must sense I need some comfort – he follows me
about as I first fill the kettle, then change my mind and extract a
bottle of white from the fridge, making a mental note to replace
it. I pour a glass – a large one – and take it to the sofa. He jumps
up on my lap, settles himself on my chest, eyes looking into mine.
Half closed, purring, as I stroke him, glad of his company.

Should I tell anyone about the notes? Should I call the police? I can't see them being interested. Saying I'd regret it if I go back to Philip can be read in two ways: as a threat, or that whoever wrote it thinks it is a decision I would regret. Going by my past experiences with the police, there'd be no point. They didn't believe that my stalker was a threat back then, so why would they interpret it that way now? They weren't much help in more recent interactions, either. When Flick was seventeen and I thought she was missing, they came when I called but treated me like a hysterical woman who needed to be soothed. That was reinforced when Flick came in late while they were still there, wanting to know what all the fuss was about.

There were other times when I was convinced someone wanted to hurt me or my children and I was proven wrong, again and again. I've cried wolf too many times for them to take me seriously now.

Should I tell Iona that there has been another note? As much as I want her take on things, I can't. She'll worry, both about the recent notes and the effect they may have on me, given how much I struggled to move on years ago. She might cancel her trip, and I can't let her do that. I'll keep the second note to myself for now.

As for the rest, I'm back to feeling numb. Is Philip right – is it just hurt feelings that have me pushing him away now? Even if it is – I don't care. I can't accept his recent behaviour, and so many other things about our lives, too. But even as I think that, I know the other stuff wasn't just Philip's problem. It was me, too, accepting the way we were together on his terms, never challenging him to be different. No wonder he's surprised now. And maybe that was part of the reason why he strayed – to find someone not just younger but with more spirit.

That's not all. I can admit to myself at least that I've been thinking about leaving Philip for a long time. But it was more in an unreal, fantasy kind of way, like the way your mind drifts and you think, *what would happen if* – a daydream, when I'm pushing a trolley around the supermarket, say, or driving to the station. Thoughts wandering to alternative lives I might have lived if I'd done or said what I wanted to at certain key points of my life. Like Gwyneth Paltrow and a sliding train door: what was the point of no return? When, exactly, did I change?

I know the answer, but I can't go there, can't think about it. Not now. Anyhow, even if I could rewrite those moments – rewind my life – I couldn't do it. I can't wish my children out of existence, the three brightest lights in my world. The fourth now also, with Lachlan.

Iona joins me, a glass of wine of her own to hand. 'I wasn't sure you'd come back,' she says.

'Neither was I.'

'Do you want to talk about it?'

I shake my head. 'Not yet. But thanks. For everything.'

She puts on the TV – images of pretend lives on the screen in some drama. Is that all we were, Philip and I, at least recently? Actors. Living pretend lives, together, while all the time there was another side of his life I knew nothing about?

He thinks he knows me, inside and out. But there are parts of me he never knew about either.

9

FREJA

I'm half asleep when my phone rings late, well after midnight. I glance at the screen. It's Philip – finally. I've been so worried, agonising about whether I should or shouldn't message him, even though I was sure it was best to leave it to him. But calling me at this hour? As much as I want – *need* – to continue our relationship, he'll have to try harder than that. I ignore it.

A few minutes later my phone rings again – it's an unknown number, likely Philip on another line. This late, he's almost certainly at home – is it his landline? He's never done that before.

I hesitate, press answer.

'Hello?'

'Hi, beautiful.'

'Hi, Philip.'

'It's so good to hear your voice.' A sexy lilt to his words, relaxed and just slightly slurred. Late-night whisky alone, perhaps? She's still out of the picture. I try to keep the smile out of my voice. Less eager always works best with Philip.

'Oh? If you wanted to hear it, you could have called sooner.

And earlier, too; I was asleep. Why are you calling so late? Is everything OK?'

'It will be if I can see you.'

'I thought you wanted to cool things.'

'Let's just say I've had a change of heart. Are you free for dinner tomorrow night?'

'It's after midnight; it's Saturday already. Do you mean tonight?'

'Yes – Saturday night. Tonight.'

I pause. He's not sure what I'll say and as long as he feels like that, he'll be more keen. Best to keep him that way. 'I do have plans. Sorry.'

'Are you seeing someone else?'

'Would it matter?'

'Of course it would.'

'But you have been seeing me and going home to your wife at the same time, so that's hardly fair. Unless there is some news there?'

'We've agreed to separate, if that's what you mean.' I fill in the words he didn't say out loud, *for now*, but it is still a good step towards where I want him to go.

'Was that what she wanted, or what you wanted?'

'Both.' Liar. 'So, are you? Seeing someone else?' he says.

I pause, not sure if competition would make him want me more or pull away. I go for the truth. 'Not at the moment. Only you.'

'I'm glad to hear that. So, please... change your plans. See me tonight.'

I relent. 'Hmmm... perhaps you could persuade me?'

'All right. Ah... how about I take you out for dinner in a lovely restaurant?'

Other than a few places where he feels we are either unlikely to be spotted or there is a private dining room, something he rarely agrees to.

'Whereabouts?'

'Somewhere new. Let me surprise you.'

I eventually agree. We say goodbye soon after.

Too awake now to easily get back to sleep, I get up. Make some mint tea. Take it back to bed, pull my blankets up around me. There is a book next to me for these moments but I'm not in the mood for reading tonight, so I turn off the bedside light. My flat does better in half-light like this. It's harder to see where some past tenant has punched holes in the walls; the mould on crumbling cornices. The cracked sink. I can imagine it all away because I'll be out of this miserable studio flat, soon enough.

I smile, stretch like a satisfied cat. Things are back on track.

10

LOU

The next morning, I'm making my first cuppa when my phone rings. The number isn't in my contacts, and I hesitate, not sure if I should answer. All the business with the notes has me on edge. But it's probably just a phone company, or – in that way they have a sixth sense about these things – a dealership, wondering if I'd like a new car. One without all the scratches and dents.

Curiosity makes me answer.

'Hello?'

'Hello there, Lucy.' A familiar voice and not many besides my mum call me by my given name any more; I've been first Lulu and then Lou for years. It only takes a moment for me to realise who it must be.

'Is that Steve?'

'One and the same.'

'It's been a long time,' I say, and it has. Steve was my boyfriend before Philip. They were in the Met together, so many years ago, before Philip left to go to law school.

'You're probably wondering why I'm calling. I heard about

you and Philip. I just wanted to check in and make sure you're OK.'

I'm surprised. 'You heard? What did you hear? How?'

He pauses. 'That you've split up. And you know the grapevine.'

I do. They say women gossip but back then that bunch were all in each other's pockets and knew everything about each other. But I'm still not sure how this would have made it to Steve, since I doubt Philip has been shouting out about it just now, and he rarely talks with that group of old friends anyway. And the only person I've told is Iona.

'That seems unlikely. How did you hear, really?'

'Well, only if you promise not to get her in trouble. My aunt has the same cleaner as you – she noticed the mess when you were gone.'

Steve and I both grew up in Buckinghamshire – lived there when we met – and his aunt lives in Beaconsfield, not far from us. I run into her occasionally and remember now that it was her who recommended our cleaner, years ago. I didn't know they gossip like that, though. How far has this news travelled?

'Once a detective,' I say.

'You got it. So, are you? OK?' he says. There is concern in his voice and it undoes me, just a little.

'I've been better.'

'If you want a coffee, someone to talk to, you've got my new number now.'

'That's kind,' I say. 'I'm busy at the moment – so much stuff to sort out.' A vague excuse, since I haven't even started to think about any of the things I need to do. Part of me would love to see Steve again, but I'm not sure it's a good idea.

We chat a bit more and then say goodbye.

How many people already know if it's got to Steve via that

circuitous route? I need to talk to the kids, and I need to do it as soon as possible.

* * *

I pull up in front of Flick's terrace in Tring an hour later, hoping she's home. I didn't want to message first and get put off coming. I've gone over and over again in my mind what to say to her – the truth, this time. But I'm not sure how she'll take it.

I see her at the window and get out of the car.

She opens the door. 'Hi, Mum,' she says. My beautiful daughter. She's tired, circles under her eyes, dark hair so like mine but unwashed and pulled back in a limp ponytail. She's not smiling, and her eyes are wary. She must still upset about missing out on her night out, and I don't blame her. I should have been there.

'I'm so sorry about the other night, Flick.'

'I know. It's OK,' is what she says out loud, but it really isn't.

'Where's my favourite grandson?'

'He's just gone down for a nap,' she says. I know she won't want me to wake him, but I still ache to give him a cuddle. It can wait.

I follow her into the kitchen; she puts the kettle on. 'Sorry about the mess,' she says, gestures at the dirty dishes and recycling all over the worktop.

'I can help—'

'Just leave it. I can cope.'

'I know you can.' I hesitate, not wanting to go there when she's already upset with me, but I can't put this off. 'There's something we need to talk about.'

'*Don't.* Dad's already told me that you've left him. That's why you were at Auntie Iona's, isn't it? Why did you lie to me?'

I'm shocked. He's told her, already? Without discussing it with me?

'I'm sorry. I was caught unawares. I guess I kind of panicked; I wasn't sure what to say.' And that's all true, but what did Philip tell her, exactly? Does she know about the other woman? I can't imagine him telling her, but without that context, will this make any sort of sense to Flick?

'How could you do that to Dad – just up and leave him after so many years?' OK. He definitely didn't tell her.

'There are problems between us. There have been for a long time. It just took me a while to work out what was best.'

'For who? You're just thinking of yourself.'

I'm shocked, hurt, try to hide it from my face. 'Flick, you don't know everything that has gone on between your father and me. That's not fair.'

'I know that you left him. What else is there to know?'

She's indignant. A child – my child – still in so many ways, despite having one of her own now. I want to comfort her, hold her, but she's bristling with anger.

'I know this must have come as a shock. But I love you, Flick. That'll never change. I'll always be here for you and Lachlan.'

'Like you were a few nights ago?' She's blinking back tears. 'Look. Could you just go? I'm so tired; I need to get some sleep before Lachlan wakes up again.'

I stare back at her – searching her eyes for some under-standing – but it isn't there, and then she looks away. To have her reject me like this hurts so much. I desperately want to tell her why this has all happened, that it isn't my fault. But she idolises her father, and she's had such a hard time the last few years, with Andy, her boyfriend, cheating on her. She saw them together, too – not like I caught Philip, but she came across them kissing in the park near their home. She was seven months pregnant and tried to work things out for the sake of their baby, but he left her soon after. I don't want her to conflate what her dad has done with Andy. I can't inflict this pain on her, not now. As unfair as it feels to me, maybe not ever.

'Flick, I'm sorry if you're hurt.'

She's rigid, arms crossed against her chest.

'Sometimes *sorry* doesn't cut it.' She holds up her hand. '*Don't* say anything else. Just go.'

I do as she wants, not sure what else I can do or say now to make anything better. She needs some time, she'll come around. Won't she?

This is all Philip's fault. I get in my car and slam the door.

Flick is in shock, denial. Things don't line up with what she thinks she knows about her parents and of course she's upset, but it's all focused on me. Philip got in with his story first – whatever it was that he told her. We should have done it together. At least then I'd know what was said. But I came over here on my own to tell her, so is it reasonable to get angry with him for doing the same?

Reasonable or not, I don't care. I'm furious.

I message Philip.

> I've been to see Flick. What did you tell her?

> Exactly what you told me last night. That you decided to leave us and have wanted to for a long time.

That isn't quite what I said. And what does he mean by *us*? I can't believe he's twisted things around like that, turned Flick against me. I'm so angry that I'm shaking. I stab at my phone to reply.

> Not us. I left you. I take it you didn't tell her what you did?

There is a pause before he answers.

> You told me that wasn't the reason.

He's quoting me back, but it'd be more accurate to say it wasn't the only reason. It was certainly the catalyst.

> Do the twins know?

> Of course. They have a right to know.

> They do. But they also have a right to hear both sides of the story. And we should have discussed it.

There's a long pause. Is he looking at my message, wondering if that means I'm going to tell them everything?

Am I? I don't know. If I don't tell Flick, I can't tell the twins. I've been backed into a corner and the unfairness of the situation I find myself in is infuriating. He's lucky I don't have him lined up with my car just now. Finally he replies:

> Do what you feel you have to do. But keep their best interests foremost.

I slam my phone down on the seat next to me. Is that what he was doing in bed with another woman – keeping the best interests of our children in mind? I won't let him make me the martyr. But I don't want to hurt our children either. They shouldn't be pawns in their parents' game. I guess I was right with what I thought last night, that once Philip began to realise I really meant it, that I'm not coming back, 'reasonable Philip' would disappear. I just thought it would take longer.

None of our children called to ask how I am or for my side of things. Will the twins be just as angry with me as Flick? They are all over eighteen. There are no custody battles to fight. But maybe there is more than one way to steal a child.

What now? No choice, not really. I head for the twins and Brighton, glad they're both only a few hours away. It wasn't a surprise that they wanted to be at the same university – they are so close, always have been. James struggles at times. After some dark times last year, I'd have been so worried for him if he were off at university on his own. Knowing they will look out for each other – especially that Jessie will be there for James – made it easier to see them go.

Once again, I don't check first – I couldn't bear it if they told me not to come. I'm longing to see them and afraid at the same time, and I find myself in the slow lane most of the way.

Once finally there and parked, I message both of them. Jessie doesn't answer, but James does. He suggests a café to meet, says he'll be about an hour as he's got a tutorial.

I walk along the promenade. It's a beautiful day. The Brighton vibe is so different to Beaconsfield. The countryside around us there is beautiful, but the grand houses and listed properties have all but been taken over by people like us, with money. It's so homogenous and beige and boring, the opposite of Brighton's human landscape. It seems everyone here is out today to enjoy the sunshine. Happy couples, young and old, wander along hand in hand; toddlers play on the beach. The tang of the sea air mingles with vinegar, fish and chips, and takes me to back to happy beach holidays when it was the twins building sandcastles. But there are only stones on Brighton's beaches, and my mood would be better suited to rain.

I get there first. James arrives about ten minutes later. He fills the doorway as he comes in and draws glances from a group of girls. All of a sudden – or so it seems to me – he looks so grown up, and so like Philip did when we first met. It's jarring to see him that way. Regardless, he may be over six feet tall now but he's still my baby.

I get out of my chair as he approaches, wanting to reach for him but not sure, after Flick, if I should. But he's coming closer and gives me a hug. I almost collapse with relief.

We sit down.

'Sorry,' he says. 'I've been meaning to call but wasn't sure what to say. Are you all right?' He's leaning towards me, concern in his eyes, and tears prick in the backs of mine. This should be the other way around. James was always an anxious child, in need of reassurance. I miss his small hand in mine.

I shake my head. 'Don't apologise. I should have called you, but your dad got in first. And what I really want to know is, are *you* all right?'

'Dunno. It was a shock. But not a shock, at the same time.' He hesitates. 'What did he do? I know you wouldn't have just suddenly left him without a reason.'

'Of course not.'

'Well?'

I hesitate, not sure what to say, but he must read my expression.

'I knew it; he did do something, and I can guess what.' He rolls his eyes but there is pain behind the nonchalance. What will it do to the young man he has become to have his role model so tarnished?

'Whatever happens between us – we both love you. That isn't going to change.'

'I know.'

'I messaged Jessie as well and she didn't answer. Is she OK?'

'I think she's on team Dad at the moment. If you tell me what actually happened, I could pass it along.'

The temptation – it's so strong. Take all the heat off me and put it on Philip. I can't tell James unless I also tell Flick, but that's not the only reason that I hesitate. How far do I want word of this to get out? Do I want everyone in our extended family, friends, to know? As much as having Iona to confide in has been essential these last few days, I don't want everyone's pity. No. It's best to leave things as they are, at least for now.

'I think some things are best kept between your dad and me. Let's leave it at that. OK?'

'If you don't want to spill, that's your choice. Jessie will come around.'

Of my three children, James is the sensitive one, the one who generally feels things most deeply. I'd have thought he'd be the one who would be the most upset. He may well be but is trying to hide it. At least he's not blaming me like Flick did. Maybe it is the different dynamic – mother and son, not daughter. Whatever the reason, I'm relieved.

'Have you got a lawyer yet?' he asks.

'No,' I say, surprised he's mentioned it. It has lurked in the back of my mind, but getting a lawyer would turn things between Philip and I into an adversarial process, a court battle. The sort of battle he always wins. It will have to come at some point, but I'm not ready to deal with that yet.

'Get one. It's a chummy business, so make sure it's one who doesn't like Dad.'

'James!'

'Kidding, not kidding.'

We talk for an hour – he tells me about his courses, hall

mates. I tease him about the girls who can't seem to stop looking at him.

I've missed the twins so much since they started uni. Is that part of the reason why leaving Philip seems – not less momentous, because it's huge – not as wrenching as it should? Without any of our children with us at home, it's not the anchor of my life the way it has always been before. But what about summer holidays? They're only a few months away. I need to work out where I'm going to be, not let Philip have them by default.

James walks me to my car. Another hug, and he holds on a little too long and too tight – or maybe that is me. And we say goodbye.

11

FREJA

I work in the morning, then take a long detour on my way home, to go past Philip's house. I'm not sure why, he shouldn't be here – he always plays golf on Saturday mornings. I have my hair under a scarf just in case he is home and glances out the window.

There are two cars in the drive and although I don't know what he has while his Porsche is off the road, I'm sure neither is his. Closest to the road is a new BMW, but it is a dusky pink – not a colour he'd choose. The other is a red four-wheel-drive Jeep, one side of it scraped and dented. Red, like the paint that was left behind on the side of his Porsche. It must be his wife's car. My hands are clenched into fists.

Why is she here?

Has he been lying to me?

* * *

By the time I'm home the anger is gone, replaced by worry.

Going to Philip's was risky. If his wife had looked out the window or come out the front door at the wrong moment, she might have recognised me. If she'd told Philip she saw me there, I'm not sure how he'd react, but it's probably fair to say, not well. I don't want him to look at me too closely – to see beyond how I look, how being with me makes him feel.

Anyhow, I don't know why she was there today – it's not necessarily because she's back home. She might have been getting some of her things, deliberately doing so while he was at golf to avoid him. The other car could have been a friend along to help her. So, until I know she's back home, I should stick to the plan.

Now isn't the time to be careless. I need to focus.

12

LOU

'Thanks for coming with me, Iona. I'm seriously pathetic.'

'No, you're not. And you're very welcome. You can do this. Right?'

'Right.'

We're downstairs in what was, until recently, my home. Being here now takes me back to the last time I stood here, listening and afraid. How everything had felt wrong as soon as I came through the door, as if I knew what I was going to find. Did some part of me know? Did I read it in Philip's eyes, his touch, in the days and weeks before, or even longer – and just didn't want to deal with it? At least the chance of finding Philip in bed with another woman today should be slight, as I messaged him just before we arrived. I didn't want to give him too much notice in case he cancelled golf and was here. But I couldn't not let him know, either. He rarely missed golf but if there was any chance that I'd come and find them here, together, I couldn't take that risk.

I'm looking around, seeing things in a way I didn't when it was my home, as if the place is different now to how it was before. But really, the only way that it is different is the degree of mess – mugs left on surfaces. Dirty plates. A suit jacket crumpled on the sofa. If he'd hang it up properly it'd get another wear before going to the dry cleaner's, but it's not my problem. I squash down the automatic urge to put things in order.

'For someone who always looks so neat and tidy, he's really a slob,' Iona says.

'True. Though I'm guessing he hasn't been looking as tidy lately.'

'Come on, then,' she says. 'Let's do this.'

We go up the stairs and I hesitate at the top.

'Are you all right, Lou?'

'No. But I will be.' I sigh. 'It's just the last time I was here – you know. What I saw. And I know no one is here now but us, but it feels as if she is still here, whoever she is. Like she'll always be here.'

'I get it. We'll do this and then if you don't want to come back, you don't have to. Right?'

'Right.'

Down the hall. Past the kids' rooms. Past the main bathroom, the guest rooms.

And on to our bedroom door. It's ajar like it was that day. I push it open and try to school my eyes away from the unmade bed. Clothes on the floor. He really is incapable of looking after himself.

Not. My. Problem.

I open the door of my walk-in wardrobe. There are suitcases on the top shelves. I pull them down and randomly take clothes from hangers, drawers, not worrying too much about what I'm choosing or folding things properly. Just wanting to get this done as quickly as possible and then leave.

I hesitate at the jewellery box on my dressing table. Almost all of it is from Philip and tied up with memories – a bracelet for one birthday, earrings for another. Birthstone rings when the children were born. But if I leave it behind, what if this other woman ends up in my place? No. I'll take it. I can always give pieces to Flick, Jessie, if I don't want to wear them myself.

The cases are soon packed, and we fill a few bin bags that forward-thinking Iona brought as well.

'I didn't think I had so much stuff.'

'There is probably loads more you should take.'

'Such as?'

'There's a whole houseful of things that belong to both you and Philip.'

'I suppose. But I'm going to have trouble getting even this much into your spare room. I need to find my own place. Don't I?'

She hugs me. 'When you're ready. I've told you, stay as long as you want to. Though if you want to buy in London or surrounds, I'm your girl. But in the meantime, I'll pack away some stuff in the spare room, make more space for you. For now, why not take something small and symbolic? And preferably valuable.'

I think about it for a while. There are pieces of art we've collected over the years, but they were more to Philip's taste than mine. There are three works of art I do want to keep, though: photo montages of our children. Flick, James and Jessie had done them for me for Mother's Day a few years ago, though likely that was mostly Flick. Each of them as babies, toddlers. Growing to children, then teens and beyond in Flick's case. I wrap them in a blanket, feeling guilty somehow at the blank spaces left on the walls, even though they gave them to me. We take them and all my stuff down the stairs, then start to load them into both of our cars. Lucky we both drove; I'm not sure I'd have managed to get it all in mine.

'Thanks again for your help.'

'No worries. I'll see you there.'

Iona gets into her car. She starts to pull out and I walk around to the driver's side of my car to get in and follow her, but then I see a deep scratch in the cherry-red paintwork, as if someone has taken a key and scraped as hard as they could. I run my finger along it, down the length of the car. It's on the side without the dents – figures.

It wasn't there before; there's no way I wouldn't have noticed. Someone must have keyed my car while we were upstairs packing. I hope Iona's car wasn't touched – likely it wasn't as she'd have noticed and said something, not just driven off.

I frown, uneasy. If it was random vandalism, Iona's car was closer to the road – less likely to be spotted and quicker to run away than coming up the drive to my car. Though I've not heard of cars being vandalised in this neighbourhood before. It seems less likely in daytime, too.

Which means me – my car – may have been specifically targeted. But by *who*? I don't think anyone besides us and Philip even knew we were going to be here. After what I did to his beloved Porsche, I wouldn't entirely put it past him, but I know he's at golf. Anyhow, Philip's machinations tend to be both more subtle and ultimately more painful. Besides, I only messaged him that we were coming a short time before we arrived. I'm uneasy and trying not to think what this might mean – that I may have been followed.

Should I report it, to the police or insurance? My car is already such a mess, it hardly seems worth bothering.

I better get going or Iona will be wondering what happened to me.

When I pull out onto the street, I pause, look back. I spent over fifteen years in this house. The twins were toddlers when we moved in, Flick a whirlwind six-year-old. So many memories, good and bad – but mostly good – are tied up in these four walls.

Am I really leaving it behind forever? There is such a mix of feelings going through me. Regret for what should have been. Uncertainty, too: am I really doing what is right, not just for me, but for my children? Unease also, to leave what was home, sanctuary, even though it could never feel the same again. We ended up in Beaconsfield for a mixture of reasons – the schools, the countryside. Its proximity to The Buckinghamshire, Philip's golf club. I'd loved living in London when we were first married and worried it was a bit remote, but it's a quick half-hour train to London. We redecorated every room together, one at a time – though more my efforts than Philip's, as he has always worked long hours. Assuming that was what he was actually doing.

Philip should be the one who has to leave, not me. I didn't do anything wrong. But I know he'd never go voluntarily, and I don't want to be under the same roof while we sort it out. I'll get a lawyer when I'm ready and extract what is mine.

One last look and I pull away. It isn't just what I'm leaving that makes it hard to go. I'm afraid of the unknown. Being alone. Philip was right when he said that I've never been on my own – at least, not for many years. But he was wrong: I *can* do this. And I will. Or so I tell myself and hope that I'm right.

Iona is parked out front when I get to her street. She must have been waiting and gets out as I pull in behind her. I check both sides of her car to make sure it's all right. Marvelling at how she managed to get it neatly into such a small space.

'What's up?' she says. I point out the damage on mine. Her eyes open wide. 'Oh my God. When did that happen?'

'It must have been while we were upstairs packing. It wasn't there when we got there.'

'It's a really deep scratch. It'll be expensive to fix. Have you called the police and insurance?'

I shake my head. 'My car is such a mess, what's the point?'

'Time to get a new car.'

'Probably. But I need to sort out money stuff with Philip first.'

'You've not had that conversation?'

I shake my head. 'We will. But not just yet.' Am I putting this off because part of me is still hoping someone will wave a magic wand and we'll be the way we used to be together, before children, time and Philip's midlife crisis came between us? I know that isn't possible. Perhaps I'm hesitating because I know once I get a lawyer, that adding in an adversarial process can only make Philip feel backed into a corner, and that is a side of him I'd rather not deal with.

Iona helps me get everything into her flat. She leaves written instructions for how much and when to feed Ginger Biscuit, who to call if anything goes wrong with the electricity and so on. And then it is time for her to go.

I watch through the window as she pulls onto the busy street, drives up the road and is gone.

Ginger Biscuit isn't in – probably out terrorising the neighbourhood, hunting for slippers. It's too still, quiet, even with the background sounds of the city, people and traffic. The tick, tick of a clock hung over the fireplace is too loud in the silence. I put the TV on but then worry I'll miss hearing something I should and turn it off again.

Keep busy.

I start going through my clothes, finding things I'll need sooner and things that can go in a case under the bed, but as the evening draws in, my unease grows. It's not just my usual gener-alised fear of being alone. Years of therapy helped me be able to logically dismiss it, to stave off the panic attacks that came from trauma all those years ago. But this time is different. Someone damaged my car. Someone also left two notes where I'd find them. To do these things, they had to know where I was, what I was doing. Now I'm second-guessing the decision I made not to tell Iona or call the police.

I still could – call the police. Or go see them. But apart from minor property damage to my car – which they might argue was random – what has whoever it is actually done? It's not a crime to leave notes under someone's windscreen wiper. Besides, with my history, I'm fairly sure they'd roll their eyes and prepare their platitudes if they saw me coming. It isn't like they were all that helpful or supportive when I had a stalker before.

Though maybe the police would be better with this kind of thing now than they were twenty-five years ago. Leaving notes might be considered a crime if they were threatening, or a stalker was involved. Is that possible?

Examine the facts.

The first note is embedded in my memory: *IF I WERE YOU, I'D GO HOME. NOW.* It was left on my windscreen when I'd stopped for coffee on my way to London. I hadn't even decided to do this until I almost went past the coffee shop – no one could have known I'd be there. That could mean one of two things: I was being followed, or it was done on the spur of the moment when the opportunity presented itself.

The second – *DON'T EVEN THINK ABOUT GOING BACK TO PHILIP. YOU WILL REGRET IT* – was left on my windscreen when I met Philip for dinner. *YOU WILL REGRET IT* in the second could be interpreted as a threat. Apart from Philip and the unlikely chance he told someone where we would be, no one knew I'd be there. He didn't leave our table while I was there, and anyhow, it wouldn't have made any sense for him to write a note that went against the things he said – that he wanted me back.

Then my car was damaged, parked out front of our house, and besides Iona and Philip, no one knew I was going to be there. Philip only knew at the last minute.

Examining the facts was one of the things my therapist encouraged me to do, years ago – to discount innocuous things and help me stop seeing threats everywhere. It's not working today; it's doing the opposite. My breathing is more and more shallow, heart rate going off the scale. I'm heading for a panic attack that won't be pushed away, and before I can think about it any more I'm on my phone. I find Steve's number in my recent contacts from when he called. It rings once, twice, three times…

'Hi, Lucy. It's good to—'

'Can you come over? Please. Right now. To Iona's.'

13

FREJA

Dinner at a lovely restaurant, somewhere new. It was Philip's suggestion, but when he collects me in his shiny, brand-new blue Porsche, he says it needs a run-in. He drives us out of the city, pushing the speed on the M40 to see what it can do. The old one could have been repaired, he says when I ask, but something that was broken and fixed isn't acceptable to Philip. He'd always know even if no one could tell. If he knew how broken I am inside, would the same apply?

We end up in the small village of Great Milton, Oxfordshire. While it's not that far in distance from where he lives in Buckinghamshire, it's out of the way enough that it's obvious that's why we are really here.

'You told me that you are officially separated. So why hide me away?'

'I'm not hiding you away. Le Manoir comes highly recommended. I had to call in some favours to get in at short notice.' I raise an eyebrow. That may be, but I'm sure it isn't the only reason.

We pull in, park. Philip comes around to hold open the door.

It looks like a manor house so the name is apt. When we go in, I'm glad I went for this new dress even though buying it made me overdrawn. It manages the tricky double of looking both sexy and classy, and he can't take his eyes off me.

We're seated in a quiet corner.

'You look amazing,' Philip says. 'Though I like your hair down.'

I know he does. 'It took me ages to pin it up like this.'

'Maybe later?'

'Perhaps.' A seductive smile on my lips. It's a ritual – part of how he undresses me, slowly, and I can see in his eyes he is thinking of just this.

Now a waiter appears. It's a tasting menu with matching wine, and we savour every course. Philip was right – the food here is amazing. But it is to end with chocolate three ways.

'Not for me, thank you,' I say to the waiter.

'You don't need to watch your figure,' Philip says after he is gone.

'It's not that. You know I don't like chocolate.'

When his arrives, even though I don't have the small bites he offers, I can still smell it, taste it, as if I had, and I'm feeling nauseous. That tomorrow is the anniversary of one of the worst days of my life is making it worse. Maybe going out tonight was a mistake. I'd had most of the wine as Philip is driving, and now there is a dull pounding behind my eyes too.

After dinner, he drives us to a secluded spot. Parks and carefully lets my hair down. Kisses me, and it's obvious what he thinks will happen next.

'Philip, I really care for you.' Tears in my eyes, but not for the reason he may think. 'I thought I meant something to you too.'

'You do – I promise you do.'

'I don't want to make out in your car. I want to be part of your life.'

He accepts what I've said, doesn't press. Doesn't comment, either, on whether that is something he wants. We start the drive back to London and I'm struggling to maintain any semblance of the woman I am supposed to be when I'm with Philip. I just want to be alone.

He pulls in front of the block of flats in Hillingdon where he thinks I live.

I hesitate. Unsure whether to leave things as they are or try to repair any damage I may have done. But my throat feels tight; I can't trust my voice. I feel like I'm about to fall to pieces and need to be out of his sight before it gets any worse.

'Can I come in with you?' he says.

He's never been through the front door. I've told him when he's asked before that my flatmate is difficult, that it was best he didn't. I'm not sure he believed me, but I doubt he'd guess the real reason. But he still asks now and then.

I shake my head no. 'I'm sorry, Philip.'

He nods, eyes thoughtful. 'Goodnight, Freja.' A kiss – not a passionate one, not on my part.

I get out, head up the stairs around the side of the building and then out of his sight on a walkway. Wait until I hear his car pull away and then another minute, two, to be sure. Retrace my steps and walk briskly down a side street, turn at the next corner. Philip thinks where I live isn't a great area; if he only knew how much worse it really was. Reminding myself to be alert, aware, I hurry to the building where I really live.

The security door is broken – it has been since I moved in. There is graffiti lining the entranceway and the stairwell smells of drugs and piss. I run up three flights of stairs. Unlock my door. Lock it behind me, relieved to both have reached it without any trouble tonight and to get away from Philip. I couldn't have kept up any degree of the pretence I need with him much longer.

My eyes take in my tiny studio flat. It's not much, but it's home. For now. Clean, apart from some mould that keeps returning no matter how many times I scrub it off. Uncluttered, unless you count books – I don't. Reading was how I escaped when I was a child and it's still an important part of my life. Especially since I came back to London. Here, my life is narrow. Work. Philip, when he can get away from his family. That's about it. It's not enough.

Make-up off, PJs on. Latest thriller in my hand – it's gripping, a new trend I love. Female rage, they call it. But I can't concentrate.

A door slams above and the latest episode of the couple there screaming *I hate you* begins, but I have earplugs. This flat is the best I could afford on what I had. My neighbours mostly leave me alone now – they've seen I can look after myself. But the backdrop of drugs and late-night screaming matches in adjoining flats, and sirens and fights on the street, can make it hard to sleep, even with earplugs. I might have done better if I hadn't been in a hurry when I moved to the area last year, but not much – London prices are ridiculous. I swore I'd never move back here and not just because of that. But of course something important came up, and for that, I had to be here.

There is so much more. Like Philip's house. Why shouldn't I have it? A girl like me.

If he only knew. By the time he does, it will be too late.

14

LOU

I wait at the window, watching the street, trying to hold away the fear, the panic. He'll be here soon – he promised. Steve never broke a promise to me before. He won't do it now.

A distant siren comes closer, then cuts off. A dark car pulls in a moment later. It's Steve in an unmarked police car, the blue light visible on the dashboard before he cuts the engine. I rush to unlock the door and when I look in his eyes, the years dissolve. His arms open and I'm leaning into him, and they tighten around me. I lock the door, and we go in, sit down at the sofa, next to each other. I can't think when I last saw him. We – Philip and me – ran into him and his wife, Stacey, at the Chelsea flower show a while back, maybe five or six years ago? He looked just the same then as he does now. Tall. Fit. A little less dark hair, maybe, than years ago, but still a decent amount. We sit next to each other on the sofa.

His hand holds mine and I'm back even further, a child scared of the dark. I remind myself I'm a grown woman and let go.

'Tell me everything,' he says.

'I think someone has been following me – they must be.' I run through it all – the first note, what it led to. He winces on my behalf when I tell him briefly what I found at home. The second note. The damage to my car. And he listens, doesn't tell me I've got things wrong. That I'm overreacting and no one is out to get me. Things both Philip, my therapist and police officers have said to me countless times over the years.

'Show me the notes?'

I fetch them from the kitchen. 'They're definitely written by the same person. Aren't they?'

'They look very much the same. Do you recognise the handwriting?'

I shake my head. 'I wouldn't, I suppose, the way they are printed in capitals. Maybe whoever wrote them did them like that so I wouldn't.'

He hesitates. 'Do they look anything like the notes you found years ago, and in Paris?'

I shake my head. Glad he brought that up, so I didn't have to say out loud what I'm most scared of. 'Not really. They were on blank paper, too, but more like standard printer paper – this paper is thicker. And they weren't written in capitals or red ink. But that doesn't rule that out. Does it? He could have just wanted to make them look different. I don't know.'

'That was a long time ago.'

'I know. It's hard to think it isn't connected – anonymous notes, left on my car like that.'

'I understand why you feel that way, but it's not likely. Assuming not, any idea who they could be from?'

'No. Though maybe it could have been the woman I saw with Philip.'

'Like she deliberately set things up, so you'd find out?'

'Yes. To get me out of the picture, maybe, I don't know. And the second note likewise.'

'Can you think of anyone else who might have written them?'

'Nothing concrete, but I did wonder if it could be someone who knew Philip was cheating and wanted me to know, but didn't want to get involved? Either because they thought I should know, or to hurt Philip.'

'Possibly. Any suspects that way?'

'Not really.' I hesitate. 'But I did wonder, maybe Iona.' I feel disloyal to even think it, but it crossed my mind so I will tell him. 'She really dislikes Philip, always has. Given that, if she'd tried to tell me he was cheating I might not have believed her. Maybe she found out somehow and left me a note, so I could see it with my own eyes.'

'Do you think that's likely?'

I shake my head. 'No. It doesn't feel like something she'd do. Iona is always very direct, to the point. Leaving notes? No. Also, her surprised reaction when I showed her the first note seemed very genuine. And she couldn't have damaged my car, I was with her the whole time. And why would she do that? Anyhow, I don't see how she would have known where I was on both occasions when I found the notes. Or how anyone else could have, either.'

'Which is why you're worried you're being followed.'

I nod. 'You said it's unlikely to be the same person as all those years ago. What if it was *her* – this woman Philip was with? If he ends up being with her, she'll be in my children's lives. And leaving notes like this, it's, well, weird. If she ends up in their lives —' I shake my head, not sure of my words. 'I'm not just scared for me but for my children, too.'

'Did you tell Philip about the notes?'

'No. We're not on good terms just now.'

'You're really worried.'

'Yes,' I say, and I am, but after too many years of worrying over nothing I need to hear that this is for real. 'What do you think? Should I be?'

'If you went to the local station and told them all of this, this is what they'd say. Leaving notes isn't illegal and depending on how you take "you'll regret it" they're not even threatening. There's no connection you're aware of between the damage to your car and the person who wrote the notes. But I'm not your local and I won't fob you off, Lucy.'

I nod, both relieved that he's taking me seriously, and scared to have the validation at the same time. 'What can we do?'

'To begin with, I'll take these notes with me. I'll see if there are any fingerprints, though as they've been handled a bit since you received them, it's not that likely. If you find another note, don't touch it – put it in a plastic bag – call me. And likewise, if anything else worries you, call me. Whatever time of the day or night.'

There are tears coming up in my eyes and I blink them back. 'Thank you.'

'In the meantime, I'll check all the doors and windows. Don't answer the door unless you know who is there. When does Iona get back?'

'In a few days.'

'You could come stay with me. The offer is always open.'

I'm remembering now what he said so many years ago when we broke up – that once it all goes wrong with Philip, he'd be there for me. The offer would always be open, he said. Is he remembering that moment, too? And I don't know how I feel about that, at all. But I'm not the only one who is married.

'Not sure if Stacey would like that. How is she?'

'You haven't heard?' I shake my head, expecting another tale of separation, divorce. He looks down; there is a pause. 'She died a few years ago. Cancer.'

'Oh my God, Steve. I didn't know. I'm so very sorry.'

'Thanks. I appreciate that. And you're welcome to come stay.' He's looking into my eyes a certain way and all at once I'm having trouble breathing, but not because of panic this time.

I find my voice. 'I'll be fine here. Thanks. Thanks for being a friend.' He nods, as if to say, message received. I put the kettle on, and he goes outside to have a look at my car, then back in to check all the door and window locks.

'Everything is secure.'

'Thank you.'

'I saw the scratch on your car but what happened to the other side of it?'

'Well, I kind of sideswiped Philip's Porsche.'

A raised eyebrow. 'Was this by chance soon after you received the first note?'

'How did you guess?'

'Was it an accident?'

'I'm not sure I should say. Who is asking – Steve my friend or Steve the police detective?'

'Definitely the former.'

'Not exactly an accident. Especially when I reversed and did it again.'

He whistles. 'Respect. Where was Philip when your car was scratched?'

I raise an eyebrow. 'I can't see him doing that, somehow.'

'But it *was* a Porsche you damaged, and, knowing Philip, it was in perfect condition before you got to it.'

'It was. And you should have seen it after I swiped it the second time.' A satisfied grin. 'Who knew criminal damage could be so very satisfying?'

'Remind me not to cross you.'

'Anyhow, he was playing golf when my car got scratched. I've no doubt that many fine and upstanding members of his club could vouch for his whereabouts.'

I make tea while he looks at the photo montages leaning against the bookshelves, then asks me about each of my children, what they are doing. I take out my phone to show him more recent images of my brood and baby Lachlan, too.

'You and Stacey never had children?'

'No. And it's too late for me now.'

'Well, not necessarily. Men can generally have children at a much older age than women can.'

'But that would require a younger woman. Not to my taste. I like to be with someone who likes the same music, remembers the same decades as I do.'

'That's unusual,' I say, a bite in my words.

'I take it Philip was with a younger woman?'

'I really don't want to talk about it.'

'If you ever do, I'm a good listener.'

'I know. I remember.'

'Despite the reason, it's been really good to see you, Lucy.' There is something wistful in his eyes, maybe mine, too. For what might have been? Perhaps. I wouldn't normally think that way – I didn't when we ran into him at Chelsea years ago. It's only because of recent events with Philip, and that's no reason to be second-guessing decisions made decades ago. 'Are you sure you'll be all right being on your own?'

'I'm sure,' I say, and I mean it. The panic attack that was threatening earlier has gone. Having someone listen and take me seriously has eased my nerves – put into perspective that not much has actually happened, and there is no reason to assume it will escalate.

We move on to a few glasses of wine. Steve tells me gossip about mutual friends from years ago. Talking about the good old days – our glory days, like the Springsteen song – as if all the years between when we didn't see each other have just disappeared. It feels good to be at ease and laughing, forgetting the recent disasters in my life, and the ones from so long ago, too.

There's a thump of the cat flap in the kitchen door and Ginger Biscuit wanders in. He hisses at Steve, then disappears down the hall.

The wine is going to my head, making me tired after days of not getting enough sleep. I'm yawning and Steve gets up, says goodnight. I go with him to the door and there is a look in his eyes when he says goodbye. Just for a moment, I think, he wants to kiss me. And I want him to – that is what surprises me most of all. But instead, I drop my eyes, step back. It's the wine, talking about old times, making me feel that way. I'm not who I was all those years ago, and neither is he.

He says goodnight again and heads out.

After he's gone, I wonder why I didn't just let him kiss me. In that moment, it was what we both wanted. Steve is attractive. His wife is out of the frame – tragically – and so is Philip. I have every right to kiss someone else if I want to. But I still *feel* married. That's the problem, isn't it? And if there is any one man Philip would be furious to see with me, it's got to be Steve.

That'd make it even better: an unbidden thought. Unworthy, too.

No. There's just too much history between all of us for me to easily go there.

I realise now that I didn't think to tell Steve that I thought I recognised the woman in bed with Philip. If she is the one behind the notes, I should have.

Who was she?

15

JESSIE

Baby Lachlan is smiling up at me and doing his best to convince me he will be no trouble at all, but I'm not reassured. Especially when Flick hands me a handwritten set of instructions that is three pages long. I scan it. Flick never asks for help. At least, not from me. It's usually the other way around. And am I actually cleared to handle a six-month-old baby on my own, even for just a few hours? I was born without an interest in ever having one, which is just as well, as likewise without any interest in boys. Anyhow, this is what grandparents are for. She needs to sort things out with Mum.

She's looking even more worried than I feel.

'Are you sure you can handle this?' she says.

'Yes,' I lie. 'I've got all the instructions and your friend next door if I need help. And an impressive list of emergency numbers.' I waggle the list. 'It'll be fine.'

What she is wearing registers: a bit too tight dress – having a baby gave her boobs. Make-up, which I haven't seen her in since Lachlan was born. 'Are you going to tell me where you're off to tonight? Hot date?'

'Not exactly.' She looks away, straightens her dress.

It's not up to the level of twin-dar I have with James, but now I think maybe there is another reason why she didn't want to ask Mum to mind Lachlan tonight.

'You're not, are you? Seeing Andy?' It's confirmed with the set to her face. 'You *are*.' There is a jolt of guilt inside. Going away to uni left Flick on her own too much and I haven't been calling her, checking she's OK. If I could have seen this coming, maybe I could have stopped it from happening.

'I can't blank him. He's Lachlan's father.' Who messed around on her and left when she was pregnant. Only comes back now and then if he wants something, and every time he lets her down and I see the hurt in her eyes – not just for herself, but Lachlan, too – I want to kick him to next week.

'I'm not saying blank him, but dating him? Are you nuts?'

She's both uneasy and annoyed. 'I can look after myself. And I'm not *dating* him. This is just going out for dinner, because we need to talk.'

'Has he paid any maintenance yet?'

'No. But he's just starting a new job. He will soon.'

I'll believe it when I see it. I know Mum and Dad paid off the mortgage for this place for Flick before Lachlan was born and that they cover her bills, but that isn't really the point. 'Just be careful. Please?'

'I will be.' A hug.

She goes through some more Lachlan instructions for the third time. 'You'll call me, won't you, if there is anything you're not sure about? Promise?'

'I promise.'

Lachlan has been fed and she gets him down for a nap. Shows me the expressed baby milk – gross – and what to do with it. He's sound asleep now. With any luck he'll stay that way until she gets home.

Flick is in the chair by her front window, watching.

'What time did he say he was coming? Seven?'

She shakes her head. 'That's what I told you, to make sure you got here in time to go over everything for Lachlan. He said seven-thirty.'

It's ten to eight. At eight she calls him; he doesn't answer.

At eight-fifteen a message comes through.

> Sorry, babe, held up with the lads. I'll came by later.

Tight-lipped, she shows me. And answers:

> No. Don't bother.

'I hate it when you're right,' she says.

'I'm really sorry.'

'It doesn't matter for me. If he does this to Lachlan when he's older – I couldn't bear it.' She squirms in her seat. 'God this dress and bra hurt.' There is a patch of wet now on the front of her dress. Milk. Ugh.

'Give me a moment.' She comes back soon after, face clean of make-up. Trackies on. Looking more sad than angry now.

'Let's make this a sisters' night,' I say. 'Do you have anything to drink?'

'Might be some wine on top of the fridge, I think?' I reach up top and find a dusty bottle of red. 'But I shouldn't drink very much. Gets in breast milk.'

'But you expressed. Is there enough to last until it gets out of your system?'

'Probably not. But I'll do it again.' While she gets busy with a breast bump – it looks weird, and painful – I find the corkscrew. Fill two glasses and hand one to her when she is done. I hold up my glass.

She clinks hers against mine. 'Cheers!' I say and we both have a sip.

'That tastes so good,' she says, and has another. 'How about we watch a DVD?'

'What have you got?'

She gestures to a shelf, and I start going through them. It's like romcom central. I extract *Mamma Mia!* as the best of a bad lot. Hold it up.

'Yay!' she says, takes whatever was in the player out, looks for the remote, but first there is something else I need to talk about.

'A question before you press play. Do you know what the hell is going on with Mum and Dad?'

'She left him. That's all I know.'

'Have you spoken to her?'

'Briefly. She came by after Dad told us.'

'And?'

'I didn't give her a chance to say much. She lied to me, days before, about why she was staying with Auntie Iona.'

'Mum lied?' I'm shocked. 'Why would she do that?'

'She said she wasn't ready to talk about it or something like that. I don't know.'

'So, all we really know is what Dad said. Maybe we need to see her.'

'Maybe.'

'Safety in numbers? We could have lunch tomorrow or something?'

'Could we go shopping first? I need something other than trackies that actually fits.'

Shopping is the seventh circle of hell as far as I'm concerned.

But I agree. It probably won't kill me or end in disaster. No guarantees, mind.

We start watching *Mamma Mia!* for the approximate three millionth time. The baby monitor goes off.

She fetches a crying Lachlan. Face red, little fists waving.

'What's wrong?'

'He's just hungry. Maybe you should feed him? So, if I ever need a babysitter again—'

'For a non-Andy-related reason, obviously? OK. I'll try.' I hold him how she showed me earlier. She gets the bottle of breast milk ready. I hold it. He's looking up into my eyes – pale blue eyes, dark lashes wet with tears – and takes the bottle. There is something inside of me, a feeling, I don't know what. A pull. Protectiveness. My nephew needs a break, considering who his dad is. Maybe he's not so bad. Maybe he needs more Auntie Jess in his life. Or maybe I even need more of him.

'I'm sorry I haven't been around much.'

'It's OK, I get it. University and all that. You're busy, you and James.'

'I'm surprised you didn't get him in as first choice of sitter.'

She laughs. 'I called him first, as it happens. He said he had a date. Any idea who?'

I shrug. 'I can't keep track.' We exchange a glance, and both laugh. His reincarnation as popular is hard for both of us to believe. Luckily we never like the same girls or there could be trouble in twin-dom.

Lachlan falls asleep in my arms and when Flick goes to take him I shake my head. 'Let him stay where he is.' She puts *Mamma Mia!* back on again – turns it down – and I'm only half watching. When I glance over a few minutes later, she is sound asleep.

What is it with my family? Mum and Dad and whatever has happened there. Flick and Andy, and this little one. He doesn't know yet that his dad is useless. He trusts he'll be fed, held, looked after. Loved. The rest of us will step up as best we can, try to fill the gap, but he'll still feel it when he gets older.

As far as Mum and Dad go, it never entered my mind that my parents could be having problems – they've always been there together. Something I assumed would never change, could never change. Shows what I know. When Dad called and told me I didn't even believe him at first. I wanted to talk to Mum but when she messaged she was in Brighton I chickened out. Couldn't – or didn't want to – deal with it. And I keep asking myself *why*. Is it just that gradually growing apart thing, or was something more serious behind it? I need to talk to James. He's always been the closest to Mum; he might know something.

But no matter what, Flick really needs Mum. *We need to get them talking, don't we, Lachlan?* I say silently, with my eyes.

Relationships are so messed up. I'm going to stay single forever.

Then Lachlan stirs and starts crying at an impressive level of decibels, and it is all driven out of my mind.

16

LOU

My first night alone in more years than I can count. Despite feeling far more at ease than I did earlier, it's still very late before I can convince myself I should turn in. I know the doors and windows are all locked but check them again.

I get into bed. The window is open but on the latch. There are more traffic sounds than I'm used to, a combination of not brilliant seal around old windows without double glazing and being close to a busy main road.

I'm hoping I've had just the right amount of wine – enough to help me drop off but hopefully not so much that I'll wake up soon after. I'm trying to relax, empty my mind. But I can hear Iona's clock ticking. Tick, tick. Tick, tick. Once I've noticed it, I can't stop.

I finally get up, go to the lounge. Take the battery out of the clock.

I check the doors are locked once more even as I tell myself it's ridiculous to do so, then go back to bed. Lying on my back, staring at the ceiling. There is a loud thump, and I sit up, heart racing, before I realise it must have been the cat flap. A moment later, Ginger Biscuit pushes my door open and jumps up onto the bed.

Not alone, after all.

I stroke him and he stretches alongside me, solid and warm. A deep rumbling purr.

Mindful breathing: *in two three four, pause two three four, out two three four, pause two three four…*

Gradually my heart rate is slowing. Eyes closed, I'm drifting to sleep…

Tap tap.

I'm completely awake in an instant. What was that? Fear and adrenalin surge through my blood but I don't stir. I keep my eyes closed, stay still, breathing slowly, listening. Ginger Biscuit isn't next to me any more. Maybe he made the noise I heard going out through the cat flap. I'm almost falling asleep again when it happens again.

Tap tap.

Was it inside or outside?

It seemed both too loud to be outside and not the sort of sound a cat or cat flap would make.

I sit up slowly, moving as silently as I can.

Tap tap.

I cross the dark room to the window, pull the curtains to the side and look out. The street is quiet, no signs of anyone. Has the sound stopped now? I move back to my bed and then it happens again:

Tap tap.

Is it coming from somewhere inside the flat? It's too loud and clear to be one of the neighbours or something on the street. I don't want to get up and check the flat, but what else am I going to do? I could call Steve. But he's already made one trip to save me, sirens on and all. He'll be asleep and might think completely the wrong thing if I call him about a vague noise in the middle of the night.

I noticed there was a cricket bat under the bed when I was moving stuff around earlier and retrieve it now, then walk as quietly as I can out to the hall. Hold my breath.

Tap tap.

Something touches my bare leg, and I almost scream before the feeling of fur registers – it's Ginger Biscuit. His eyes shine in the dark. He's not rattled, and he would be if someone had broken in, wouldn't he? I do a quick check of every room: bathroom, Iona's room, kitchen, lounge. The hall to the front door. There's no one here.

What was it? Could it be the door knocker – echoing through the wood door, so loud at night in the quiet flat that it sounded like it was in the room instead of outside?

But who would be knocking in the middle of the night? Not just once, but multiple times.

I make myself walk across to the door. Stand there, silent, waiting for the sound to repeat, but nothing.

Maybe I should call the police, or Steve. And say, what – that someone is tapping on my door?

I look through the peephole: I can't see anyone. I stand there, undecided for a moment. Then rip the front door open all at once. Brandishing the cricket bat. The small front garden doesn't take much searching: a quick glance tells me that no one is here. I tap the door knocker lightly myself and it sounds exactly like what I could hear, but there is no one in sight. Then I remember Iona's video doorbell. If anyone came up to the door it should have recorded them doing so. But when I glance at it, there is a leaf stuck on the front of it. I pull it away and look up and down the street – no movement. Could someone be hiding behind a car or in one of the neighbour's front gardens? I can't see into the shadows of fences on either side unless I leave Iona's doorway and walk past each, and there is nothing that would make me do that just now. I back up over the threshold and lock the door.

That's when I see it – a white piece of paper half sticking through the letter box. My hand is shaking a little as I reach for it, then unfold it.

DO YOU KNOW WHERE YOUR CHILDREN ARE?

Fear rushes through my gut as I stare at the words. They are written on a white square of paper, block capitals in red ink like the others. Was someone tapping to make sure I came down and found their note?

I glance at the clock for the time, then remember I took out the battery. I retrieve my phone from the bedside table in my room. It's after three in the morning. But there's no real choice, is there?

Jessie first. It rings, rings, goes to message. I call again and still no answer, and just as I'm telling myself it's either because she's avoiding talking to me still or her phone is on silent – not that anything has happened to her, please, *please* no – a message pops up on my screen a moment later.

What?! I'm asleep.

Is everything OK?

It was until you woke me up. Go away.

Her words are so Jess I almost cry.

Then James. He answers his on the first ring. 'Hello?' He sounds wide awake.

'James, it's me – Mum.'

'Is everything all right?'

I reassure him as best I can. There is something, some note in his voice and the way he answered the phone – why is he awake at this time of night? Maybe he's not alone. Now my Mum-dar is kicking in, thinking we need to have another talk – or get Philip to do it – about staying safe. But first I have to get off the phone to call Flick.

Flick's rings once and she answers.

'Flick, is everything all right?'

There is a pause. 'Why are you asking?'

I lie. I promised I wouldn't do it again but it's getting to be a habit. 'I had a dream that something was wrong, that's all. Just had to call you. Sorry if I woke you.'

'I was already awake.'

'Lachlan got you up?'

'Yeah, I've just put him down. Mum, I was going to call in the morning, so while I've got you – Jessie is here. Do you want to meet us for lunch tomorrow?'

Despite the worry and fear over this note and the lack of sleep, this overture from Flick makes relief swell inside me. 'Yes. I'd love that.' We agree to work out when and where in the morning, then say goodbye.

I feel so apart from my children. It hurts that Jessie was up from Brighton and I didn't know. Usually, she'd be a whirlwind of washing her clothes, raiding the fridge. Telling outrageous stories about friends and lecturers that mix fact with fiction and have us laughing so much it hurts.

I miss her. The longing for all three of them to be back home with me is overwhelming. But I couldn't fit three adult-sized children and one grandchild in Iona's spare room, and what is still home to them isn't mine any more. It's half mine I guess, jointly in both of our names, but even assuming I could dislodge Philip, I don't think I want to live there on my own. But the summer holidays will be here in a few months. I need to find my own place before then, or he will have the twins by default.

Back to this note. I need to focus, try to figure out what is going on.

The facts: someone pushed a note into the letter box, then tapped on the door to make sure I found it. They also made sure that the video doorbell didn't record them doing so. Whoever they are, they know where I'm staying.

Not many people know where I am. How did they find me? And to come and do this in the middle of the night, too. If this was designed to scare me, it worked.

Who are they? Why are they doing this? Are they the same person who scratched my car? I don't know.

Are these things a stalker would do? Maybe. But I haven't noticed anyone following me around. Because of what happened to me years ago, I'm always alert, careful. Apart from the notes themselves, I've seen nothing.

None of the notes have been threatening per se. This one really just asked a question – but it *felt* threatening, mentioning my children like that. Put together with tapping on my door in the middle of the night, it was designed to upset me, scare me. Someone has been able to find me here at Iona's, out for dinner with Philip, and then, the first note, when I was just stopped at a random place for coffee. If they have been following me somehow without my notice, I've recently been to Flick's and to see James in Brighton. What if they followed me then? Do they know where my children are too?

Should I call Steve? He did say to call any time of day or

night. But it is just a note, and the children are all OK. I should leave it until the morning. Thinking of Steve reminds me that I've been handling this note when there might be evidence on it. I find a plastic bag in a drawer in the kitchen and slip it inside.

There is another problem to think about. Should I tell Philip about the notes? If there is any chance that whoever is leaving these notes might involve our children beyond just mentioning them, then I should. But I know Philip. He'll use it against me. Either he will downplay it and make me feel like an idiot for being rattled, or do the opposite, to make me even more terrified of being alone. Besides, I've got to learn not to run to him every time something scares me.

Oh my God. What if *Philip* left this note, to manipulate me into coming home? I feel sick to even think he'd go to those lengths, that he'd deliberately scare me. But that doesn't make sense. He wouldn't have written the other two, which had the opposite effect. And they look identical – they must be from the same person.

Unless being on his own a few days made him realise how much an unpaid, all-hours PA is worth.

I'm not likely to be able to sleep any more tonight. I'm tired, but it's as if my eyes have been forced open and won't close again any time soon. Might as well stay awake, keep an eye on the door – an ear out for tapping.

I make some tea, find the remote and turn on the TV. Take a blanket to the sofa. I'm just getting comfortable when a thump at the back door makes my heart race even though I logically know what it is – the cat flap. Ginger Biscuit comes in, gives me a look as if surprised to find me up this time of night. Jumps up next to me.

Eventually I doze off, disturbed by dreams of tapping noises, notes, and me, running in panic, being chased or chasing –

perhaps both. I don't know. And an image of Lachlan, red-faced and crying and needing me, but no matter how I try, I can't reach him.

* * *

Bleary-eyed, I stretch. Back sore from sleeping on a too-short sofa; head sore from red wine, worry and not enough sleep. I get up, fill the kettle. Ginger Biscuit is glaring at me from next to his empty bowl and I fill it. Sunshine beams in through the edges of the blinds and I open them. A beautiful morning, but the fear from last night is casting an uneasy shadow. I make tea. Once I've reached a decent level of caffeination, I realise what I should have by now. If anyone stuck a leaf over Iona's video doorbell before tapping and leaving the note, it should have recorded who it was.

I message Iona.

> Can you check the video doorbell recordings?

> Why? Is something wrong?

I don't want to worry her with all the rest while she's away, so I'll limit this.

> It's just I noticed there was a leaf stuck over the camera.

> It was probably lodged there by the wind, but I'll check. Something must do first so give me a moment.

I make tea while I wait. I know she'll check it properly, and I'm jumpy, nervous at what she might find.

My phone pings.

> I couldn't see anyone there sticking a leaf on the camera. It was just suddenly there.

> Does that make sense?

> Yes. It only takes an image every so often until movement triggers a recording. So, if a leaf blew in from the side, that could be what happened.

A pause.

> Get the app and check it yourself if you like. I'll message you the password. Are you OK?

> Yes. I promise.

> If you want to go stay with your mum or somewhere else, GB is fine on his own overnight.

> I'll be fine. Thank you.

And I do actually mean it. Being able to check the front door camera will help. I *will* be fine.

I download the app and enter the password when she sends it, then work out how to go back through the recordings. I see my comings and goings, Steve's as well. A few times people walk past on the pavement and their movements are recorded. Much later, the view is suddenly cut off – covered by the leaf. No one coming or going. But someone was there, tapping on the door. Putting the note through the letter box. And I don't accept they were just lucky enough that a leaf covered up what they did. I go outside with the app on, go as far to the side as I can. Wait until the recording I triggered ends. I reach from the side, put my hand over the camera. The view disappears but there is no recording of me doing this.

So: if someone came through the gate as usual, the camera

would have been triggered. If they came from the side, maybe not. They could have gone into the neighbour's front garden, clambered over and put a leaf on the camera.

So now I know *how* it was done. A way to find out who, though, eludes me. Though if Steve can find fingerprints on the latest or past notes, that might be the answer.

I call him. It rings once, twice.

'Hello, Lucy,' Steve says. I feel easier just to hear his voice. 'I'm hoping you're calling because you're missing me.'

'Well, of course. But also, because I got another note.'

'Tell me.'

I explain about the tapping on the door, the leaf over the video doorbell. That there is no recording that shows who it was. The note pushed through the letter box. *DO YOU KNOW WHERE YOUR CHILDREN ARE?* That I checked on them all late last night and everyone was fine.

'Someone was there late last night, tapping at your door? I don't like this.'

'I'm not crazy about it either.'

'You should have called me when it happened.'

'Once I found the note, the tapping stopped. I think they just wanted me to find it.'

'I'll come get the note, add it to the others for fingerprinting.'

'Thank you, Steve. I did touch it when I first found it, but then put it in a plastic bag.'

'Perfect. I'll come around this afternoon.'

'I'll be out soon. I'm meeting Flick and Jessie for lunch.'

'How about tonight, then. I'll bring takeaway – pizza? About seven.'

'Sounds good. Thank you.'

After we say our goodbyes, I sit a while, still holding my phone. That note in his voice – when he said he hoped I was calling because I missed him. Was he flirting, or is it just that he is worried about me and that's his way of making things less fraught? I don't know. But I do know there are other things I should be thinking about just now.

He's coming over because he's helping me – that's it. Isn't it? What it most definitely is *not*, is a date.

17

FREJA

I'm so tired. After that dinner with Philip last night and all the memories it stirred up, I barely slept, and not just because of the shouting in the flat above and on the street, the sirens that followed. Have I wrecked things with him – the way I was? He's not seen me be anything but what he wants me to be before now. It was right to say no to having sex in his car; I need him to see me as more than that. But the way I was afterwards – upset, withdrawn – I don't know how he'll take it. But I can't change what is done.

I try to put it out of my mind. There is something I need to do today.

There is a very upmarket florist I love near work. The kind of place where you can choose each flower with care to make a beautiful bespoke selection, not one of the sad already made-up bunches from a services or supermarket. I'll go there first, and then face this day.

18

JESSIE

'Auntie Jess! Auntie Jess!' A comedy voice pulls me towards wakefulness. Unless Lachlan learned to talk overnight, it must be Flick. I open one eye and soon regret it as she deposits Lachlan on me while she goes for a shower. In her defence, she did bring a cup of tea, too. He's in happy mode, grinning and gurgling. Eyes wide open. Once the tea is gone, I scoop him up and wander into the front room, to the play mat on the floor. Lay him down and he's grabbing at dangling baby-type toys and giggling. Wish I was so easily entertained. I tickle him and he smiles up at me, grabs my finger and tries to put it in his mouth.

'If I didn't see it with my own eyes, I wouldn't believe it.' I glance up at Flick in the doorway, wet hair and a dressing gown. 'I couldn't get you closer than halfway across the room when he was born.'

'He's all right for a baby. I suppose.'

'Breakfast – then shopping. You promised, remember? I want to go to Westfield.' I mime cutting my throat and collapse on the floor. 'Then lunch with Mum.' She toes me to make sure I'm still alive.

I sit up. 'Oh yeah, Mum,' I say, glad Flick has agreed. 'Want me to call her?'

'Already sorted. I messaged this morning and she's going to meet us there.' She sits next to me, reaches for Lachlan. 'Something a bit weird happened last night. Mum called in the middle of the night. She said she had a dream and had to check we were all right.'

'She called? I thought I dreamt that.' I look at my phone, and there are the missed calls and messages afterwards.

A dream, she told Flick. Could she really be that freaked over a dream that she had to call us at the time and not wait for morning?

I'm uneasy, and not just because of the moment of insanity when I agreed to go shopping. Aren't I supposed to be the irresponsible teenager? It feels like Flick and Mum really need me. I'm not used to things being this way around.

We head out after breakfast. I soon see why Flick needed someone along to go shopping. All the stuff for Lachlan and Lachlan himself in a buggy is a lot to manage; even with both of us, getting on and off a bus and then two trains is a challenge. We arrive at the centre for consumerism of Flick's choice, and I settle into my role. Push the baby around. Thumbs up or down at whatever Flick tries on – not that she pays any attention to what I think, despite the fashion icon that I am. Stuff parcels in the basket underneath and glare at any shop assistants who think I might need help or who want to fuss Lachlan. He's about as excited about shopping as I am and is soon sound asleep.

Mum messages to ask where we are as Flick gathers more dresses. She is back in the changing room when Mum finds us.

She smiles to see me, but looks tired – pale, dark under her eyes.

'Hi,' she says. 'Didn't know you were coming this weekend.' A chiding hidden under the words that I should have reported in.

'Yet here I am.'

'Well, it's good to see you now.'

I remind myself of my personally appointed role of peacemaker. 'Sorry I didn't answer you the other day. I was kind of in shock.'

'It's OK.'

She's bending over sleeping Lachlan now, literally cooing, when Flick emerges and goes to the three-way mirrors. She has another dress on that, unless I'm mistaken, is the same as the last one but in blue instead of red. I give a weary thumbs up.

'That's a lovely colour on you,' Mum says, and Flick turns and sees her now.

'Oh. Hi.' Awkward, much?

'Thanks for suggesting lunch,' Mum says.

'It was Jessie's idea.' She disappears back into the change rooms. Mum sighs.

They need some time on their own, or so I tell myself. Maybe it's more that I need to get out of this shop before I scream. Or even, both.

'Can you take over?' I gesture at Lachlan. 'Want to go check out the bookshop.'

'Of course. Go.'

19

LOU

Everything will be fine, I tell myself and Lachlan. We'll have a lovely lunch, and I'll apologise again for lying to Flick and handling things poorly, and try to make both of them understand – that whatever happens between me and their father, I'll always be there for them. That we can find new ways to make our family work.

Lachlan is stirring and I itch to pick him up, to hold him. Instead, I wheel him around the shop in case the movement soothes him back to sleep, so Flick can have some more peace. He soon settles. I spot a jumpsuit that would be so cute on Flick. Look through for her size but it's not there. There are some on a display and I check that – find one folded underneath. Perfect. I gather it up and turn back and – the buggy. Lachlan. Where are they? I look all around, disorientated, as if I thought I went left instead of right, but no matter which way I look, he's not there.

Confusion then fear rush in my gut. He was just here, behind me – I know he was. I rush up and down each aisle of the shop. An assistant spots me.

'Is something wrong?'

'My grandson – in his buggy. He's gone.'

Her eyes widen. The manager starts to call security and the assistant to check through the shop.

This *can't* be happening. Maybe Flick has him. I rush to the change rooms just as she steps out.

'Have you got Lachlan?'

'What? No. Where is he?'

'I turned around and he was gone.' Her eyes are on mine. Disbelief, then fear, and anger, too, and it is my fault – my fault – if anything happens to him. My dream last night, of Lachlan crying and not being able to get to him. And now he's missing?

'He's here,' a voice calls out – the shop assistant. We rush across. The buggy is just where I left it, around the other side of a display. But it wasn't there when I looked before—

Flick gathers him up in her arms, holds him close. She is crying and he starts to cry, too, a hungry baby wail that I am so glad to hear.

A security guard is here now. 'Ah. The missing baby, I take it?' He's on a radio, passing along that he has been found. Jess steps in now, looks around.

'What's going on?'

'Mum forgot where she left Lachlan. Someone could have taken him for real when you left him alone!' Flick spits out the words, furious.

'I didn't – I turned to look at something, and then he was gone. Someone must have taken the buggy with him in it and then put it back.'

The security guard is exchanging a look with the shop assistant, one that says they don't believe me.

'Maybe someone took him and lost their nerve,' I say.

'And put him back where you left him?' Flick says. 'They'd be more likely to be caught doing that – why wouldn't they just have left him wherever he was when they changed their mind?'

'I know what happened. I'm not making this up.' I turn to the security guard. 'You need to do something – find who did it in case they do it again!'

'Mum! Drop it,' Flick says, jiggling Lachlan up and down, trying to soothe him. 'Thanks for your help. We're fine now.' The security guard and shop assistant go, leave us.

Jessie clears her throat. 'Don't know about you two, but I'm hungry. I think Lachlan is, too. Lunch?'

20

JESSIE

So, this Jess-the-peacemaker effort isn't going as well as I'd like. Flick is angry and Mum is still insisting someone took Lachlan. Flick doesn't believe her, and OK, while Mum does look tired it seems unlikely that she could actually have forgotten where she left him. It doesn't make sense.

I half drag them to Zizzi's, the restaurant we booked, not sure if keeping them together to sort things out will make it all better or worse. But I wasn't lying when I said I was hungry. Flick is sorting her clothes to feed Lachlan, who is wailing even louder and waving his fists. Instant peace descends when he starts to feed. We're tucked away in a corner, but it is still a weird public activity in my view. Weird just generally, being a walking feeding station, but he can't cry and eat at the same time, so that is a plus. And with the reduced decibels Flick is looking calmer, too.

'Mum, you've got to stop being so overprotective,' Flick says. 'You're always imagining threats.'

Mum shakes her head. 'It happened, just like I said. I didn't make a mistake.'

Flick raises an eyebrow. 'It doesn't make sense that someone took the buggy and then put it back where they found it a minute later. Why would anybody do that?'

'Maybe it was like a sick practical joke,' I say.

'You haven't told Jess, have you?' Flick says.

Mum shakes her head.

'Told me what?'

'I think you should.'

I'm uneasy, getting the vibe that there is some Big Thing I don't know about, and it somehow relates to what happened today.

'You realise I'm now both worried and dying of curiosity?'

Mum turns to me, takes my hand across the table. 'Don't be worried. It's about some things that happened a long time ago.' She sighs, hesitates, looks around as if to make sure no one is near enough to hear whatever she is about to say. 'When I was a little younger than you are now, I'd just made the move from Juniors to the WTA tour – travelling and playing tennis. Singles, and doubles with Iona. I had what today you'd call a stalker. They always seemed to know where I was, how to upset me. I tried going to police in the UK and abroad, but no one believed it was anything more than an overzealous tennis fan. But it got worse. Notes left in places no one could figure out how anyone could access. And... I had enough. I quit the tour and came home.'

'Did they get whoever it was?' I say.

She shakes her head. 'He's still out there.' Her voice is quiet.

'Do you know for sure that it was a man?' Flick rolls her eyes at my automatic question – the way people assume whether someone is male or female based on their actions or who they are attracted to drives me up the wall.

'I suppose not,' Mum says.

I knew about Mum's tennis, of course I did. It is mentioned

now and then by people; I've seen photos, trophies. I know she and Auntie Iona won the doubles at Wimbledon, so they were right up there. But it never occurred to me to ask when or why it ended. Thinking about it now, she seemed to change the subject whenever her tennis came up. Maybe this is why. To think someone did that to her when she was younger than me – scared her so badly that she gave up something she was so good at, must have loved? There is a core of anger in all the disbelief and shock inside of me.

'And that's why Mum has always been so overprotective,' Flick says. 'She was always scared someone would hurt us or take one of us. And why she freaked when she lost sight of Lachlan for a moment. She told me a few years ago. She'd called the police when I was late getting home one night. And they were there when I got home. They were... funny with her. It was obvious they didn't believe anything she said. Dad got home before they left. He convinced her to tell me why. She has, you see, called the police many times. If one of us were late, if she thought she saw someone look at her or us the wrong way.' As she says that I'm remembering odd moments from our childhood that make more sense now. And also that when Dad was away, she'd always have a friend or her mum come and stay. She was never alone with us overnight.

Mum is shaking her head. 'I've learned over the years to assess things I see and hear more logically, with less fear. And I'm telling you – Lachlan was missing today. Briefly, but he was.'

'He's safe now,' Flick says. 'Let's order some lunch.'

FREJA

Not a day for being underground, I take the bus. I see the glances, assumptions. A beautiful woman, lovely flowers. Who gave them to her? Is she out on a date tonight? While I don't know what, if anything, I'll be doing tonight, they couldn't be more wrong about the flowers.

I get off the bus a stop early. It's a glorious day – sunny. Just like the day Mum died. Twenty years ago today.

I walk up the road to the cemetery gates. It feels wrong to be here when I'm not sure where things stand with my plans; I usually only come when I've got good news to share. But I couldn't miss the anniversary. I can update her another time.

I kneel in the grass next to her grave, arrange the flowers, each chosen for her in the reds and purples that she loved. A sharp prick in my thumb draws a few drops of blood – from thorns on the stem of a deep crimson rose. The flower – the blood. The colour of both. I'm swept back, to so many years ago. I don't try to fight it. I need the pain. It helps me focus on what I must do.

The house was quiet when I got home from school – no radio

or TV, no lights on. I wasn't immediately alarmed. Sometimes Mum was in bed when I got home – some days she stayed there all day, and that had been happening more and more often lately. I took the moment to raid the chocolate biscuits while she wasn't watching. Brushed the crumbs away and went upstairs to her room. But her bed – it was empty.

'Mum? Mum!' I called out, but there was no answer. I looked in my room. My bed was made, and she'd done the washing – school uniforms neatly folded on the end of it. These things meant it was a good day. But where was she?

By now I was getting scared. What if she went out and doesn't come back?

The bathroom door was ajar. In my memory it took forever to walk down the hall to the door, to push it open, but it couldn't have been as long as all that. Only a few steps. It's because I don't want to look through the door. See the razor blades. The full bath, still running. Starting to drip, drip, splashes of red on the floor. Mum's eyes, open, staring.

I was only eight years old. I didn't know people had so much blood inside of them.

I was sick, again and again. I could never stand the taste of chocolate after that.

Mum and me – both of us: we were collateral damage. No one meant to hurt us, but they did. Mum never recovered from Dad's murder. It may have taken her two years to kill herself, but she was dead long before that. Then I went into foster care, but the word *care* didn't belong to what happened to me there.

I was a fast learner, and not just at school. I learned to protect myself. To carry a knife. Sleep with it under my pillow. Early lessons never forgotten, even now, though I upgraded the knife years ago.

Maybe I'm much the same as Mum was now – dead inside.

But there is something that keeps me going. A goal. My plans. If I keep my eyes open, opportunities will present. Like they did today.

If Philip doesn't want me around any more, there are other ways to get what I want.

When we get to Flick's she's going through her bag but can't find her keys. Mum has a spare, opens the door.

'Your bag was on the buggy handles. Could the person who took Lachlan have taken your keys?' Mum says, her voice sharp with fear. 'Maybe they realised they couldn't get him out of the mall with all the CCTV but are going to try again.'

Flick dumps the contents of her bag on the table to make sure she didn't miss them. No keys.

'You're sure you had them when you left?' Mum says.

'I must have. The dead bolt was locked just now – I couldn't have done that without my keys.'

Mum is worried; Flick and I exchange a glance. 'What if she's right?' I say.

Mum, phone out, calls Westfield. Asks to speak to someone in security. Identifies herself from earlier, says Flick's keys are missing and she's worried they were stolen when someone had the buggy, and – she stops abruptly. 'I'm on hold,' she says.

Flick puts the kettle on. Mum is getting more and more impatient.

'Hello? Oh. Hang on.' She passes her phone to Flick. 'They've found some keys – want a description.'

'Hi. There were four – no, five – keys on a double ring. A London bus charm, one of an angel with a baby photo. Exactly, thank you. Hang on a sec.' She turns to Mum. 'They're mine. Can you pick them up?'

'Of course,' she says.

'My mum will collect them. Yes. Her name is Lou Kingsley. Thanks very much. Bye.'

'See? Nothing to worry about,' Flick says.

'Were our house keys on your ring?' Mum says.

Flick opens a kitchen drawer, shows her a bunch of keys. 'They're separate. See?'

We have a cup of tea. At least Flick and Mum are talking again, but it feels weird, like the world has gone upside down. Like they've swapped roles, and I can't stop thinking about what Mum told me. To leave her tennis career behind like that, she must have been terrified. Would just finding notes be enough to do that? Maybe there is more to the story, something she won't tell us.

A bit later Mum is cuddling Lachlan while Flick sorts some washing. I'm on the periphery, picking up my things, my laptop. Putting my boots back on.

Mum notices. 'Do you have to go?'

'I've got an early class tomorrow morning.'

'I'll drive you to the station.'

'No – stay with Flick. It's not far.'

Before she can comment or say anything else, I'm out the door. Running down the street. Needing space. Realising after I've left that the thing we were meant to be talking about – the situation between Mum and Dad – wasn't addressed. I'm hoping Flick and Mum can sort things out between them.

I shouldn't be running away when they both need me. But I felt like I couldn't breathe in the same room as them any more, that I needed time on my own to think. And the more I do, the more certain I become that there was some part of the story that Mum wasn't telling, that there was some other reason why she quit – that she is unable to talk or even think about without shaking. I'm not sure I want to know what it is.

There is only one person I need to be with right now. I call James once I'm on the train to Brighton, but he doesn't answer.

23

LOU

Lachlan is in his cot, cheeks flushed in sleep when I go to say goodbye. I gently kiss his forehead, then watch the rise and fall of his chest with each precious breath. Before he was found, my mind came up with the worst imaginable things that could have happened to him in an instant. He's so small, so fragile. To even think that someone might hurt him – I understand how murder can happen. I'd have done anything to get him back safe. And then going from the fear and panic to the relief when he was found a moment later, unharmed? The flood of emotion, fear then joy, almost unhinged me. And telling Jessie about the past – did she really need to know? If I hadn't told her, Flick probably would have done so. I felt cornered – much like I did when Philip insisted I tell Flick a few years ago. It's not something I can easily talk about. Even thinking about it makes a panic attack threaten. Jessie hearing that, about her mum, and a stalker – it feels like I've taken some of her innocence away, knowing things like that happen not just to other people, but in her own family.

Nobody believed me today about Lachlan. Were they right? Could I just have got confused about where he was? I am sleep-deprived, which is never good for clear thinking, but I can't believe I got things so wrong. If no one believes me, it's up to me to work things out. I have to focus, to think everything through.

What are the possibilities?

We were in a clothing store. Maybe someone innocently moved the buggy because it was in the way of something on the display next to it that they wanted to look at. But no one was there when I noticed the buggy was gone, and surely they'd have moved it back again when they were done.

Next up, perhaps a random stranger spotted my inattentiveness, and either thought it would be funny to scare me by moving it away for a moment, or decided to take him and then thought better of it. Though as Flick said, if that were true it seems unlikely they'd put him back where they found him – they'd be more likely to be caught than if they just left him wherever he was when they changed their mind.

The final possibility is the one that scares me most of all – that someone targeting our family took Lachlan. If so, the danger may not have passed. Maybe they realised that with all the CCTV cameras in the mall they'd never be able to leave with Lachlan without being recorded and identified, but they might try again somewhere else. And what if they took Flick's keys, copied them and then left them where they would be found afterwards? Then they're not safe.

As to who it could be, one perhaps obvious option is Lachlan's father, Andy. But given how little he wants to have to do with his son, it seems unlikely at best. Who else?

Someone who wants to hurt Flick, Philip, or me. Flick gets on with everyone, with the occasional exception of me. I'd ask her if there is anyone she can think of who would mean harm to her or Lachlan, but I could imagine her reaction if I raised it. It hurts that she doesn't believe me. As far as Philip goes, as a barrister, it's probably fair to say that anger is directed at him regularly by clients of opposing counsel when he wins. He deals with big commercial cases mostly so it is more about money than depriving someone of their freedom, but huge sums can be involved.

But it's hard to imagine someone taking Lachlan because of losing some complicated commercial case Philip was involved in. Greed can be a motivation, of course. It can lead to crimes of theft; murder, too, if the prize is big enough and someone is in the way. But this feels more *personal* than that.

And then there is me. There is the recent sender of notes and scratcher of cars – could they have escalated up to stealing my grandson? If so, they must have been watching me or my children, waiting for an opportunity.

Who would do such a thing? There are two options: either it is someone new, messing with my life. Or *he's* back.

If so, I had no idea who he was then, and I still don't. It has been over twenty-five years since the last note he left me. Perhaps his fixation was on me as a tennis player, because it all stopped when I quit tennis. Given that so much time has passed, I can't see what would have brought him back now.

Whoever took Lachlan today, the thought that someone might have deliberately put my grandchild in danger – my rage is stronger than any fear now. I won't sit back and wait for something even worse to happen to any of us. I *will* find out who they are.

As far as any enemies of Philip, there'd be no point in asking him or involving the police, because barrister–client privilege would prevent Philip from discussing case details. I worked as his PA for years; as such, I didn't have access to his case files. But I'm friends with his senior clerk, Janice. She always liked a drink and gossiped more than she should about clients, so I could try her.

As far as the current writer of notes, Steve already said he'd take the last note, check it for fingerprints. Maybe he can check it for DNA, too – maybe whoever wrote the notes is already known to the police and can be found from DNA or fingerprints.

I'll ask Steve. And I can tell him what happened today, ask him if there is anything else we can do. Even though I don't want everyone knowing our business, I'd go directly to the police if I thought it would do any good. People knowing Philip was having an affair isn't important in comparison to any threat to my grandson or children. But I know Steve will listen to me and help if he can; the police are unlikely to take it seriously if I approach them officially. Flick is right – there hasn't been anything recently, but they must have records of me going back, making complaint after complaint.

There is one thing I can't understand, though. Despite the notes and the scratch on my car, it's hard to imagine that there has been someone following me around. Given events when I was a teenager, I'm vigilant. I notice people looking at me or being in the wrong place. Like Flick said, I see threat when there is none, and I've seen nothing recently until the notes began to appear.

Think. If it isn't my stalker from years ago, then who could it be?

The first note sent me home a few days ago. I flinch but make myself go back to what I heard, saw. The look in the eyes of that woman in bed with my husband – staring back calmly – assessing, judging. The second note said I'd regret it if I went back to him. So, one note caused our separation, and the second sought to reinforce it. Who does that benefit? Only one person I can think of. Perhaps she isn't content with adultery and wants to have Philip all to herself. Maybe she saw my car and was angry I was there, damaged it out of spite. But as far as today goes, I can't see a reason why she would have briefly taken Lachlan.

I still feel like I recognised her but can't work out *why*. It feels like an old memory, but she's too young for me to have known her long ago, unless as a child. Philip obviously knows who she is, not that he'll necessarily tell me or believe it has any bearing on what happened to Lachlan. Not that I can tell Philip about that. He'd be like Flick: not believe a word of it, and undermine my efforts.

There is only one way to find this woman, and work out if she is the threat. I have to be close to Philip. This will also make it easier to go to his chambers and see what I can glean from Janice. There is no other way.

After I collect Flick's keys from Westfield, I call Philip's number. It goes to message. What to say...

'Hi, Philip. Can we talk? Please call.'

I'm meeting Steve at Iona's – I'll head there now, before I take Flick's keys to her. As I drive, my mind is still turning things over, unable to stop my thoughts going where I don't want them to go. What if recent events have nothing to do with that woman or Philip's work? It doesn't matter that logic tells me my stalker from so long ago reappearing is the least likely answer: that is what is really stopping me sleeping at night.

I spent so many years deliberately excising that time from my thoughts, leaving it behind, but I can't do that any more. I have to remember every detail and see if there is something that was missed back then that will lead to discovering their identity.

Where – and when – do I start? When the police were looking into things years ago, they started at the first note. Maybe that was wrong. Maybe I need to go further back to find him. I really only hit the public eye enough to attract that kind of attention when my tennis career started taking off.

It all begun with my first year at Bisham Abbey, the top British centre for junior tennis at the time. It was such an exciting time, being selected as one of the very best tennis players of my age to train there. I was fourteen. We lived there, went to school in the morning and trained afternoons and weekends. Iona, a year older, was the golden girl that everyone wanted to be or to beat. We didn't know it yet, but we needed each other.

Who was I then, before so many things went wrong?

It's hard to remember back so far. I've avoided thinking about it because of what followed, but I do know that I always loved training. When the ball going out didn't mean the match was over, the fear was gone. The focused effort, the perfect winner on the line – not a fluke. I could do it again and again. The euphoria that came with the endorphins from pushing myself as far as I could go.

But the joy didn't last.

24

LUCY

When the last whistle says we're done with drills for the afternoon, most of the girls look ready to collapse. I'm disappointed. It doesn't matter that I'm tired, sweaty kit stuck to my skin – I'm buzzing. I could go on and on.

'Lucy! And Iona. I need a word with both of you.'

I glance at Iona, uncertain why Coach would want to keep us back together. She's one of the posh girls, golden and not just in hair colour – all the right clothes and kit, comes from a top private club. I'm inches shorter, boring brown hair and barely held together by last year's end-of-season bargains. It's my first term at Bisham Abbey; Iona was here last year. We've never really spoken. I've seen her play. She's one of the ones everyone says will make it. She's had junior wins, wildcards up; she's won qualifiers, even a main draw match at Nottingham. She gives me an evil look; the last winner I hit was to her. I'm getting used to all the petty behind-the-scenes bitchery from other players when I best them. I smile in return.

Coach must catch this. 'Ah good, friends already, I see. I have a problem with both of you, and it's been discussed. I believe we have the perfect solution.'

'What sort of problem?' Iona says.

'You are opposites, yet both could make it as pros – you each need something the other already has. I want you to share skills.'

Iona's eyes are wide with outrage as she glares at me and then Coach.

'Try to listen for a change,' she says to Iona, who crosses her arms, raises an eyebrow. I'm just baffled.

'Iona, you have competition in your blood. You fight and fight and somehow find a way to beat players who are better than you. Lucy, the way you train and practise has you both fitter and technically a far better player than Iona.' She holds up a hand to Iona to keep her quiet. 'In training you wipe the floor with all of the other players, but as soon as we put you in a match situation, it doesn't happen.' I'm both shocked and warmed by the praise, despite the criticism that followed, but Iona's hands are on each hip. I think her nostrils are actually flaring.

'Our solution is this,' Coach says. 'You will play doubles together. Learn from each other.'

'But I'm a much better singles player—' Iona sputters.

'I'm giving you an opportunity to grow as a player. To lift your game to another level. That will translate to singles.'

'Is this a suggestion or an order?' Iona says.

'I don't make orders. But along with not giving training your full efforts, failure to follow a reasonable suggestion would be noted.'

A grant from the LTA is funding none of us can do without, even Iona. And our places here, at the top training school in the UK? She won't dare argue.

When I get into the change rooms later, Iona is there, her back to me. Talking to a friend.

'I can't believe she's making me play with Lucy the Loser.' She holds her hand in an L on her forehead. Her friend sees me and her eyes widen. Iona turns.

I'm not backing down. Hearing Coach say that I'm a better player, even if winning eludes me? It's given me confidence I didn't have before. 'I'm not too thrilled about this, either. But you heard Coach – I'm a better player than you. Maybe you'll learn something.'

'That's not quite what she said—'

I raise an eyebrow. 'You heard her.'

'Whatever.' She turns to her kit bag.

* * *

In training the next weeks, Iona is more committed than she has been. In the gym, whatever weight I use, she goes one higher. Let her injure herself, I don't care. On the practice courts she is more focused, too. Maybe she thinks if she redeems herself there she'll be rid of me? But on the last day of term, there is a doubles tournament. Single set matches. Losers play losers, winners play winners. And her good behaviour goes unrewarded – we are told to play together.

'I don't like to lose,' Iona says. 'Try not to rub off on me.'

Her face when my first serve doesn't clear the net – so scathing. She shakes her head, dismissing me with a glance and a flick of her blonde ponytail, and it does something inside of me – flicks a switch. Lights a fuse to red-hot. All the put-downs and catty remarks of the last days and weeks from her and others like her, which I've ignored or even smiled at because at least they noticed me enough to bother? That's it. *Enough.* I'll wipe that smirk off her face and I'll do it *now*.

I throw the ball up high for my second serve – it's a little too forward. Catch it. Calm myself, breathe, bounce it a few times. Throw it up again. I swing and throw my weight into the hit and follow through. It's sound. Unreturnable. An ace. A glance to Iona – she's surprised.

Every return, every volley, serving again, too – I'm buzzing like I do in training. My body and racket are one. Each time I hit the ball it does what I want, goes where I direct it to go. We win 6–4, then follow that up with a 6–2 win in our second match.

Our third opponents are more of a challenge. We all hold serve and get to 6–6. We win the tiebreak after I hit a killer return.

'You *can* play,' Iona says, a bit grudgingly, maybe.

One more match – us against the only other undefeated team. All the other players and staff are watching when we begin. It's end of term, so parents are arriving to take us home for the weekend; some of them have come to watch. I search the faces – my mum isn't one of them.

I make a few errors and lose my serve. We're down 3 games to 5. We dig in and break back to make it 4 to 5. I'm struggling to find how I was playing before and it's not fatigue, it's something else. Iona is serving. She is overly aggressive, double faults at the crucial moment. We lose, 4–6.

We're shaking hands over the net. Iona, distracted, looks to the spectators. A woman there is so like her, must be her mum. She doesn't look happy, scowling and shaking her head.

We head to the change rooms together.

'Well played,' I say.

Iona gives me an incredulous look, slams her kit bag down on the floor. 'We *lost*.' I shrug. 'That is why you're not winning matches at tournaments. You don't care!'

'That's not true! Besides, *you* lost the last game when you double faulted.'

'I did,' she says, through gritted teeth. 'But if you hadn't had your serve broken, we could have won.'

'So, it's my fault?'

'I'm not saying that. I'm saying there were points you should have won. You came over all nervous again. Why?'

And I don't know what to say. It's true.

'You're both right.' Coach has come in, unnoticed; she must have heard what we said. 'You did play well together. Lucy, being nervous took the two of you down a break. Iona, being down a break made you play wildly, with too much aggression, which dropped your accuracy below what it should be.'

We exchange a glance, Iona and me, and I think I get it. Why Coach wants us to play together. Does Iona, or is she so convinced she can never be wrong that she can't see it for what it is? I don't know.

We head out.

Mum waited in her car. She's frowning, looking at the time. 'You're late,' she says.

'There was a tournament today – doubles. I was in the final. You could have come and watched.'

She's closing her laptop, puts it aside and starts the car. 'I had work to do to pay for all this.'

I don't bother to point out that LTA sponsors cover my place here; I know my parents have made sacrifices to get me to this point. Even with funding I'll need their help to progress, to go on tour.

'Aren't you going to ask if we won?' I ask.

'OK, then. Did you win?'

'No.'

We pull past Iona and her mum, standing by a car. Iona is looking down, body slumped. Her mother facing her, face like thunder – much like Iona's when Coach first said we should play together. They get into the car and Iona's mum slams the car door shut.

25

FREJA

'You're looking beautiful as always,' Philip says. He takes my hands. A warm kiss and then he pulls my chair out for me to sit down. He'd waved away the maître d' who showed me in, leaving us alone.

'Thank you.' I hesitate, uncertain still how to play things after last night. I'd been so relieved when he called, asked me to meet him here, at one of our favourite London restaurants. It has a number of small private dining rooms like this one, which he says is so we can be alone. I know it is more for him to avoid being recognised, seen with me, but I was so relieved when he called that I didn't point out that he shouldn't be worrying about that any more. 'About last night—'

'Let me go first. You were right. I was out of line with the car caper. Though it would have been... amazing,' he says, his eyes on my lips and then back to my eyes.

'Do you have... an alternative in mind?'

'Well, yes. I've checked into a suite at Blakes. We could even go straight there, unless you're hungry?'

I raise an eyebrow. 'I am, a little.'

'Damn.'

'Though couldn't we go to yours? And maybe even through the front door.'

'This is an apology, so you get the full luxury treatment.'

Hmmm. He is saying some of the right things, but he still doesn't want us to be seen in public or me to be seen at his home. There is work to be done there still. But I'm mostly relieved. I really didn't know how he was going to take being turned down like I did last night, but things seem to be back on course.

A waiter appears with wine Philip must have already ordered. He pours a taste. Philip defers to me.

'Sensational,' I say. I wasn't lying – I am more than a little hungry. An empty stomach has the wine going straight to my head, warmth in my veins as his foot against mine under the table and a hand on my knee helps it spread in my body.

We order. He glances at his phone; a perplexed look crosses his face. 'Sorry, I need to make a call.' He gets up without another word, goes through the door.

I have another sip of wine. Judging by his face as he walks back into our dining room a few minutes later, it looks like dinner and the hotel suite will need to wait.

'Something's wrong. What is it?'

'Family stuff – with my daughter,' he says. 'I'm going to have to go. Have dinner – it's taken care of.' He gives me a key card, the hotel suite number.

'You'll come later?'

'If I can. I'm sorry.' A quick kiss on the lips and he's gone.

I hold up my wine glass, a silent toast to my mother. A promise to her that her daughter will succeed where she failed. For now, beginning with three courses and this lovely wine.

Followed by a long soak in the no doubt huge bath of the posh suite.

I'd rather he'd stayed, either that the summons never came or that he decided to ignore it and stay with me, instead. But still – this dinner, the suite – they tell me we are back on track.

Not such a bad day, after all.

26

LOU

Steve is already here, pulled in front of Iona's when I arrive. He gets out of his car as I park, pizza boxes in his hands.

'I'm so sorry I'm late. Long story.'

'I just got here; they're still hot.' I unlock the door, and he follows me in. Ginger Biscuit is sprawled on the sofa. He stretches and sits up, miaows imperiously with a narrow-eyed look that says dinner is late.

'That's me told.'

Steve follows me into the kitchen. I tell him where to finds plates and so on while I get the cat food sorted.

'I've brought some wine also; you look like you could use a glass. Tough day?'

'You could say that. But I can't have any wine, I've got to drive back to Flick's.'

'Shame,' he says, with a smile that says he had hoped for more than just pizza tonight. How it makes me feel is confusing. Philip called me back while I was driving. I said I'd meet him home later tonight. His voice, when I said it – he knows, or thinks he does, that he was right. That I can't live without him. But until I go back to him – I'm free. Aren't I?

I can't tell Steve; I need his help and don't know how he'd react. But it's true about going back to Flick's – I told her I'd bring her keys by tonight.

He's opening the wine. 'Half a glass then,' he says, and pours two glasses that are more like three-quarters full.

'Aren't the police supposed to be against drinking and driving?'

'Under the limit is OK.'

We set the table. 'Pizza looks good, but I'll confess I'm not that hungry. Had a big lunch out with Flick and Jessie.'

'How are they with all the changes?' My face must give me away. 'Not great, then.'

'It's not that. Something else happened.'

'Tell me.'

'Eat, first.' He accepts that. Tells a few tales from work that show that London's finest aren't always as fine as we'd like, and has me smiling, almost laughing. I pick at a few pieces of pizza while he has most of the rest, then he clears the table while I put things in the dishwasher. He holds out the bottle of wine and I hold my hand over my glass, shake my head.

'OK, out with it. What happened today?'

'We were at London Westfield. Flick was trying some stuff on; I had Lachlan. I was distracted for a moment and when I turned back, he was gone, buggy and all.'

I tell him all the details, how he was found a moment later where I'd last seen him, but he wasn't there before.

'You believe me, don't you?'

'I believe that is what you think happened,' he says, carefully. 'What would someone have wanted to achieve by doing that?'

'I don't know, other than upsetting all of us. But then there were Flick's missing keys.' I explain about how they were missing and then found.

'So that's why you're going to stay with her.' I don't set him straight.

'You must see why I'm worried. What if someone took her keys from her bag on the buggy, copied them and then left them where they'd be found? And then I thought, what if it is the same person leaving me notes? Hang on – I'll get the latest one.' I fetch it in its little plastic bag and pass it to him. 'Look – it's the same kind of paper, capital letters, red ink, as the other two. It mentions my children, and then the next day someone kidnaps my grandson? It can't be a coincidence!'

'Let's talk it through.' He gestures at the sofa. We sit down. 'I will get this note and the others checked for fingerprints tomorrow. But as far as the rest of it goes, if someone did briefly take Lachlan, it's unlikely to be the same person who wrote these notes. By far the most likely explanation is that it was just a random act – someone moved the buggy for some reason and then moved it back. It might even have been some kind of practical joke, and they never meant him any harm.'

'What if whoever it was does it again, and this time we don't get Lachlan back?'

He's considering my words, doesn't reject them out of hand. 'How about this. I'll mosey over to Westfield and see if there is any CCTV around that shop, see who was coming and going. Give me the details.'

I tell him what time we were there, the shop and what is around it.

'With the notes, my fingerprints would be on them. How do you know which prints to focus on?'

'Yours are in the system. We took them for elimination purposes for the notes you received years ago.'

'Can you check the note for DNA – and the handles of Lachlan's buggy?'

'His buggy that you've all been handling since then? Not much point. Anyhow, I'll be calling in favours to get fingerprints done. I can't slip in DNA tests without an official investigation.'

I absorb that. 'Does that mean we need something concrete to shift this into an official investigation?'

'Even then, resources and lab time are limited. DNA tests are expensive and are rationed to solve or prevent the worst level of crimes.'

And by then, it could be too late. But I know Steve is doing what he can. 'Thank you for believing me.'

He takes my hand. 'I'm doing this to put your mind at rest. What you went through all those years ago was horrific. It's left an impression. I understand that.'

Tears are threatening, but I blink them away. I refuse to cry. Whether he helps because he believes me or, as he said, to put my mind at rest – same result, and I'm grateful. And it *was* horrific. I was too terrified to ever travel on my own again. It ended my tennis career before it really started. Then I got pregnant and married Philip, and it was the perfect escape from all that came before. I needed him so I could feel safe. But having children meant there was more than just me to worry about, and it took me a while to stop seeing threats everywhere. It's long enough ago now that sometimes I can forget, days, weeks, months, at a time. But even talking about it as tangentially as we just did makes the darkness beckon.

I *refuse* to disintegrate. My family needs me.

I nod. 'You'll let me know if you find out anything at all?'

'Of course I will.' He's still holding my hand – his eyes on mine – and I know what is about to happen, and that I shouldn't let it. That he won't understand if – *when* – I end up back with

Philip, even if temporarily. It isn't fair. But his lips are on mine and my body reacts, pulls him closer. Down on the sofa on top of me and his hands are in my clothes and I'm pulling his jumper off over his head. He pulls away a moment, his eyes on me as he takes off his jeans. All at once he's inside me, my fingers are curling into his back, and we're moving together as if the years are gone, and we remember just how we fit together. This isn't making love, if it ever was with Steve – it's more primal than that.

After, what should be awkward, isn't. We get dressed. I pack a few bags – I'll get the rest of my things another time – and Steve helps me load them into my car, then gives me a kiss that makes me want to go back inside with him. He sends his best wishes to Flick and Lachlan.

I'm in my car, trying to pull myself together before I start the drive to Flick's when my phone beeps.

It's a message, from Iona.

> Ooh la la.

Ah. The video doorbell.

> Stop spying on me.

> Is that what I get for checking when the app beeped because I was concerned? Was that Steve?

> Yes and yes.

> Interesting development. I'll be home midday tomorrow btw, so no need to rush back to feed GB if you've got a better offer.

I pull onto the road, bemused. That *interesting development* was a bad idea for so many reasons, so why did it feel so good?

And now Iona knows, or guesses. She was always going to have trouble understanding me going back to Philip – now, even more so.

I drop the keys at Flick's. Convince her to keep the chain on the door at all times. And then drive home to Philip, going slower and slower until drivers behind me are getting annoyed and overtaking.

Time is moving too fast, swirling around me and mine.

I can't delay. It has to be tonight. I have no choice.

27

FREJA

I had all the courses for dinner, and a lovely long bath in the suite Philip booked. There were roses and champagne waiting on ice. I can't let that go to waste. I am on a second glass when Philip finally calls.

'Hello there,' I say.

'Hi.'

'So...'

'I can't make it tonight. I'm sorry.'

'Is your daughter all right?'

'Yes, she'll be fine. She needs us just now.'

Us?

A slip-up that I don't challenge. Instead, I murmur how much I miss him, his skin on mine. And we say our goodbyes.

Phone down, I throw my glass against the wall. It smashes, champagne dripping down on shards of glass.

* * *

A few hours later I'm wearing dark clothing, my hair covered. Outside Philip's house – trees across the road provide good cover that I've made use of before. It's chilly and I'm thinking of that comfy warm bed in the suite that I left behind, or even the one in my flat.

Philip's new car has been parked in the drive since I arrived. Nothing to see, nothing to report. I'm about to give up, leave the trees and walk down the road when another car approaches. I stay put.

It's *her*. His wife, Lou, in that red Jeep with the dents and scratches. And she's not just here to say hi or get more of her things – she is getting cases from the back seat. The front door opens. Philip walks over to her, wraps his arms around her. A kiss, not for long but it wasn't just a peck, either. No sign of the daughter who supposedly needed him, is there? He helps her carry her things in and the door closes. He is inside with his wife; everything and everybody else shut out, kept apart by walls, doors and locks.

I punch a tree so hard it hurts. I shake my hand after, knuckles bloody.

It looks like it's time for plan B.

28

LOU

I step over the threshold to the home I said I never wanted to return to. The trauma the last few times – with Iona to pack, and before that, seeing Philip in bed with *her* – is still fresh, yet its impact seems less than I thought it would be now. Was that the hidden reason for what happened between Steve and me, this evening? To reset the slate. You cheated; I cheated. Now that we are even, we can try again.

No. That's not why I'm here. I'm only here to find out what I need to know to keep my family safe, and then it's over.

Philip locks the door behind us. 'You'll never guess what I've been doing since we spoke earlier,' he says.

'Let me think. Counting your lucky stars? Making a list of your faults?' I look around and realise that downstairs is tidy, much more so than when I was here with Iona. 'Have you been *cleaning*, Philip?'

'Guilty as charged. Cleaner isn't here for a few more days. I did the hoovering and all.'

'Tell me you didn't just throw all the dirty dishes in the bin to avoid dealing with them.'

'Dishwasher is running. Plus, hand-washed what wouldn't fit.' He takes my hand, leads me to the sofa. We sit down. 'There are a few things I need to say.'

'I'm listening.'

'I didn't get it right when we had dinner the other night. I've done a lot of thinking since then. There isn't any doubt at all, Lulu. You are the only woman I've ever loved, that I want to live with for the rest of my life. The depth of my regret and pain at what I put you through – it will never happen again. *Nothing* is more important to me than you, and our children. Can you find it in your heart to forgive me – to move on? Can you do that?'

His words are the right ones, said with conviction, but how many times have I heard him speak just like this in court? Today, I am the judge and jury. He may even believe what he says, but I'm not sure I can.

Again, I remind myself why I'm here. But it wouldn't be believable if I agreed to just step straight into our lives as they were before.

'Words are cheap, Philip,' I say, finally. 'You have to prove they are true, day in and day out. Can you do that?'

'I swear it. I love you, Lulu.' He hesitates. 'Can I hold you?' The uncertainty, the words used – not assuming, said with longing – do more for his case than those before.

There is a feeling inside me, as if walls have broken. Releasing emotions I've been trying to hide, and not just from Philip. From me, too.

I move closer as does he until my head is nestled against his chest, his arms around me. He doesn't make another move; he's waiting for my lead.

My blood is quickening. Two sofas in one day? No.

I disentangle myself, step towards the stairs. Gesture for him to follow. Unsure how I'll feel when we get to our bedroom, but then there is another surprise. New bedspread and pillows on our bed. Does he think that will make the memory of what I saw go away? I hesitate on the threshold.

He gently draws me into our room and into his arms. No matter who or what he is now and the things that happened these last days, what he said before is true for me – he is the only one I've ever truly loved. The father of my children. The half-formed plan I'd had before I arrived, to find a way to tell him that I've changed my mind and want to try again, and doubting I could pull it off without him suspecting my motives – all melts away. He holds me and just now, in this moment, I feel loved. Safe. Where I am supposed to be. The place I first fled to all those years ago.

But is it sanctuary, or am I hiding from the things I can't face – was that why I married him in the first place?

I don't know.

29

LUCY

Iona truly is the new golden girl of UK tennis. By my second year at Bisham, she wins the national junior championships, but that isn't enough. She also pushes, cajoles and bullies me through the whole junior doubles tournament, all the way to the final, and we win that as well. I'm equal parts deliriously happy and terrified when we get a wildcard to the main draw doubles at Wimbledon. Iona is given a wildcard to the singles qualifiers as well.

The pressure, preparation and training is intense. I'm in awe of Iona aiming for both singles and doubles, glad I'm not. I play better when we play together.

Then one day, Coach calls us both off the training court. 'I've got some news. It's about Wimbledon.'

We exchange a glance.

'Tell us already!' Iona says.

Coach turns to me. 'Lucy, you've got a wildcard to singles qualifiers.'

My mouth is hanging open. I shake my head as if to shake sense into it. 'But I only made it through the first round of singles in junior nationals—'

'Doesn't matter. This is recognition of your potential, Lucy.'

'But—'

'You idiot – look happy! This is amazing!' Iona grabs my hands and spins me around and I can't help thinking that it's amazingly... terrifying. But the money even just in singles qualifiers, put together with the doubles main draw – it's what I need to keep playing. A grin is taking over my face. And the points for any wins will get me up the rankings, into more tournaments. Iona's right: this IS amazing!

'That's not all.' An even bigger smile. 'Iona – your wildcard in singles has been upgraded from qualifiers to main draw.'

* * *

We're celebrating together that night – Iona insisted. Mum and even Dad come to Iona's; he's visibly uncomfortable, looking around at their grand house. Mum is pretending not to be. It's in Wimbledon and conveniently very close to where we'll both be playing soon.

Iona's mum pours champagne for everyone, makes a fuss about having chosen it herself at a vineyard in France. She gives me half a glass, something my parents don't approve of even though I'm sixteen now. Thankfully they don't say anything, but I'll hear about it later.

She raises a toast. 'First, to Lucy for going to qualifying at Wimbledon.' Then she turns to Iona, beaming. 'And to Iona. I knew this day would come. Main draw! It's a first step through a door you were always meant to march through. You have to take this opportunity – grab it by the throat and show the world of tennis who you are!'

We all clink glasses. Bubbles tickle my nose, and I sneeze.

A bit later, Iona draws me up to her room.

'Sorry,' she says.

'What for?'

'For Mum. We've both got our foot through the door now – right?'

'I suppose.'

Now I'm actually thinking about what it'll mean. Playing at Wimbledon. Even in quallies. I can't fail; I need the money, the sponsors that could follow. Better kit and physio and coaching. Even with backing from the LTA, I won't be able to travel to enough tournaments to get the points to get into better-paying tournaments, to earn enough to keep going. All I want – all I have *ever* wanted – is to play tennis. Since my auntie gave me my first racket, age five, and took me to Halton, her tennis club, there was nothing else. Somehow I convinced Mum and Dad to help me continue after she moved to Canada a few years later, but I need to start earning my way to continue.

Iona can see through me. 'Don't you *dare* come over all nervous about this now.'

'I can't help it.'

'*I* can help it – and I'll get you through this. Plus, we've got doubles in mains! You and me, together.'

'Don't you ever get stressed by all the pressure?'

She shrugs. 'I do, but I'm a winner. I fight my way through it.' Words she believes and says with effortless confidence.

It must be easy to feel that way when you've always had everything. She can't imagine not getting where she wants to go. Neither can her mum. There is a path at her feet and she's rushing down it as fast as she can.

She's spinning me around, looking at me from all sides.

'I think I see the problem. You need to change who you are.'

'How?'

'Start by changing your name. You are no longer Lucy the

Loser – now you are half of Iona and Lulu! Together and apart, we are invincible!'

Now I'm grinning, seeing us through her eyes. 'We're a team.' We high-five. 'We are... team Lu-ona?'

'Or Ion-lu.' She makes a face. 'It doesn't roll off the tongue and sounds like a soft drink. Lu-ona it is! Everything is coming together for us – you'll see.'

* * *

'Iona's mum is a bit OTT, isn't she?' Mum says, in the car home. 'Just do your best, darling. That's all that matters.'

Best isn't good enough, not for Lu-ona. And not for Lulu, either. I want to win.

* * *

The name change – and being there with Iona – helps. Qualifiers in singles one, two, three: all victories. And not just that, I win them fairly easily. The adrenalin and effort combine to something magical, my body and mind in harmony in a way they've never been before. Nothing can stop me.

Next I'll be in the main draw, along with Iona and the best players in the world. Her drive and focus are infectious: we're both going to win and go all the way. But then our castle-in-the-air dream to reach the final together bursts when the first-round main draw is up: we have to play each other.

Much is made of two locals, best friends, competing against each other in their first grand slam main draw match. The media doesn't tire of staging photos of us, the things that are different – my dark hair and brown eyes, her blonde-streaked hair and hazel eyes; the things that are the same – ponytails, smiles. Iona had me practise it until I could smile on demand for the camera. Kit sponsors want us to be in the same kit, not that in Wimbledon white there'll be much difference either way. Mum and Dad are coming and even my auntie who gave me my first tennis racket is coming over from Canada.

But the more excited everyone gets, the worse I start to feel.

In the dressing room before our singles match, I feel physically sick. I'm leaning over, hyperventilating, when Iona comes in.

Her hand is on my back. 'It's all right, Lulu. It's just you and me going out there. Right?' She tells me I can do this, I can do it well, and I listen to her voice and start to feel a little better.

We're walked to court by security. It's an outer court but one of the bigger ones, and the seats are packed for two locals. I find the players' area – my parents. My auntie who started everything for me is with them is smiling, nodding – saying encouraging things I can't hear. There are so many people here, watching – so many eyes. I focus on Iona through the warm-up. It's a practice match, that's all, I tell myself. She wins the toss. Serves first. We both start a bit tentative and then get into our groove.

After the run of wins in quallies, I'm in the form of my life. I know her game inside and out. I capitalise on both. Play one point at a time. One game at a time. Iona wins a first set tiebreak. But she's tiring, I know this, and make her run from one side of the court to the other when I can in the second. I win my games more easily, but it is another tiebreak; this time, I win. It's one set all.

The third set begins. I've forgotten about the spectators, the photographers, everyone on the court around us. It's only me, Iona, the chair umpire. Win one point, another. One break, another.

I'm so focused on one point at a time that I'm almost startled when the chair umpire says, game set match, Lulu Cooper.

All around – applause. Iona is breathing heavily, leaning on her racket. I run over to her. Give her a hug and she hugs me back.

'Well done,' she says, and she smiles, but not with her eyes. She gathers her kit, ignores kids wanting signatures and leaves the court.

Then there is media work, on my own for a change. A sea of faces, questions.

'Congratulations, Lulu. How does it feel to both qualify and then win your first main draw match at a slam – at Wimbledon?'

The smile Iona had me practise is in place. 'It's amazing. I still can't believe it.'

'How does it feel to knock your best friend out of her first main draw match as well?'

'I wish it could have been anyone else,' I answer truthfully, then follow it with something I've heard Iona say, many times. 'But it's a competition and I play to win.'

This time, I know it is true. All the other stuff doesn't matter, the petty rivalries along the way, the doubts at home. This win is mine and no one else's.

30

LOU

'Good morning, Mrs Kingsley.' Half asleep, I open my eyes. Philip has a mug of tea in his hand – my favourite mug that the twins got me on a school trip to Italy a few years ago. He's dressed for work. He puts the mug on the bedside table.

'Thank you. But you should have woken me; I'd have made you breakfast.'

'Didn't want to disturb you. You looked out for the count.'

He sits next to me; a soft hand brushes hair from my eyes. I've slept well for the first time since – don't think about that now. He leans down to kiss me, and I put my hands around his face, pull him closer.

He pulls away. 'Stop that. I'm due in court.'

'Hmm. Shame.'

'Bye.'

I drink my tea slowly, bemused. Last night – it was incredible. Has it been a while since things have been like that between us? I think back, trying to remember, and can't. Is that what was missing, so he went looking for it elsewhere? Or maybe he's learned things from *her*.

Well. That thought has completely spoiled my mood.

I give myself a shake. Remind myself why I'm here. Last night was a good performance, to convince him that all is forgiven. That's all. I'm only here to identify any possible threats to my family.

I get up, head for the shower. Have some breakfast. Then it is time to get started.

First up, who is the woman I found in bed with Philip? I'll begin by looking for any clues to places they've been or things they've done, and see where that takes me.

I start with Philip's dressing table, then move on to the washing to check his pockets. I find numerous yet innocuous things that shouldn't go in the wash, like tissues, pens, one of his many spare pairs of reading glasses, sorting piles into washing and dry cleaning as I go. I'm looking for something, anything, I don't know what, that will lead me to *her*. He knows I do this so he's unlikely to leave anything incriminating in a pocket, but it's worth checking anyhow. Then I move on to check pockets of various coats and jackets he might have worn; even go to the garage, check his golf bag. Find a half-eaten, mouldy banana – ugh. Into the bin.

His study next. It's his domain and I rarely go in, other than to collect half-drunk cups of coffee and other mess. It's tidy now. Nothing much on the surface of his desk but a to-do basket of correspondence, bills. I flip through and find his mobile bill. I scan it and note any numbers I don't recognise. There isn't a pattern, though – as in, none of the numbers repeat regularly. If he was messaging her though, or calling from something like WhatsApp, which is encrypted, I could only look at that if I can get into his phone. His, like mine, operates on facial recognition. I don't know his password. He might have a second phone, hidden away. If so, it's more likely to be with him or at work, but I start checking behind books on the shelves, backs of drawers, when my phone pings with a message – from Philip.

For a moment I think he somehow knows what I'm doing, that he's going to demand an explanation – but how could he? My guilty conscience is making me feel that way. Anyhow, if we're going to grade sins, his are worse.

I open the message.

> Something is being delivered for you now. It's out front.

I head downstairs, open the front door.

'Mrs Kingsley?' A smiling man, a clipboard.

'Yes?'

He hands me a key fob and key card. Gestures to a car next to mine on the drive – a yellow Mini. Shiny and new, this year's plates.

'Sign here. Enjoy your new car.'

'Thank you.'

He's taking the old car away too. I fetch the keys for him, then watch it disappear up the road. Was my damaged car the last outward sign of the day I caught Philip and that woman in bed? Now it has been tidied away, erased.

Philip knows I love Minis, but with three kids and their gear to cart around it was impractical. Other than carting stuff to uni, that happens less and less often now, but still. I walk across, open the door, sit behind the wheel. It's got that new car smell and it's perfect.

Another message beeps on my phone.

> What do you think?

I don't even know. Is this on his list of ways to say sorry – is it a kind of bribe?

This gesture would have melted me a week ago. He's waiting for an answer, but I can't say anything about all of these conflicted feelings. I need to keep him onside.

I love it. Thank you.

You're very welcome.

I'm blinking back tears as I go back through our front door. I wander the house, looking for anything out of place; anything that may hold an answer. But there is nothing.

I make a shopping list. Grab the dry cleaning, my new key fob and head out.

31

FREJA

These things are so easy now. If social media and the rest had been more prevalent twenty years ago, maybe Mum would have sorted things out back then and I wouldn't have to do this now.

I search for Lou Kingsley to start. She's not very active on socials, but I find a fan page about her tennis days. Not in much current use but someone is bound to notice a new post. I use a spare profile, set up with an email made for this purpose, to post a comment on her fan page.

> Have you heard the latest about Lulu? Her scumbag husband has been cheating on her.

I add a photo of Philip for good measure – one he doesn't know I took. He's lying back in bed. Eyes half closed, naked, cropped just enough to stop it being taken down on decency grounds. To make it even better, it was taken in *their* bed. When he finds this post – and I'm sure he either will at some point or someone will show it to him – he'll have to think who took it: me, or his wife? And it'd be more likely to be her calling him out for cheating. I link the post on X and other platforms for good measure. That is bound to get back to both of them.

Next up: Jessie Kingsley. James Kingsley. I find their profiles, recent photos. Where they are both studying – Brighton – and what subjects. Going back further, I find Jessie with a girlfriend – perfect. She's likely either bi or gay. Philip never mentioned that, not that he talks about his children much to me. I go forward again to now. Pub photos, in Brighton. She's checked in to one particular pub many times, so that will be a good place to start.

I study her face. There is something about her, even just in photographs. A girl – an almost woman – who doesn't care how she looks, what anyone thinks. She is just resolutely herself.

She could be fun.

32

LOU

'Steve. Hi. Thanks for meeting me.' I'd called him after the dry cleaner's, hoping he might have news. Knowing I had to tell him about Philip and me and dreading it.

'No problem, I was about to call when you did.' A waitress comes over and we order coffee.

'If you were about to call, does that mean you've found something?'

'Afraid not. There are no fingerprints on the notes you gave me besides yours. Whoever it was must have been wearing gloves. And I've been to Westfield and had a look at the CCTV. There might be movement that backs up what you said, but it is indefinite. There is a gap in the camera coverage. I can see you and the buggy moving along, then you both vanish – in the gap of camera coverage. You emerge, looking at some clothes. Then I see you spinning all around, looking for the buggy. From the edges of what we can see, it looks like someone may have been there just before, but you can't clearly see who they are or what they were doing. They managed to be in just the wrong place.

The right place, if they didn't want to be seen. In short, it is inconclusive.'

'So, you can't tell for sure that someone took Lachlan?'

'Or that they didn't.'

I think for a moment. 'It's Flick's keys that are worrying me. Do you know where they were found?'

'It was near the same shop.'

'If they fell out of her bag, would you be able to see that?'

He half frowns, thinking. 'Resolution might not be good enough. I could have another look. Though there are other things I'm meant to be working on, you know. Now. Why did you need to see me?'

He's looking into my eyes and there is an intensity there, a feeling, as if he somehow knows or has guessed what is coming.

'The thing is that Philip and I have decided to try to work things out.'

He shakes his head. 'After what he did? Lucy, I'm really worried about you.'

'I appreciate that.' And I'm relieved, too – that that is how he is framing it, rather than jealousy, even as part of me – my pride, maybe – wants him to argue, to want to keep me in his life. But we were always more friends with benefits than the real deal. He must know that.

'What was yesterday about then? Was it your tit for tat with Philip?'

'No! Of course not.' At least, not consciously, I admit to myself. 'It was what I wanted at the time, very much. But it can't happen again.' At least, not yet, but I can't tell him why I'm really back with Philip.

He's raising an eyebrow. 'You don't owe me any explanations. It's your life. I've got to get back to work.' She's bringing our coffees as he gets up, leaves.

He's upset and I can't blame him. I sigh. I don't want to lose our refound friendship. I wish, like I have so many times in my life, that I could go back. Change what happened.

I'm an adult, not a teenager. I should have had more sense. Years ago, when I left Steve for Philip, I didn't handle it well at all. As far as more recent events go, I didn't think what happened between us on Iona's sofa was the kind of thing that he'd expect was going to lead to anything serious. Maybe, instead, it was a reminder – of past pain. I'm sorry for having caused it.

What makes me feel even worse is the thing that upsets me the most is not being sure if he will still go back and check the CCTV for Flick's keys. I can't be certain, so I need to do something about that. Something I should have done yesterday.

I sip my coffee and check locksmiths online. Make a few calls and find one who can do it today.

Time to call Flick.

'Hi, Mum. Before you ask, I left the chain on, no one tried to break in and we're alive and well.'

'Glad to hear it. But hear me out. There is something I need you to do for me.'

'What's that?'

'I've found a locksmith who can come by today to change your locks.'

'Seriously? I've got my keys back.'

'But what if someone took them, copied them, then left them where they'd be found?'

A pause. 'Sounds far-fetched don't you think?'

'Please. It'll set my mind at ease. Otherwise I won't be able to sleep.'

A sigh. 'OK, fine. When?'

'They'll be there in an hour.'

'Huh. What if I'd said no?'

'Wouldn't happen. Because I know that you're a lovely, kind person who would do this for me.'

'If you say so.'

'I've got some other news.' I pause, not sure how to broach this after the trouble it caused before. 'The thing is, I've moved back home. With your dad.'

'Really?'

'Yes.'

'Well, I'm glad to hear it.' She doesn't fill in that she's glad I've come to my senses, and I wish I could tell her everything, so she'd understand – that I'm doing this for them. Or is that even true, or is that the justification for doing what I wanted to do? If Philip truly is committed and never sees her or anyone else besides me again, why would I want to leave? I love my comfortable home, knowing where I fit in my life and my family. Even this new car. I shake my head. Am I so easily bought?

We say our goodbyes. I should call the twins too, though I know Flick will tell them. What will James think? He more or less guessed what the problem was, told me to get a lawyer. I don't know how he'll react now.

I can't dodge this and let someone else tell them, like happened before with Philip. I have to face it.

I call Jessie first. It rings and rings, finally goes to voicemail. I end the call, not sure about leaving this in a message.

Now James. He answers on the first ring.

'Hi, Mum.'

'Hi, James. Glad I caught you.'

'I'm just on my way to a tutorial. Is everything OK?'

Do it, I tell myself. *Just dive on in there.* 'I've got some news. I've moved back home with your dad.'

A pause. 'Seriously? After whatever it was you wouldn't tell me that made you leave in the first place?'

'It's the right thing to do,' I say, which is technically true, but not the way he'll interpret it. I wish I could tell him everything, hating that I'm not being honest.

'Oh. Are you sure? Do you want to talk things through?'

'What about your tutorial?'

'I can skip.'

'No, you can't! Love you.'

We say our goodbyes, and I stare at my phone in my hand, put it down on the table. He sounded first worried, then confused, and back to worried. I hate that I'm not being honest with my children, but I don't know what else to do.

At least Flick agreed to have the locks changed. That gave an almost instant sense of relief.

Which diminishes as I remember the other thing that I've been dreading – facing Iona.

33

JESSIE

My phone vibrates in my pocket in the middle of organic chemistry lab, and I sneak a look.

It's Flick.

Give me a call, I've got news.

And I see now that there is a missed call from Mum, too. What's going on?

I'm about to message Flick when the lab assistant catches me with my phone in my hand.

'Pay attention to what you're doing, Jess! We don't want a repeat of last month.'

It was only a small explosion. I get back to work. When the experiment is finally finished, no fire extinguishers have been needed today – success? Though, as I weigh and test the product I have at the end, I notice mine seems to be a different colour than most. I glance at the chemical store. Maybe mix it with something random to change the colour?

But I've been spotted. 'Don't even think it, Jess,' he says.

'Think what?'

A raised eyebrow and he scans my report. 'As it turns out, despite being in the minority – your results appear to be correct.'

Excellent.

I pack up and leave. I've got a tutorial soon but should answer Flick. As I take out my phone to do so, another message from her drops in.

> Are you OK?

I don't know what to say. Between Mum and Dad's split and the stuff Mum told me, everything feels wrong.

I finally send back:

> I'm OK. Just on way to a tutorial.

Flick answers:

> I've got some news... drumroll, please... Mum and Dad are back together. She moved back last night.

Seriously? That must be why Mum called. With all the fuss about Lachlan and Flick's keys, I never managed to talk to Mum at all about what was going on between them. And now they're back together?

> For real?

> Think so.

I shake my head as if to knock some sense in it. If they were so sure about splitting up, this could be temporary – is that only obvious to me? Or was the split the temporary thing? There's no way to know, not yet.

I message James.

> Have you heard the news?

About Mum and Dad?

> Yeah.

Mind officially boggled.

> Can we talk later? Come to the pub.

OK. Let me know when you get there.

My mind is wandering in my tutorial. While having my family together is good as far as me and my siblings are concerned, I'm less sure about Mum. With what she said at lunch, I'm realising I don't know her as well as I thought I did – not as my mum, but who she is, apart from that. If she had all these secrets, who knows what else there could be.

34

LOU

'Have you really thought this through, Lou?' Iona is watching as I gather the rest of my things from her flat. And I can see she is struggling not to say all the other stuff she is thinking, like what a mistake I'm making. That I'd be better off without him. Once a cheater, always a cheater. Et cetera.

'I know it's hard for you to understand, but it's right to do this for my family.' I did consider telling her everything – that my motivation isn't what it appears to be on the surface. I'm only going back to Philip to work out if the threat is from someone near him – whether that woman, or someone from his work. But then she'd try even harder to talk me out of going back to him. She'd be convinced my fears are unfounded, that I'm still processing what happened so long ago. Just like the police would be, Flick and Philip, too. I need to do this my way and tell no one.

'What about what's right for *you* – is this what you want? And then there's Steve.'

'That was just a moment. A moment versus a lifetime.'

She raises an eyebrow, not convinced.

She helps me take my things down the stairs, looks about for my car. Then I walk up my new one. Open the door with the key fob.

'Nice. No scratches or dents. But is it worth it?'

'I didn't go back to Philip to get a car, Iona!'

'I didn't mean that—'

Now I'm the one raising an eyebrow. 'The car arrived the next day, all right?' I realise something then. He must have already ordered it – unlikely he could have arranged a new car to be delivered that morning. Maybe it was meant to be a bribe and all the things he said were second thoughts.

'It *is* beautiful. Like a bumble bee! Don't lose your sting.' She gives me a hug.

'Thank you for everything.'

'I'll be here if you need me,' she says. 'I'll even try not to say *I told you so.*'

'You'd fail. But thanks.' I hug her back and it's hard to let go, tears unexpectedly pricking the backs of my eyes. 'I'm sorry that I'm always disappointing you.'

'Don't say that!' But it's true. Isn't it? And we both know it.

I get into my car and pull away – she's watching me go. She waves and so do I, blinking back tears that won't be banished. I hope this closeness we've found again will continue, but I'm not sure it can, not when I'm not being honest with her. I've never been good at that. Unlike disappointing her, at which I'm champion.

35

LUCY

It's today: Wimbledon, main draw. Second round.

'You have to win this for both of us,' Iona says. 'I mean it! If you lose and I could have won, I'll never forgive you. And I know you can do it. It pains me to say this.' She looks both ways, making sure no one is close enough to listen. 'You are a better player than me.' I'm shaking my head, denying. 'Don't be an idiot. You know it; I know it; our coaches always knew it. They put us together so I could teach you how to win. I've done that now. The rest is up to you.' A fierce hug. I know it cost her to say what she did. She'd do anything to be in my place. She leaves to go to the player box while I wait to be called.

The applause when I step out from the tunnel as they announce my name – I know it's not for me, not specifically. It's because I'm the local kid, the new sensation everyone is talking about. But even knowing all of that, the sound lifts me up instead of scaring me. Maybe Iona is right.

We warm up.

I take one point at a time. One game at a time. My service is broken early on, but I break back in the next game. I'm on form now, buzzing with the effort and power, the joy; hitting every shot where I want it to go. With each point there is a surge of belief, confidence, and now I'm the one up a break. I belong here. I can do this.

I hit a winner to nail the first set, then glance to my player box. Iona is there, standing – a huge grin on her face. 'Come on!' she yells, and I can hear her over everyone. Mum and Dad, too, are applauding. Mum never thought I could do this, really compete, did she? I'm going to prove her wrong.

A few games into the second set, I pass my towel back to the ball kid, grinning as I do so – he is doing what I did, not many years ago. Then his eyes shift over my shoulder – wide, alarmed – I spin around as there is a collective noise from the crowd and a man runs into me and throws his arms around me, pawing at me, and I'm struggling to push him away. People are yelling and there are footsteps and now someone is grabbing hold of him and trying to drag him away from me, but his hands are clutching at my kit and don't let go, pull my top off over my head as they drag him away. He's being held on the ground, more security coming.

The other player runs over with a towel, wraps it around me. 'Are you OK?' she says. I'm shaking. Not really taking in what happened or is happening now. Who was he? How did he get on court?

He's being taken away and there is sound, eyes everywhere, looking at me and now I can't breathe. Everything spins and I'm falling.

There's a medical timeout. A doctor. I'm helped off court. They're checking my blood pressure, blood oxygen. I fainted, that's all. I'm fine now. I say over and over again, that I want to play – four automatic words, but are they even true or what I am supposed to say?

It's not far but walking back onto court, each step takes effort.

I can't stop my eyes darting all around, looking for that man, even though I know he's been taken away.

The crowd applauds to see me. They're willing me to serve. To resume the match and win it. In the midst of so many strangers are Iona, Coach. Mum and Dad, too. Iona's lips are moving. Even though I can't hear her this time, I know what they are. *You can do this, Lulu.*

Breathe, in, out. In out. Throw the ball up but it is off kilter. Catch it and do it again. My first serve is straight into the net. The second sails wide. Double fault.

My rhythm is all wrong.

I fight to get it back, but the games are slipping away, then the set. When the third set begins, I try to rally. I really do. Even though I just want it to be over, to get away from all these people and be alone.

I lose.

Afterwards, there are calls for a replay, people saying it wasn't fair. And it explodes in the news. He was some superfan who said he just wanted to give me a hug, but I've been hugged before and that isn't what it felt like.

That night, every time I start to fall asleep, I can feel him pressed against me, his hands, that moment when he's ripped my top off and I'm standing there in a sports bra, in front of so many people, cameras. I'm exhausted.

Our next doubles match is tomorrow, but just thinking of stepping out on the court has me shaking again.

I don't think I can do it – I tell Iona the next morning.

'You can and you will, because I'll be there with you,' Iona says. 'That idiot won't come back. He's been arrested. He's in jail. If there are any other idiots around, security has been increased.' Her eyes hold mine and I try to listen to what she says, to believe it.

'Most of all, I'll be in your corner, Lulu. No one can get through me – right?'

'Right.'

Somehow I let her draw me out onto the court. The applause, to see us both there, together – it's overwhelming. Iona hugs me and we both wave to the crowd. We warm up and the match begins. Gradually my game starts to come good and somehow we win that match. My form is almost back for the next one, and the next. And so on, all the way to the final.

Centre Court. The feeling to step out on that court together, against the top seeds? For the first time since the court invasion, I don't look around for threats. This moment, I want to bottle it – to keep how I feel right now, forever. It feels inevitable that we will win, like nothing can stop us when we are together. And we do: we're doubles champions at Wimbledon. Our first grand slam, and we won.

It's a triumph, everyone says, that I recovered my form and managed this. But they give me more credit than they should. Without Iona, I'd never have managed to step back on court.

36

LOU

Between what Iona said about my car and thinking about the past, I'm not in a good place when I get home. I've got to stop thinking and start doing – begin with the things I know and go on from there. One possibility for anyone targeting me and my family has to be enemies of Philip's from his work as a KC. And a good place to start will be Janice Gidney, senior clerk at Philip's chambers.

Janice was there from the beginning. We're about the same age and were instant friends when we met at a work party, reinforced when the twins were born within weeks of her son. We used to lunch now and then, though not so much recently. I haven't seen or spoken to her since the Christmas party.

If anyone knows of any worrying recent cases or threats, she will. All I have to do is persuade her to tell me. She shouldn't – anything she may have managed to glean is under barrister-client privilege – but I should at least be able to get a sense from her reaction if there is anything to be concerned about.

I make the call.

'Hi. Janice? It's Lou. Lou Kingsley.'

'Lou! It's lovely to hear from you. How're things?'

'Great, thanks. I was just wondering – we haven't had lunch in so long. I'm going to be in the city tomorrow. Are you free?'

'Let me check.' A moment, another. 'Can it be late – say 1.30?'

'Perfect. It's my treat and I'll book. I'll stop by chambers first.'

* * *

Philip gets home from work earlier than usual – at six. I've done the shop, planned dinner. We make it together, a glass of wine to hand. Eat, then load the dishwasher. Watch some TV. Nothing unusual from many other past nights, but it feels... odd. Like we're not who we were and aren't quite sure how to be with each other now, and until we work that out there is this strange politeness in how we interact. Have we ever really known each other, inside and out, like I thought we did? Is that even possible, with anyone? When a relationship begins, you put your best face forwards – even if just subconsciously, trying to be what you think this new, desired person in your life most wants. Somewhere along the way that changed. I relaxed my guard – it's hard to be anyone but yourself during childbirth, for example – but there are always hidden corners, things we don't share. Maybe more than I realised.

'You look deep in thought. Is everything all right, Lou?'

'I don't know.' The truth, at last.

He takes my hand, pulls me closer. Holds me. Kisses me and draws me upstairs to bed. And while it lasts, everything retreats. But it lies in wait, ready to creep out again.

Once he's asleep, I stare at the ceiling, remembering so many things. Like a virtual photo album, flipping pages in my mind and questioning if things were the way I thought, or if he has been living a double life all along. Has there always been a part of Philip I knew nothing about?

If he's brought a woman into his life who is a threat to our family, I'll never forgive him.

37

JESSIE

By the time I'm done for the day, I've had enough of my own thoughts. I want noise and friends to fill the space. I get to the pub, pause out front and message James and a few friends that I'm there. James pings back that he'll be a while; the others say they're on their way.

I go in. It's busy but I see a break in the queue at the bar and go for it.

Lager in hand soon after, I look around for my friends but there's no sign yet. I spot a table where a group look to be standing up, leaving, so I head across to it. But another girl reaches it at the same moment.

Well, she is maybe a fraction of a second ahead of me.

I shrug. 'You have it.'

'We could share?' I'm not sure she looks like someone I'd hang around with, or more to the point, that she'd have anything to do with me. She's, well, gorgeous, and I probably not only smell like chemicals, I'm also scruffy, deliberately so. Tired of telling eager teenage boys to piss off. She doesn't look to be wearing make-up, and her pale skin is flawless, and those eyes –

blue, but not a shade I've seen before; somehow both deeper, darker. Is she wearing coloured contacts? I can't see the tell-tale ring around her irises. And her hair – it's so beautiful, a pale blonde shade and obvious with her colouring that it is the real thing. Then she smiles and I realise I've been staring, feel warmth in my cheeks.

'Please,' she says, gestures at a chair and I sit down. She does also, moves her chair a little closer to mine. 'What's your name?'

'Jess.'

'Hi, Jess, I'm Ella.' She offers a hand – who shakes hands at a pub? – but I slip mine into hers. Warm, soft skin. Her grip is first firm, then loosens, but she doesn't let go. Being so close to her, touching her hand, I can feel my heart racing. She's flirting with me. Isn't she? I'm not imagining this, and I don't know what to do, what to say. She's so far out of my league it's like a different sport entirely. *This* doesn't happen to me. She finally lets go of my hand but stays close.

She smiles, a low throaty chuckle. 'Um, come here often?'

'Only in days ending in *day*.' She laughs, asks what I'm studying, and I'm telling her about the broken beaker award that I won for nearly blowing up the lab: an honour no other first-year chemistry student has ever achieved, for hitherto unreached feats of danger to life and property.

'I never really got chemistry in school.'

'Chemistry is like cooking: mix A and B, add C. Stir, heat, add some more stuff. See what happens.'

'An explosion?'

'Not usually.'

Now that I've started talking, it's like I can't stop. I'm so focused on her that the rest of the crowded student bar disappears along with all the family worries. I'm half aware when my friends arrive but they must get the vibe and stay away. No sign of James as of yet.

Ella smiles. Leans in. 'Let's go somewhere we can be alone,' she says, voice low, breathing so close I can feel the warmth of it on my skin.

Seven words, like a stone dropped on still water, that ripples out from a centre point – changes what was there.

I find myself making an excuse, saying I've got to go, and almost run to get away. Glance back from the door. From the surprise in the bluest of blue eyes, rejection probably doesn't happen to her often.

I'm back at halls soon after, angry with myself. Why did I do that? I haven't had a girlfriend in almost a year. I was completely attracted to her – I don't think I've ever felt that strongly drawn to someone I've just met before. It's almost like it was *too* much – too intense – to be real, so she couldn't be for real. But if she wasn't, why? What possible motive could she have to pretend to be into me if she wasn't?

I'm telling myself I was right to be cautious, but the truth is that I was scared. *Admit it:* I ran away, because I was scared.

I wonder if she'll be there again, some other night?

Huh. If we are both ever there at the same time, after that she'll keep well away from me. I'm not sure how old she was – from a distance she could be a first year like me, but up close, not signs of age as such, she felt older. More together or something. I realise now that she steered the conversation to me and never said anything about herself.

Doesn't matter. She probably thinks I'm a child now.

I'm an idiot.

38

LOU

'It's so lovely to see you, Lou,' Janice says, between air kisses and an almost hug. 'You look amazing.'

'Thank you.' I'd gone to some effort this morning, with a beautifully tailored dress that shows me to advantage. I don't always wear make-up, but the smudges of darkness under my eyes after a night of poor sleep demanded it. Besides, if anyone here knows Philip has been cheating, I'm not going to cringe and blend into the background.

'Is Philip in?' She nods towards his door; it's ajar. He closes it if on a call or in a meeting. I tap on the door, open it further. The wood panelling, the bookshelves, the faint smell the place has always had, of dusty books and leather sofas – it takes me back. His chambers are in the heart of the traditions of Temple and the Inns of Court, here since the Middle Ages.

He looks up from his computer screen, eyes wide in surprise. I don't know why I didn't tell him I was coming in today – no particular reason, or to see what I could catch him at or with? It's highly unlikely at work.

'Hello. What brings you in?'

'Lunch – with Janice.'

'Ah, I see.' Likewise, he's not sure why I didn't mention it. Games of guessing and second-guessing; move and counter-move.

'Will you be home for dinner?'

'Barring the unexpected, probably about seven.'

'All right. Hope to see you then.'

He gets up and pulls me in from the doorway, closes it. Gives me a kiss. 'Do you remember what we did on my desk when I started as a junior at these chambers?'

'Vaguely. I think the twins appeared nine months later.' He holds me for a moment and I'm remembering those times, not the desk so much but the excitement of new beginnings. The plans he had swept me along with him. It all started when he'd been wrongly accused of causing the death of a protestor when he was in the police. Although exonerated, that led to his decision to leave and study law. He was going to defend the innocent, bring more justice to the world. That changed early on when he realised how much more money was involved in commercial law. Now his clients are mostly huge corporations, the very rich. Not the downtrodden, at all.

Not just idealistic, we were young – in love. Is there any way to go back, and be who we were all those years ago?

* * *

Janice smiles widely when I lead her to the French restaurant I've booked. Cord is amazing and well above usual lunch from work level. I was lucky to get a reservation at such short notice.

'What a delightful surprise!' she says. 'What's the occasion?'

'No reason at all other than I haven't seen you in ages, and fancied it.'

'How lovely. Thank you!'

It's a tasting menu, with matching wine. Only small glasses at lunchtime but I've already spoken to them, instructed them to give me only a taste of each wine – and more to Janice. It sounds like a seduction trap, but all I want is information.

We stick to family news – her new granddaughter, how the twins are settling in at university – for the first few courses.

'Any good gossip going around work?' I ask her. Soon I hear which clerk was seen coming out of which barrister's London flat; who got sacked for what.

'What about cases – anything juicy on the go recently?'

She shakes her head. 'Deadly dull, the lot.'

I hesitate. 'Have there been any credible threats made to Philip recently that you know of? He's seemed worried, preoccupied. And I saw him looking into alarm systems.' A fabrication, but something we discussed recently. In the unlikely event she mentions it to anyone and it gets back to Philip, easy enough for him to discount.

She shakes her head. 'Nothing that I know of, I promise.' She changes the subject and while I believe her about the lack of threats, something else is going on. Nothing I can quite put my finger on in what Janice has said or how she looked as she said it. A reticence, perhaps. Has she been feeling conflicted because she's been covering for Philip?

I face it head on.

'Is there something wrong, Janice? You don't seem quite yourself.'

'Not at all. It's just been a busy few days.'

Despite her words, I'm *sure* there is something she isn't

saying. I could press her, even tell her some of what has happened to get her to spill what she knows, but it would be too humiliating.

If Janice either knows or suspects what Philip has been up to, does that mean everyone else does, too? Maybe it goes beyond his workplace. Friends, neighbours, acquaintances. Does everyone know but me – have they been feeling sorry for me and saying nothing? Well, until whoever it was left the first note. There is a twist of embarrassment and bitterness in my gut.

After we've said goodbye and I'm heading to my car, I'm thinking about my suspicions. If there is any truth to everyone but me knowing Philip was cheating, surely I'd have been aware that something was going on, even if not what it was. Perhaps I'm being paranoid – natural in the circumstances, I suppose. These thoughts aren't helpful. I need to deal with facts, not guesswork.

Shallow or not, I feel a sense of satisfaction when I walk up to my new car. A bumble bee, Iona called it. I glance at the windscreen before opening the door – an automatic part of getting into this car or the previous one since I found the first note. My eyes have turned away before what they see can even register.

My gut twists as I look back again. A piece of white paper is tucked under the wiper. I look all around. No one is paying the slightest attention to me as they rush along the pavement, the car park. I reach for it, unfold it. It's like the others – capital letters in red ink gouged into a square of white paper.

I TOLD YOU THAT YOU'D REGRET IT IF YOU WENT BACK TO PHILIP. YOU SHOULD HAVE LISTENED.

I get into my car, lock the doors. Shaking and feeling sick inside. Who is doing this? And it's a threat – it must be. You did what I warned you about; you should have listened.

I'm sliding back to a dark place just when I most need to keep it together. Maybe that's the point of the notes, rather than representing any real threat to me or mine. But I can't stop myself going back in time.

39

LUCY

It's been months but I still haven't wanted to try my hand at singles again. We're continuing to rack up wins in doubles – and more than a few titles – and that has given me both confidence and occasionally enough funds for my new coach and physio to travel with me, but it's hard to think of stepping out onto the court, alone.

But then I'm offered a wildcard to the singles main draw at the US Open. I can't turn that down. Even with our doubles wins, the travel costs for me and my team are so high that I'm barely breaking even. Even if it ends in a first-round loss, this is big money.

Iona hasn't quite cracked the top one hundred in singles, so she has to qualify. Her mother, travelling with Iona as usual, is not impressed. Some people are saying I only got a wildcard because people feel sorry for me, after what happened at Wimbledon. I do my best to ignore that, and the hype around my return to singles. The photographers at training courts and endless requests for interviews that I mostly deflect. I tell myself that I need to keep away from all of that to focus. I tell myself that I'm ready.

On the morning of my first-round match, I'm actually pumped, excited. I'm on a training court for a light session on serving with Kristina, my new coach. She's amazing, has my serve regularly over one-ten now and I'm buzzing more and more with each toss of the ball in the air.

When we're done, I see a box on the bench next to my kit. It looks like flowers; I bet they are from my aunt. But when I go to look all it says on an envelope taped to the box is *Lulu* – a delivery from Canada would need a bit more info than that.

I open the envelope. There is a folded piece of white paper inside. I unfold it. Handwritten in blue ink:

I'll be watching you. Better be careful.

Nothing else, nothing about who it is from, and who would say be careful like that?

I open the box – flowers, red roses – but all the stems have been broken. The flower heads cut off and the petals shredded. What the hell? I ask if anyone on the sidelines saw who left them; no one noticed.

Kristina sees my face, comes over. I show them to her.

'Someone is just trying to distract you. Ignore it,' she says, and I say I will.

When I step out onto the court a few hours later, I look around at the crowd. There are so many people. Is one of them the one who left that box? What if it is the man who ran on the court at Wimbledon? Maybe he's going to try to do it again.

Be careful. As if I'm one of the roses and can be broken.

I lose.

40

___

LOU

After finding the note on my car, it's a while before I'm calm enough to drive home. When I get there and pull into the drive, I look all around – see no one. I get out and walk quickly to the front door, unlock it and go inside. I'm relieved to lock it behind me, but what if someone has broken in? I check the rest of the house and that the back door is dead bolted, then start to feel a little better.

I take out the note, read it once again. Wanting to call Steve, but not sure if he wants to hear from me again, let alone do anything to help. Though there wouldn't be much point in fingerprinting this one, given the lack of prints on the other notes – as Steve said, whoever it is has probably been wearing gloves. I was parked on a busy road in the city when the last note appeared. There are CCTV cameras just about everywhere in London. Could Steve access them, see who left the note?

I might as well call him. The worst he can do is not answer or say no.

I put the kettle on for a cup of tea first, but then realise more caffeine isn't what I need right now. It's only mid-afternoon but feels like the perfect time for a glass of wine.

I find his number and hit call. It rings once, twice, three times – he's not going to answer, is he? – but then he does.

'Lucy. Hi.'

'Hi.'

'I'm in the middle of something. Is it important?'

'I found another note on my car.' I read it to him and tell him where it was parked.

'And you want me to check CCTV.'

'If you can. It's a yellow Mini now – my new car.' I tell him the plates.

'Got it. I've gotta go.'

'Bye, Steve. And thank you.' But he's already gone.

OK. He was abrupt but he was busy, and he still answered. He didn't cut me off when I gave him the details or say that he wouldn't or couldn't check CCTV, so I'm sure that means that he will.

In the meantime, I'm jumpy, nervous. Scared what might happen next. And even though it seems unlikely that it is the same person from so many years ago, if it is – maybe we'll finally have a visual on who they are. A first step to catching him and putting an end to my fear.

The only identified suspect back then was the man who got past security and grabbed me on court at Wimbledon. The police were completely sure he wasn't involved in anything that followed. He was on remand and locked up for part of it, and nowhere near the rest, so unless he had one or more accomplices, it wasn't him. And the police thought that extremely unlikely. The kind of actions of someone who sends notes and means to scare someone, follows them – in short, a stalker – is by definition an individual.

Please, Steve. If there is even a chance of identifying the person who wrecked my life, don't let me down.

41

FREJA

It is nearing the end of my shift when Philip calls. I slip into the stockroom to answer.

'I've only got a sec – I'm at work.'

'When would be good? We need to talk.'

The four most-dreaded words in a relationship: *we need to talk*. Is he actually going to come clean about his wife moving home? Will that come with a goodbye?

I don't think so.

'It's good to hear your voice,' I say. 'But *sound* is only one of the senses.'

A pause. 'Oh?'

'Well, we have sight. Taste. Smell. And my personal favourite – touch. There are so many... variations... with touch. I'm finished work in an hour. Meet me at the usual place?'

Another pause. Is he working out what to say? I hear the *click, click* of Yasmin's heels approaching.

'I've got to go.' I hang up before he has replied. Phone slipped in my pocket, I head back out to the floor with a few items in hand to restock before Yasmin opens the door. It's busy and I'm caught up helping someone get the right shade of foundation – obvious that she's an idiot, what she came in wearing was way too dark. Then another woman endlessly deliberates on what shade of lipstick would suit her best. All the while I'm thinking of Philip's call. What he said, what he didn't.

I dodge a customer who comes in a few minutes before the end of my shift. Yasmin frowns as I disappear into the back room, take off my name badge, fix my hair and emerge with my bag. March off with a wave while she is helping the customer I avoided. I'll hear about that tomorrow, but right now, I don't care.

Will Philip be there? Will he still want to talk, or move on to all the senses?

Because that is the thing with touch. As I said to Philip earlier, there are so many variations – blurred edges between pleasure and pain. If he turns up, he won't forget tonight.

I get to our pub – the one near my work where he meets me sometimes. Watching the door, not entirely sure if he'll show or call with an excuse. Five minutes, ten – and there he is. I watch him search faces until he finds mine. I smile when he reaches me, kiss him before he can say anything.

'I'm glad you came. I need to be alone with you.' I can see the struggle, just under the surface veneer. If I didn't know, would it be so obvious?

I pull his tie, release it. 'Come on.' I walk towards the door, glance back over my shoulder. He follows.

42

LOU

I'm savouring another glass of wine and about to start dinner when my phone pings – a message from Philip.

> Sorry, late meeting – don't wait for dinner. I'll grab a bite out.

It could be a last-minute meeting with solicitors or a potential client. That happens often enough, but I can't stop thinking that he's lied to me. That he's gone to meet *her*. Who is she? How long was she on the scene, and, despite Philip's promises, is she still there?

I couldn't find anything the other day, checking Philip's study, pockets, everywhere I could think to look. Is there another way? Bank accounts: I can check for any unusual expenditures.

I log in to online banking, scan through months of statements of our accounts, credit cards. Nothing strikes me as out of the ordinary, but then I'm not really expecting to find anything. Philip is too smart for that. He's good at what he does because despite being rather a slob at home, he is meticulous. He's all about the details.

Surely he wouldn't put expenses through work accounts. That could get him into trouble with HMRC.

Though maybe the reason I can't find anything is because she was inconsequential and transient, like he implied. Or maybe they go to hers, so there aren't any sneaky hotel bills to track down. I sigh, then go to fill up my wine glass, realise the bottle I started this afternoon is almost empty.

What else? I haven't checked our landline for calls. He's too clever to be caught that way. Unless... there was the night, just days ago, when we met for dinner and I told him it was over. If he was upset – whether he believed me or not – maybe it was enough for him to let down his guard. I might as well check. I log in to our phone account online, scan through our call history for that day.

I sigh. There is nothing. I'm about to close the screen when I see it. He did make a call, but it was so late that it was actually the next morning so shows on the next day. Who would he be calling after midnight? It's her. It must be her.

I finish the wine. Enter the number into my mobile phone. What will I say if she answers? I don't even know, but I can't stop myself. I think just in time to withhold my number. It rings once, then goes to voicemail.

'Hi, this is Freja. Please leave a message.'

There's the beep.

I hesitate, then hang up.

OK, Freja. I have your number; I know your first name. It's a start. You better watch your back.

43

FREJA

It's a few hours later. Philip's arms are wrapped around me. He's sated, starting to drowse, but then, as if he remembers who he is and where, wakes himself up. Disentangles himself and starts getting dressed. I watch him, eyes half closed.

'Don't go,' I say.

'I have to. Early start tomorrow.' He turns back to me, cups a hand around my face. Kisses me. He pulls away and his face – it's like an addiction. He can't get enough of me, even though he knows it might destroy his life. Perhaps he wants me even more because he convinced himself to end it, then couldn't go through with it. Or maybe he's so ego-driven he can't accept it could all come tumbling down. After all, in Philip's world, everything and everyone always behaves according to his wishes.

That may have been true in the past, but not for much longer.

I wrap a sheet around me, stand and kiss him again. Then pull away, run one finger down his face to his lips. He kisses it.

'Philip, wasn't there something you wanted to talk about?'

'Hmmm?'

'When you called earlier, you said we needed to talk.'

He shakes his head. 'No. We're good.'

He's lying, getting in deeper and deeper, and he doesn't know what to do.

If he were anyone else – someone I didn't hate with every fibre of my being – I'd feel sorry for him.

44

LOU

Philip is very late. Tired and uncommunicative. When I ask he says he's worried about a case, but Janice said there were no big things on just now. He heads for the shower and I'm in bed when he comes out.

'Goodnight,' he says. A peck on the cheek.

How would he react if I asked him straight out: were you with Freja? It's tempting. If he wasn't so late that I had some time to sober up, I probably would have done it. But I'm not being that jealous wife, not unless I have proof. And not until I find out if she is the dangerous one.

He rolls over and is snoring almost instantly. I'm staring at the ceiling. Remembering what I saw of her the day I walked in on them here, in this bed. Thinking of them being together, I'm eaten up by anger and jealousy and a lifetime of being who and what Philip wanted me to be.

I tell myself that I don't *know* he was with her tonight. No doubt there is a long list of reasonable places he could have been and people he could have been with that have nothing to do with her or any other woman, for that matter. But somehow I can't believe it.

Time ticks slowly by. I slip in and out of dreams, fleeting visions left behind. In one I'm looking in through our windows. Freja is in our front room, laughing at me. Philip is lying on the floor – asleep or dead, I don't know. The doors are locked and I'm hammering on them, and then, everything reverses. I'm inside the house and can't get out. I can hear my children crying, alone, outside, and I can't get to them. In another I wake up and when I open my eyes, there are folded pieces of white paper everywhere – on the bed, floor, stuck on the mirror. I'm trying to step on the floor without touching any of them, but they keep moving when I put my foot down. Then the floor turns to grass – a grass court. Wimbledon. Laughter echoes all around, discordant and harsh, the sound gradually turning into Philip's morning alarm.

I keep my eyes closed, pretend to be asleep, until he's gone.

I'm losing it. Aren't I? Completely. Jealousy and the fear that has reappeared in my life with the recent notes have combined, and I can't think straight about what it all means. I wish I could talk to Iona, but while she'd no doubt agree all my suspicions about Philip are right, she'd be convinced that I'm completely wrong about the rest of it.

Maybe she'd be right. Maybe it's jealousy and that is all it is, and there is no bogey man – or woman – to be afraid of.

But I can't take that risk.

45

JESSIE

It took me a few days, first, to think of it, and second, to stop talking myself out of it, but I finally search Mum's name before she got married. And there it is: a long list of links under both Lucy Cooper and Lulu Cooper, her nickname then. It's weird, but although with everything these days the first thing I think to do if I want to know something is search it online, doing that with my mum's name just felt very odd. As if she's so old nothing would be there, though I know that isn't true. Or she's so just my *mum*, that it's hard to believe that her life was in the public eye enough before we came along that anything would be out there. Not so. She's even got a Wikipedia page and I start there.

It has all the usual basic bio stuff – date of birth, parents' names, schools she went to. Then it's mostly all about her tennis career. There are links to what is described as a fan incident – a man ran on court and grabbed Mum. There are photos, even another link to footage of what happened, and she's so young, so scared. I'm furious to think what this idiot did and all the consequences it led to.

But I thought she said they didn't know who the stalker was? Or even whether it was definitely a man.

I read on, follow more links, and soon realise that it wasn't him. There are old news snippets – stories like tennis star Lulu Cooper terrorised by unknown fan. Little in the way of detail beyond mention of a few notes and deliveries of mutilated flowers. Ick.

There is a fan page for her, too, mostly all old posts. But *WTF*? There is a recent post by tennisbunny3246, saying that Lulu's husband is cheating on her. And a photo of Dad, in bed, eyes closed, bare chest, with a kind of half-smile that is just gross to see on your father's face.

This just *can't* be for real. He wouldn't. Would he? I'm shocked, but even as I'm denying it, calling it impossible... it would explain why the split between Mum and Dad seemed so out of the blue. If she found out somehow, that could be why she left him. But then why were they back together again so soon afterwards? If it's true, as much as I'd like my family all in one piece, I don't get why she'd think she should leave him over it and then change her mind such a short time later. And she *shouldn't*. That isn't the kind of thing that I could ever forgive. How could she trust him after that?

Maybe they don't know this post and photo are out there. Maybe Mum didn't even know he was cheating – assuming that he was – and there was some other reason she left. I look at the post again. A photo of only him isn't exactly *proof* of anything, but it looks suss enough.

Assuming they don't know about this... should I tell them? But which one – Mum or Dad? Or even both of them. Maybe they can get it taken down somehow. But I haven't got a fucking clue what I should or shouldn't do.

I keep digging. I find a website that has tennis gossip going back enough years. There were rumours of a stalker in connection with Mum, but they make it sound like it was nothing, or maybe didn't even happen. As if she made it up. Why on earth would she do that? There are some snarky comments calling her Lucy the Loser. Nice. Saying that she couldn't handle the pressure, that she made up a stalker as an excuse to leave tennis behind. Others say she did it because she liked the attention. FFS. Someone else says she couldn't manage to play without Iona always there backing her up. I already know why Iona's career ended abruptly – there was a car accident. Injuries that took her out of sport. I didn't realise that they both stopped playing at about the same time.

Mum looked so rattled at Westfield the other day. She really thought someone had taken Lachlan, might do it again or something else. The fear isn't something she made up. And it was like there was something else that she wasn't telling us, something that was even worse.

Enough. I'm afraid if I search any more I'll find more things I don't want to know.

What do I do now?

I want to talk this out with James, but I'm not sure I should. He's not great at dealing with emotional stuff sometimes, and I don't want to send him spiralling backwards. He's been doing so great in Brighton, as if getting away from the secondary cesspit was just what he needed. But it also feels wrong to not tell him something this big. We always talk about everything.

Back to this post and photo of Dad. I want to leave it, pretend I never saw it – run from it like I run from everything else. But I'm worried, and want to hear Mum's voice, know she is OK. Then I'll decide whether or not to mention it.

I hit call before I have time to change my mind. It rings once, twice.

'Hello?'

'Hi, Mum it's me. Jess. How're things?'

'Fine. Thanks. You?'

'Ah, good I guess. Sorry I didn't call you back.'

There is a pause, like she's putting things together. 'Do you know about your dad and I?'

'That you've moved back home? Yes. Flick told me. Is everything OK there?'

'Of course.'

I chatter on a bit about uni and friends, the usual stuff. She doesn't sound like herself at all. But I'm not sure I can tell how she really is over the phone, and I want to go there. She's not responding like she usually would.

'Mum, I'm worried about you. Are you sure you're all right?'

'Aw, Jess. I am, I promise. What's brought this on?' Her voice is more hers now.

'You know. Stuff. Like with Lachlan and that.'

'It's fine. It was probably all overreaction, but I convinced Flick to get her locks changed. Just in case. So, nothing to worry about there.'

We talk a little longer about nothing much, and I'm no closer to deciding if I should tell her about the post. We say goodbye.

What now? I could get on a train and go see her, but I still don't know if I should tell her. I could call Flick – she's both nearby and likely more able to get Mum to talk. But I'm not sure how she'd take seeing that photo, or any of this. She's always been a Daddy's girl.

I think, right now, what Mum needs is a friend to talk to. With us she'll always be more focused on how anything affects us, trying to protect us.

There is only one choice, really. It'll have to be Auntie Iona.

46

LOU

Jessie tried to hide it at first, but she was really worried. When she finally admitted it, I did my best to reassure her. There is nothing she can help with, and I want to keep her as far away from all of this as I can.

What next? I'm too tired to do much of anything. I try to sleep, but it's impossible. The nightmares come back every time I close my eyes. What I need to do is to find this Freja, work out if she is the one who is a threat to me, my family. But I have no idea how to do that, and maybe it isn't just tiredness stopping me. There is a feeling that I'm looking in the wrong place.

The doorbell rings and I'm about to get up to see who is there when I hear a key turning in the lock. An automatic rush of fear has me on my feet, ready to flee, when the front door opens.

'Hello, Mrs Kingsley.' It's Ana, our cleaner.

I try to school my face back to normal. It's her half-day with us; I forgot.

'Hello, Ana. How are you?'

'Good. You?' She looks concerned. No doubt she can see by how I look that things aren't right, but I'll give her a reason.

'I haven't been feeling well. A cold coming on, I think.'

'I'll make you some tea, with honey?'

'Thank you, but no. I'm fine, really; just tired.'

Ana's eyes shift over my shoulder and to the window. 'You've got a visitor,' she says.

It's Iona, pulling in behind Ana's van. I go to the door, wait for her to get out of her car.

'Hi, you,' she says.

'Hello there. I wasn't expecting you.'

She gives me a hug, sees Ana, who has started dusting.

'I was going to invite myself in for lunch, but how about we go out instead?'

As far as I can remember, Iona has never driven all this way – about ninety minutes from Islington – without arranging it with me first. Something must be up and I'm not sure I can handle having anything else to deal with just now. But I don't want to be in the house with Ana all afternoon, either.

'OK. Give me a few minutes.'

I go upstairs, to my dressing table, and look in the mirror. I do look shocking. I change out of trackies to something more acceptable, then dab concealer under my eyes, a quick brush of blush and foundation. I study myself critically. If it wasn't for the worry around my eyes, I look almost normal. But I still have the smile Iona made me practise for the press that I can call upon at will, and I do so, now. That's better.

I say goodbye to Ana and join Iona in the front room. 'Shall we?'

'You're parked in; I'll drive. Where to?'

'You choose.'

We head out. In contrast to my dark thoughts, it's another sunny day, showing Beaconsfield and the green hills beyond our leafy neighbourhood at its best. As much as I like London, the

lack of space gets to me. Wherever you go, even running in a park, there are always people everywhere.

Iona pulls into a nearby pub we've been to before. It's weekday quiet. She asks for a table that is in an alcove on its own – one made for confidences. We order wine and are left with menus, but she doesn't even glance at it.

'Tell me. How are things going with Philip?' she says.

'Fine.'

'Ha. The way you said *fine* means not fine. I'm not trying to be nosy or disruptive, I promise. I'm worried about you.'

Tears are stinging in my eyes and I'm blinking them back. I have to reassure her so she'll go away, and I can focus on what I need to do to make my family safe.

'The day I came home, he said I'm the only one he's ever loved, that he's sorry and regrets it more than he can say, and it'll never happen again.'

'Do you believe him?'

I hesitate. I don't want to out-and-out lie to her. Plus, if I do, she won't accept it and will want to chip away at it bit by bit. I can't deal with that right now.

'I believe he meant what he said when he said it,' I say, finally. 'And time will tell.'

She nods. 'OK. That sounds fair.' She's looking back at me like she is searching for words, what to say next. There is obviously something going on, whatever it was that brought her all this way out of London.

'Go on, Iona. Spit it out. What's on your mind?'

'I'm afraid I have something to show you that you aren't going to like.'

What could it be this time? I can't even guess. Whatever it is adds to the ball of tension, anxiety, in my gut. 'That sounds ominous.'

'There is a fan page somebody set up for you, years ago.'

'Assuming it is the one I remember from before, I've seen it. Though not recently.' It was mostly photos of me playing tennis. People making comments, good and bad, when I left the sport. The police looked at it at one point, in case someone involved in it was sending me notes and so on, but found no one of interest there.

'Someone put up a post a few days ago that you should probably see.' She reaches for her phone, taps on the screen, and my nerves are going up a notch. What could be so bad that it led to her to come all this way to show me, in person, instead of just messaging a link?

Wine arrives now. 'Have a drink of that and brace yourself, hon.' She hands me her phone, the new post on screen. A photo of Philip – he's lying back in bed, eyes closed. Nothing on but cropped at about his hip so almost decent. The words with the post are swimming in and out of focus so much that it takes a moment to read them:

Have you heard the latest about Lulu? Her scumbag husband has been cheating on her.

What the actual? I look again, the date it was posted – it was after I came home. I look more closely at the photo, zoom in. See details of the bedhead, the bedding.

Iona's eyes now – the sympathy. The pain at being the one to show this to me. She reaches for my hand when I put the phone on the table, face down.

'That was taken in our bedroom.'

'I take it you didn't take the photo?'

'Of course not. Who's the poster?'

'Looks like a troll account. I mean, one just set up to post that one post.'

'His eyes were closed – he wasn't looking at the camera,' I say. 'He probably didn't even know it was taken.'

'Don't imagine he'd have allowed it if he was aware.'

'No.' I let go of her hand and reach for the wine glass, have what is more a gulp than a sip but it tastes like acid. 'If I didn't take that photo, there is really only one other possibility. It must have been her – that woman I saw him with.'

'That seems likely. I'm so sorry, Lou.'

Who has seen this? Is everyone laughing about it behind my back? I feel sick to even think it, but it doesn't actually go against what I said to her earlier.

'Look. This doesn't change anything between Philip and me. He's admitted what he did—'

'—no choice when you saw it.'

'I know. But this photo could have been taken that day, or before then,' I say, though it sickens me to think she might have been there more than once. 'And Philip said it was nothing, that it's over now.' That is what I'm saying out loud but inside, what about last night? Where was he? Just a girl, he said. A girl with a camera and some kind of agenda. This isn't happening.

'Lou? I've looked into it. You can request the photo be taken down for privacy reasons – hopefully the post as well. But I think Philip would have to do it. Since the photo is of him.'

I wonder if he's seen it? But if he had, no doubt he'd have done that already.

I convince Iona to talk about something else, anything else. We have lunch. I finish the glass of wine, have another. This drinking in the daytime thing is starting to be a habit, one I don't think I can break.

She drives me home. I'm relieved that Ana's van is gone when we get there. I couldn't handle trying on another mask, making polite conversation about the weather or whatever else.

Iona gets out of her car, walks me to the door. 'What are you going to do about that post?'

'I don't know. I need to think about it some more.'

'Call me if you need me, need anything. To talk or to come get you. Any time of day or night, OK?'

'I will,' I say, but she can't help me this time. Some things have to be faced, alone. But it is still tempting, so tempting, to just go with her and leave this mess behind. She says goodbye and I watch her go, wave when she does. And go through the front door.

It's a relief to be home, alone, door safely locked behind me. Despite saying I need to think about it some more, I know what I must do – I just don't want to face it. I have to show this post to Philip, get him to have it taken down. I'm afraid when I do I'll see something in his eyes, his face, that confirms all my suspicions. Including where he was last night. But I can't just leave it out there and hope no one notices. Who knows who might have seen it already? What if one of the kids stumble across it? It may be Philip, not me, who is shown in a poor light, but I couldn't bear it. The gossip, the pity. False and otherwise.

Should I call him? Message the link? No, that doesn't feel right. It'll have to be when he gets home tonight – we'll have to face this, together.

I have to look again. I can't stop myself. I find the fan page. It was a new post so it should be on top, but it isn't there. Maybe other posts have been made since or older ones have gone above it because of new likes or comments. I scroll up and down, then again. There are no new posts, no new interactions with old ones. It simply isn't there.

Maybe the page admin took it down. Maybe the person who

posted it had second thoughts. Or maybe Philip found it, requested its removal.

Why do bad things travel in packs? It's like the saying: bad luck comes in threes. I don't even want to count how many I'm up to now but think that number is an underestimate.

And it all started with one note. Just like it did all those years ago.

47

LUCY

There is a box on the front step when we get home from the shops.

'It's for *Lulu*,' Mum says, reading my name on the box in a disparaging tone – she doesn't like me using Lulu instead of Lucy. It's my birthday – my eighteenth – tomorrow, and it looks like the kind of box that contains flowers, but instead of happy anticipation I'm full of anxious dread. Since the broken roses delivery, I've had note after note, left in all kinds of places at tournaments – practice courts, hotel desks, pushed under my hotel room door. None threatening exactly but unsettling, and whoever it is seems to keep doing it without ever getting spotted by anyone. My stomach twists when I see there isn't an address on the box, just 'Lulu'. If it's from him, he knows where I live when I'm at home.

I take the box inside, put it on the table. Open it. There is tissue paper inside – black tissue paper. I push it aside to see what it contains, and my hand, it's stung. I pull it back. Inside the black paper are nettles, other weeds. Dead flowers. And a note that says only two words: *happy birthday.*

Mum comes over. 'Why would anyone send you this?'

'I don't know,' I say, and burst into tears. I haven't told her about the rest of it. My coach Kristina said whoever it is wants to be noticed, so ignore him – tell no one. Tournament security were informed and that was about it.

Mum is surprised – I never cry where she can see me. Not any more. She gives me a hug. 'Ignore it, it's probably someone's idea of a joke.'

I shake my head. 'It's not just that.'

'What's going on?' she says. She generally has little patience for weakness, but she is looking at me and not the tears.

I'm wiping my eyes, trying to keep it together. 'Somebody has been leaving me notes all over the place where I'll find them. I think they've been following me around on the tour. And that this came here? It means they know where I live.'

She asks me some questions. And then calls the police.

Two arrive, hours later – a red-haired detective in a suit, a younger man in uniform. By now mum has had the whole story from me, starting with the broken roses and all that followed. They introduce themselves as DS Power and Constable Fitz-patrick. Mum starts telling them everything; DS Power interrupts her, wants to hear it from me. I tell them all I can remember. Most of this hasn't happened in the UK, they note – they want to know if other police forces have been notified. I shake my head. Tournament and sometimes hotel security knew. Everyone thinks I should ignore it, that it's just a fan.

Mum is furious. 'Stinging nettles now, what will be next? There was that man who invaded the court at Wimbledon and assaulted my daughter last year. It must be him.'

'I'm aware of that incident,' DS Power says. 'We'll check into his whereabouts.' We're given a card.

I retreat to the sofa while Mum demands this and that of the detective. The younger one follows me.

'Are you OK?' Concern and a smile and something *else* that makes me smile back.

'I don't know. It's weird.'

'Anything else scares you, anything at all, call.' Despite the fear, my earlier tears, there is something about his eyes, his smile. And he's totally fit.

'Should I call you, or the police?'

'Same thing.' He slips me a piece of paper when Mum and the detective are looking the other way. A phone number – a mobile. *Steve* written next to the number.

Mum notices my smile after they've left. 'What's got into you?' she says.

I shrug. Message Iona.

48

JESSIE

My phone rings – Auntie Iona's name on the screen. I pounce
on it.

'Hello?'

'Hi, Jessie.'

'How'd it go?'

'I drove down there – took your mum out for lunch. Showed
her the fan page post.'

'How'd she take it?'

'About as well as you might expect.'

'And?'

She hesitates. 'We spoke in confidence. I can't tell you every
detail.'

'Fair enough. You didn't tell her I've seen it?'

'No, and I won't. I promised, remember?'

'Do you think she's OK?'

A pause. 'She's going through a tough time. You did the right
thing, telling me. I've made her promise to call me if anything
else happens or she needs someone to talk to.'

'Is she going to tell Dad?'

'I think she must have done. I checked just before I called you, and the post has been taken down.'

'Thank you.'

'You're welcome. Now get back to blowing up the chemistry lab, partying all night or whatever else students get up to these days. I'm on the case. I'll keep an eye on her.'

'Thank you.'

We say our goodbyes.

That was quick to get a post taken down. Iona is on the case – I've done the right thing. She said so.

Sorted.

49

LOU

The doors are locked. I can smell smoke – there is a fire. I'm trapped inside. I try to turn the key in the lock, but it won't turn no matter how I try. Then it snaps – it has broken off in the lock. I have to get out of here. I'm pounding at the door. Coughing. I step back, look for something heavy to smash a window to get out, but the house is empty. No furniture, none of our things. Empty. I'm sinking to the floor. There are sirens in the distance.

Please help me, please...

The sirens are getting closer, louder, ringing in my ears. I open my eyes.

Not sirens. It's our fire alarm – it's still going. I'm on the sofa. I must have fallen asleep – dinner?

I get up and rush to the kitchen. There is a pan on the stove – I'd started a stew to slow-cook later. What is left of it is smoking. I grab an oven glove and take it off the burner. Open the kitchen door and a window. Wave at the smoke with a towel and finally the alarm stops. The pan is ruined and so is dinner.

It's early still; Philip won't be back for a while. It's been hours since I had wine at lunch with Iona; I'll be fine to drive. I lock up, find my keys, phone. I'll get a takeaway, heat it up later.

I'm heading for the front door when my phone rings.

Steve's name is on the screen. I swipe to answer.

'Hi. Steve?'

'The one and only. I've got an update on the CCTV. The time the keys were found was noted by security, so I found that on the camera. I then rewound to just after you left and checked the same spot. No keys. Which suggests they didn't fall out of Flick's bag when you were there.'

My eyes widen. 'So, somebody could have taken them, copied them and put them there after we were gone?'

'I can't rule that out.'

'Could you see who left the keys where they were found?'

'That's the odd part. They slide into view of the camera, as if someone was deliberately keeping out of range of CCTV and slid them across the floor.'

'This is proof. Isn't it?'

'Slow down. Someone could have picked up the keys, dropped them again.'

'Why?'

'I don't know, a kid, maybe? They might have been kicking them around. There is no proof of anything.' His voice – that tone. The one that says I'm overreacting. I'm glad I had Flick's locks changed.

'How about the CCTV for my car when that last note was left?'

'Had a look. The front of your car wasn't on camera – couldn't see anything. The only visual of someone by the side of your car was you, coming and going.'

I'm so disappointed. But grateful he took the time to look into it, despite everything else. All at once I'm longing to see him. 'Thanks for checking. Are you OK?'

'Me? I'm always OK. I'm more concerned about how you are. Are you? OK?'

'Yes,' I lie. Tears run down my face as I say it.

A pause. 'I've got to go,' he says. The call ends.

I wipe my face on my sleeve. I know he's not happy with the situation – that I went back to Philip. That he still went out of his way to check CCTV – that's Steve, through and through. Maybe I didn't appreciate him enough all those years ago. Somehow, I'm sure he'd never cheat on me, either back then or more recently, if we'd got back together properly; that he'd never be the one to take up with a younger girlfriend. Qualities I maybe didn't appreciate enough.

I head out. Get my favourite takeaway from an Italian restaurant not far from home.

When I get back to my car, a bag of boxes of pasta to hand, I almost don't look – as if I don't see it, it can't be there. But I do and there it is. Another note, under the windscreen wiper of my car. I didn't even decide which takeaway I was going to go to until I left home; no one would be able to guess where I was going. I spin around, past caring if I look crazy. No one is looking that I can see. I put the bag on the passenger seat. My hand, shaking a little, I reach for it. Unfold the square of white paper, red capital letters as always. But not pressed so much into the paper – less anger?

IF I WERE YOU, I'D LOOK UNDER YOUR FRONT DOORMAT.

What the fuck?

Some of the words are the same as in the first note – *If I were you*. The same action suggested, basically – to go home.

The fear is still there, but this time, there is more anger. Who the hell is playing with me? It is tempting to crumple it up and throw it to the nearest bin. Ignore it. But where else can I go but home? And I need to see what is there.

I drive home on automatic, not watching to see if I'm being followed. What is the point? They always seem to know where to find me.

I pull in. Open the car door and walk to the mat, looking around as I do so – are any strangers watching? Any neighbours wondering what I'm up to? No one that I can see.

Under the mat is an envelope. A4 sized. I scoop it up, unlock the door. Go in and lock it behind me.

OK. It's an envelope. It's too thin to hold a ticking bomb. How bad can it be? But I remember a box of gloves – left over from pandemic paranoia. In case I want whatever is in there to be checked for fingerprints, I put them on and then rip it open.

Inside are photographs. The first one is of Philip. He's facing away from the camera, on his way into what looks like a pub. I almost miss what is in the corner, slightly out of focus – it is yesterday's newspaper. A date, to place the photos in time.

Next photograph, a blonde woman. I know who she is – Freja. I recognise her from our bedroom. She is the woman he swore he'd never see again. Yet following behind her? It's Philip. There is a sick twist inside of me. I don't want to know, don't want to look.

Next photo – they're in his car. Kissing.

Then there are more photos. The front of a hotel. They are checking in together. The time – a clock on the wall. Later, another of photo of Philip, leaving the hotel alone. The time on the clock a few hours later. He looks pleased with himself, doesn't he? And about an hour later, he came home to me. He had a shower when he got home. Was he trying to get the smell of her from his skin? I run up the stairs to our room, the laundry bin. Find the clothes he was wearing yesterday and take them out, and yes, there is a definite smell. Sweat and semen and a particular something else I can't quite place until I shake out his shirt. A few thin streaks of brownish-red. It's blood – bloodstains. Do they play rough? Was it her fingernails digging into his back? Did he think I wouldn't notice?

I'm angry – furious – shaking. His betrayal so soon after he said he'd never do it again is a red-hot pain, so intense. I'm skewered by it and want to scream, to slam him into the side of our house with my car for real this time.

Who took these photos, left them and the note for me? Did she set it up – have an accomplice there, taking photographs, so I can see what he's up to?

And what now?

I'm sure what I'm supposed to do is follow the wronged wife script – scream at him and run away. So I'll do nothing. See what happens next.

Besides, if anyone is leaving our home, it's Philip. If she thinks I'll just step away and leave her to the spoils, she couldn't be more wrong.

It's going to take a hell of an acting job. Am I up for it?

I don't know.

I get through the evening. We eat pasta and he doesn't comment on the unexpected takeaway. He's probably too busy thinking of *her* to notice. Before he said she was just a girl, no one important, yet he goes to a hotel with her just a few days after telling me I'm the only one he's ever loved and it will never happen again. The only *never* in this situation is that I'll never believe another word he says.

I'm consumed with wanting – *needing* – to know everything. Every detail of their relationship – when it started, how. How long it has been going on with me being a trusting idiot. I've searched through the house as much as I can. What I need is access to his phone. His, like mine, unlocks with facial recognition. Would a photo of his face work? If not, maybe a video? I hunt through my phone looking for a good face shot, then a section of video where he is staring at the camera. Send them to my laptop so they can be the right size on the screen.

I go to bed early. I pretend to be asleep when he comes up, gets in the shower. I open my laptop and get his phone.

First I try the photo. Nothing. I tilt it around a little to see if it will unlock if I change the angle. No. Video next. I play it, holding his phone about the right distance for his head to be the size it'd be if he was holding the phone to unlock it. Nothing. I try again, several times at different angles, but get nowhere.

Then the water cuts off – he'll be out of the bathroom in a moment. I put his phone back where it was and go to my side of the bed, face the wall and pretend to be asleep. Listen to him moving around the room, then getting into bed. Switching off the bedside light.

If he *dares* to try to reach for me, to touch me – I'll lose it. But whether he gets the cold shoulder when he feels it or is just too worn out by her to bother, he settles into bed and stays on his side.

It's not long before even breathing says he is asleep. That he can sleep so peacefully, with the things he has done?

He has no shame.

50

FREJA

Philip would barely recognise me like this. Minimal make-up. Hair loose and brushed shiny. Jeans and low-cut jersey top. I inspect myself critically in a mirror in the Brighton station bathroom. I could easily pass for years younger than my twenty-eight if it wasn't for my eyes. They are too wary and have seen too much. Is that what scared Jess away the other night?

I try for a more wide-eyed look. Imagine I'm one of them, that Mummy and Daddy have paid to send me to university, that nothing worse than the bumps and scrapes of childhood has ever happened to me in my short, privileged life.

Better.

I head out. I was delayed by a cancelled train in London so it's later than I meant to be, but things are still lively. There are a half dozen student places I'll try first. The laughter, warmth. Crowds of bodies, eyes drawn – *who is she* a few say to their friends, but they're not who I've come for. I fall in with one crowd and another, blending, flirting, seeking.

And finally, there he is. He's even taller than his father. He has his dark hair, a bit longer and curling around his ears. If you didn't look closely he could pass for closer to my age. A drink in my hand and good timing: he knocks into me, and it spills.

'Oh, sorry,' he says.

I sigh. 'That was the last of my monthly allowance and still the whole week to get through.'

'Let me get you another.'

'You don't have to—'

'I insist. I'm James, by the way.'

I smile. Hold out a hand. 'I'm Lucky.' I don't know why I said that this time, it's an improbable name, but on the other hand, tonight, I'm sure it fits. A drink is bought and another, and his friends exchange glances with him and move away, leaving us alone.

I remember how things went wrong with Jess. Tonight, I will take things at his pace.

After a while, he holds my hand. A long while, and it did take me brushing his hand with mine.

'I love Brighton,' I say. 'Don't you?'

He nods. 'More and more. What are your favourite things about it?'

'Let's see. Brighton rock.'

'You've got a sweet tooth.'

I run my tongue over my upper lip. 'Oh, yes.'

'What else?'

'The sea. I love walking on the beach at night.'

He takes the hint. We stand, head for the door. He slips his arm over my shoulders as we walk down to the beach. We stop under moonlight, and I'm smiling into his eyes. He leans down and kisses me. Then we sit on the beach and he's kissing me some more.

I haven't got all night, so suggest it first. He seems shocked but sneaks me back into his halls readily enough. His room is small, basic. Single bed.

Somehow we cope. More enthusiasm than finesse. He's stroking my hair afterwards, a look of wonder in his eyes and I make mine a mirror.

'I should go; my flatmates will be worried,' I say, finally.

'Message them.'

'It's not just that. I've got an early start tomorrow.'

'I'll walk you back.' I shake my head, stand, his eyes on me as I get dressed. For a moment I'm thinking, I wish I could be who he thinks I am. Just starting out. Not weighed down by all that came before.

'Can I see you again?' he says.

'Maybe.'

'I don't know anything about you.'

'What is there to know?'

'Your phone number would be a good start.'

I take a pen off his desk and write it across his arm. Kiss him and leave him with a smile on his face.

It won't last.

51

LOU

I've stared at the ceiling for so long, listening to Philip's soft snoring, when it occurs to me: would his sleeping face unlock his phone? I listen to his breathing – even, steady – and get out of bed slowly, carefully. I walk around to his side of the bed.

There is enough light from the digital clock on his bedside table to see his phone next to it. I pick it up and the screen comes to life. The screen is so bright. I hope it won't disturb him, but I have to try. I hold it in front of his face at about arm's length – it doesn't work. Maybe it has to be closer? I move it in a little closer and try again. Nothing. A little closer—

He stirs, he's waking up. I freeze. How can I explain this? His eyes flutter open part way, then he yawns, turns. He's breathing evenly again. I didn't realise I was holding my breath until I release it. I'm about to replace his phone when I glance at the screen. It's unlocked. Was it having his eyes part open that did it? I don't care how it worked; I'm in.

I tiptoe across to grab my phone and laptop, then out our bedroom door. What next? I'm itching to go through his social apps and calendar, but this is an opportunity to get into Lex, his legal software. Then I'll be able to go through his clients and work schedule. I'll do that first.

I tiptoe down the stairs to his office. Go in, shut the door and put on the desk light. I know the password to his computer – I have used it now and then, as it is connected to the printer. It's easier to use his if I need to print something quickly.

I log in to his laptop, get his passwords for MS and Lex from his password manager. Then log in to it on my laptop and use his phone for two-factor authentication, then delete notifications sent to his phone and email about the new login. Now I can go through Lex on my laptop another time.

I creep back up the stairs, to a guest room. Into the en suite and lock the door. I start with his social media apps. I don't see anything of interest in his messages in the first few. Then I go into WhatsApp and scan the list of chats. There is one that stands out as not having the name of the person or group involved like all the others – this one is just initials, FL. Could F be for Freja?

I select the chat. See the most recent messages, then scan back further.

It is her, and it's so much worse than I imagined. Most of it is arranging times and places to meet. Occasional photos of Freja in various stages of undress. Interspersed with things like, *miss you. Can't wait to hold you.* The words he has sent to her stab into my heart.

I keep reading and, as I go, take photo after photo of the screen on my own phone, not even sure why I'm doing this. For a future divorce lawyer, perhaps, or to cut myself repeatedly, a small death with every endearment?

I go all the way back. To the first exchange. It was almost six months ago – it's been going on as long as that? He never answered when I asked him how long he'd been seeing her, that time when we met for dinner. He implied with things he said then and since that it was nothing, meant nothing. But *six months* isn't nothing.

Alphabetically, FL is just above a chat with our daughter, Flick. It seems so wrong that they are next to each other on his phone.

His very first message to Freja.

> I can't stop thinking about you.

I'm shattering inside, tiny pieces with jagged edges. So sharp that they cut deep.

But I'm not the only one who will suffer. I'll make sure of that.

I sit there, cold, alone. Hour after hour. Going through every message, again and again, somehow unable to stop myself. I'm startled when the time registers. It isn't long until sunrise. I can't let Philip wake and find his phone missing. I slip back into our room. He's still sleeping soundly. He's moved across a little, one arm flung across my side of the bed. When he's asleep like this, he looks younger. I can see traces of the twenty-something man who fell in love with me and me with him. How could he have done these things?

I take a dressing gown, go downstairs to where I've hidden the photos that were left under our mat. I should be exhausted, but I'm strangely wired, alert. I look at them again, one after the other. She could have an accomplice who took these for her, and the whole point was to get me to leave Philip. Maybe she'd tried to get him to end things with me and he wouldn't, so she had to try to find another way. But there is something about the photos that doesn't seem quite right for that. They are like surveillance photographs, or images taken from CCTV. The resolution isn't great as if they were taken from a distance, often at odd angles – taken in such a way that neither Philip or Freja would notice. If she'd known the camera was there, would she have glanced towards it, or positioned Philip more clearly in its path?

Maybe there is another player in all of this. One who not only forced me to face the painful truth, but also chose to do it in a way that terrified me – using anonymous notes. My past isn't exactly a secret – anyone who wanted to find out about it probably could do so online. But *why* would someone do this?

Then there is the photo of Philip in our bed that was there and then gone on that fan page. It was a close-up, suggesting she took it herself. Why? Was it to alert me, or upset Philip? To cause distress to our family? If these were the goals, some of these other photos – of them kissing, and going into a hotel – would have done a better job. Which makes me think she definitely didn't have access to them.

There is too much going on that I don't understand. But I *do* know that someone is stalking and manipulating me – *trying* to manipulate me, that is – and I won't let them do it any more.

I'll stay put. And I'll hunt them down.

52

JESSIE

I see James across the quad at lunch and go to join him on the grass. I realise it is the first chance we've had to talk on our own since Mum and Dad got back together. I haven't told him about that post on the fan page, either, and keeping secrets from James, even with the best intentions, feels, well, wrong. It is also possible that he knows, and hasn't told me – and that feels even worse.

'Do you know what's been going on with the parentals?' I say.

'Dunno. But that's got to be the shortest break-up in history.'

I look at him closely. 'You know something. Don't you?'

He shakes his head, but he's hiding something.

'Tell me, or I've got secrets of yours going way back.'

'You're such a child.'

'I'm two minutes older than you.'

'Don't I know it – you never let me forget. I don't *know* anything. I guessed something and Mum didn't deny it, that's all.'

I study his face; he squirms. I'm sure of it; he knew. 'So, one of them had an affair.' Despite having seen that photo of Dad, it hurts to have it confirmed. 'In which case I'm not sure that getting back together minutes later is, well, healthy, for either of them.'

'Days, not minutes, but who knows? Let them live their lives and hope they let us live ours.' This doesn't sound like James usually would. There's something else he's not telling me.

'I thought you were going to show at the pub last night. Where were you?'

'Sorry-not-sorry. Got waylaid,' he says, with a certain kind of grin as he says the last word.

I'm instantly on alert. 'You met someone. Didn't you? What's her name?'

'Good work on the twin-dar. Can you tell what I'm thinking now?'

'Yes I can, and I won't keep my nose out of your business. So, I repeat. What is her name?'

'Lucky.'

'So, what you're actually telling me is that you got lucky with Lucky?' I'm laughing. 'Is that a real name or did she give you an alias?'

'Enough with the puns. And a gentleman never tells.'

'You *did*; don't deny it. I can see it all over your face. You only met her last night, and then that? Seriously? Hope you used protection. With a girl like that you might catch something.'

'Jessie! It wasn't like that.' He's looking properly annoyed now.

'So, set me straight. What *was* it like?'

'Our eyes met across a crowded room and everyone else just vanished.' He sighs and lies back on the grass.

I thump his arm. 'James, get a grip. That dopey look on your face is making me nauseous.'

'I think I'm in love.'

'Sure you are. You've known her, for what – how many hours?

Love at first sight is such a crock.' That's what I say, but I'm the one who can't stop thinking about Ella, and how long did I know her? More like minutes than hours.

'You're just jealous.'

'As if. What else do you know about her? Apart from that she has questionable taste. Is she a student? What subject? Her surname? When you will see her again?'

'None of that matters, except that I *know* I'll see her again.'

'When?'

He shrugs. 'Soon.'

'So, you know absolutely nothing about her apart from a mystical connection that says you will see her again.'

'Well, and this.' He sits up and shows me his arm, a phone number written across it.

'Tell me you plan to wash that off at some point. Have you called or messaged her already, so she knows how desperate you are?'

'So, she knows how much I care, you mean?' he says. 'I've messaged.' A shadow crosses his face, there and gone quickly but we're so in tune I know what it means.

'But she hasn't answered.'

'Not yet. But she will.'

'Be careful, James. I don't want you to get hurt.'

'I know. But I won't be.' Said with complete confidence. Maybe he's right and this is the real thing, and one day they'll be telling their grandkids about it.

But I doubt it.

Even when we were fighting over toys we have always been so close. It's like we got mixed up in the womb, as if some of what I am and some of what he is in each other. If he hurts, then so do I. James has always been so open, trusting. As if I'm overcompensating, I'm more the opposite. We'd average out fine, but maybe either way isn't a great way to live. At least he went for it and didn't run away like I did.

James messages me later.

> She's messaged back and we're meeting up tomorrow night, ye of little faith.

I'm pleased that he is pleased, but maybe less damage would have been done if she'd ghosted him now instead of later. I answer:

> Try to find out her full name etc this time.

He responds with an eye-rolling emoji.

53

FREJA

It was only 8 a.m. when James' messages started. It's afternoon now and I'm barely awake at work after getting the late train back to London from Brighton last night.

> I can't stop thinking about you. What are you doing tonight?
>
> When can I see you again?

I don't answer. Leave it until my afternoon break. Then tap in a reply:

> Who is this?

A pause – hurt feelings?

> It's James.

> James who?

> From last night?

> Oh, of course!

You were teasing.

> Sure. Let's go with that. *winking face*

So...? What are you doing tonight?

> I'm busy. Sorry.

I'm not busy, not unless Philip calls. But it is best to keep him uncertain, off balance. And he must be, because he doesn't answer for a while.

How about tomorrow night?

I string him along into the early evening, messaging maybe once to every four or five from him. Then finally agree to meet him tomorrow night.

Soon after there is a message from Philip.

I miss you. How about we get together at lunch tomorrow?

Lunch? Is he worried about getting caught if we go out in the evening?

> That'd give you indigestion.

Willing to risk it.

> No. I'll be at work.

How about tomorrow night?

I pause, thinking how to play it. It might be time to make him jealous, to make him take more risks.

Sorry, can't. I have another date.

I smile. And think how shocked he'd be if he knew who with.

54

LOU

I had all the answers at 4 a.m. but as the day wears on, all my certainty goes with it. All I really know is that Philip is cheating and lying. Freja may have some kind of agenda, and she might or might not be responsible for the notes and photographs. It is all guesswork. I'm exhausted but can't close my eyes. I need to talk it through.

Part me of me wants Steve. To call him, tell him everything. He's a detective. If there is something obvious I'm missing in all of this, he might see it. But I don't trust myself alone with him. Part of me just wants to cry and scream and then be held, protected, but isn't that how I ended up with Philip in the first place? And I don't want to use Steve like that. No. I have to rely on myself, and I will, but I still need someone to talk things through.

There really is only one choice.

Iona answers on the first ring. 'Hi. What's up?'

'Ah. I – well. Can we talk in person?'

'Hang on a moment.' I wait what feels like a long moment, then another, not sure if this is the right thing to do or what I should say to her. I just need a friend, another point of view. But she's not exactly a neutral ear as far as Philip goes. Maybe this is a bad idea.

'Sorry, I just had to reschedule something. Do you want to come here?'

I do, if I could blink and be there, but if I've learned anything it's never drive when you are upset. 'Can you come here? I'm not sure I should drive.'

'I'm on my way.'

'Wait. You must promise me something first.'

'What's that?'

'That you won't tell anyone what I tell you. And you won't push me to do something I don't want to do.'

'Those are pretty big promises.' There is a pause. 'You've got the first one. As far as the second one goes, I can tell you what I think, but I won't push you. Is that enough?'

'Yes.'

It'll take at least an hour and a half, likely longer, for her to get here.

I'm pacing, actually wringing my hands until I notice and make myself stop. I'm dizzy, too – it's the lack of sleep, I think, then realise I haven't eaten anything yet today. Nothing in the fridge appeals. In the end I get out the chocolate biscuits that I keep on hand for James. The pack is half gone when my phone beeps and I'm afraid Iona is delayed, but instead, it's Steve.

> Hey, how are you doing? Thinking of you. Call any time if you want to talk.

What is he, psychic?

> Hi, I'm OK. Iona is just on her way over.

I'm not anything approaching OK and I'm glad she is on her way over – otherwise I'd have called him by now.

Offer is always open xx

Tears prick in my eyes, and I blink them back as I reply:

Thank you

I need to distract myself, think of something else. I get my laptop and sign into Lex. Soon I'm ensconced in Philip's schedule, his current and recent clients. I note names to search, find the cases they've been involved in and their opponents, but don't find any likely prospects.

I've calmed down by the time Iona arrives, but she still looks alarmed when I open the door. I must look a state.

'Thank you for coming,' I say, gesture her in and close the door against the world.

'You know that I'm always in your corner, hon. What's happened?'

I don't know where to start, but they say a picture is worth a thousand words. I show her the photos of Philip, Freja. The hotel.

Her eyes are wide. 'Where did you get these?'

'The anonymous writer of notes left them under the doormat.'

'You've been getting more notes?' I nod. 'You should have said.'

'I didn't want to worry you. And Steve took some of them to check for fingerprints, but nothing came up. He said they must have been wearing gloves.'

'So, what now? I'll help you pack.'

'No. I'm not leaving. Don't you see – whoever it is, that is what they want me to do.'

'What about what *you* want? Did you talk to Philip about any of this? By talk, I mean scream and throw things.'

'No.'

'What about that photo on the fan page? I saw it was taken down – I assumed you'd told him.'

I shake my head. 'I was going to – decided I had to – but I looked again before he got home, and it was already gone. I assumed he had it taken down.'

'Did he say anything about it to you?'

I shake my head.

'He should have. You don't know who might have seen it, where it might pop up again.'

'I know. But he didn't.'

Iona is shaking her head, distressed on my behalf. I can't give in to her sympathy or I'll lose it completely and there are more things to say.

'That's not all. I got into Philip's phone. He's been seeing Freja—'

'You know her name?'

'I'll get to that. He's been seeing her, frequently, for six months. And these photos are from after I came home, so it is still going on.' I show her the paper and its date on the first one.

'You must leave him, Lou. You don't deserve the way he's been treating you.'

I shake my head. 'I can't. There's more going on here.' I explain all the things I've thought through – that Freja, or some shady other character, has an agenda – not just to take Philip, but to act against me and our whole family. That there must be more involved for it to all make sense.

'If you really think that – go to the police. Or maybe Steve. Call him and see what he thinks.'

I shake my head. 'I can't involve him any further. It wouldn't be fair – I'd be using him. I won't do that. And I don't think the police would listen to me. They never helped me before, so why would they now? There's no point.'

'So, what are you going to do?'

I tell her how I got Freja's name from her voicemail, that her initials are FL on Philip's WhatsApp. That I'm sure I remember her from somewhere, so must have come across her before. That from their messages, I have all kinds of details of places Philip has met her in the past. I'm going to go through it all, try to find her.

'Then what?'

'I'll work it out.'

'There is one thing that worries me in all this.'

'Only one?' I half-smile.

'You're focusing on Freja as being the bad actor in all of this. Maybe she's just an innocent—'

'Innocent?!'

'*Listen.* Maybe she's just a woman who has fallen for a married guy – won't be the first, won't be the last. The one who has been lying to you, deceiving you, is Philip. You need to get out of here. Get away from him.'

'I won't. I can't. I'm staying until I've got it all worked out and I know my family is safe. And I'm not only focused on her; I'm looking at other possibilities.' I explain how I spoke to Philip's senior clerk and that I've been going through his recent clients, looking for anyone else who might hold a grudge. That I've been thinking through the past, too. In case my stalker has come back on the scene.

She's silent a moment. 'I'm so worried about you,' she says, finally.

'But you won't tell anyone or push me to do anything. You promised.'

She shakes her head, glances at her phone. 'Sorry. I rescheduled some things, but I have to go soon. Will you be all right?' I nod, even though I'm far from sure. 'You'll let me know if anything else happens – more notes are left or anything else?'

'I will. I promise. Thank you for coming all this way, Iona. You really are the only person I trust completely.'

She turns to the mirror, straightens her hair.

Gives me a hug and says goodbye. The look on her face as she goes – she's uneasy, worried. Maybe I shouldn't have called her, told her all these things. Despite her promises, if she thinks I'm in any kind of danger or losing the plot completely, would she tell someone? I don't know.

* * *

That evening, instead of applying more make-up to hide the sleep I haven't been getting and an acting job I'm not sure I'm up to any more, I tell Philip I'm unwell, that I'll sleep in a guest room. He manages to look concerned, to make his own dinner and offer me some.

I'm in bed early. I pretend to be asleep when he comes to check on me a few hours later, on way to bed himself. I'm so glad I thought of this. I couldn't bear the thought of being in the same room with him any longer, let alone the same bed.

I can't stop thinking about Freja. Why did I recognise her? There is an odd feeling to it, a sense of both dread and time having passed. Though if I'm right that she's in her twenties now, it couldn't be too long ago.

I slip to uneasy dreams. A small blonde girl, eight or nine years old, staring at me with an odd smile, a maniacal look in glowing eyes – like a child from *Village of the Damned*.

Every time I turn around she is there, staring.

55

JESSIE

I'm on a bench under trees with a view of James' halls entrance, watching for him. Far enough away that he's unlikely to spot me. I'm struggling to sit still, full of nervous energy and unsure if I'm doing the right thing, lying in wait for him like this. But I really need to talk to him.

When I called, he said he had another date with Lucky-who-he-got-Lucky-with the other night. I'm hurt he didn't get how much I needed to see him. The more I think about Mum and everything that happened to her years ago, the more worried I am about her. I need to tell him the things I didn't before and get his take on all of it. He's more intuitive about people than I am. Usually. Unless it's a beautiful girl and then sense goes out the window. That he's prioritised seeing Lucky over me adds worry about him to the worry about Mum, and it's all just too much.

He comes out just after seven. I hang back and follow. This is completely wrong for so many reasons – I get that – but I'm anxious, beyond just worrying he'll get hurt if it goes wrong, and I don't know why. I'm closer to James than anyone. If anything is wrong with the other we just know, without being told, and there is something about what is going on that just feels beyond *wrong*, in my gut.

He goes into a pub, not one of the usual student ones. I slip in after a while, behind some other people going in. Good thing they're blocking his view as he's sitting at a table watching the door. I go to the other side of the bar. He won't see me here unless he turns around.

He's waiting. Looking at his phone, sending a message. Waiting some more. She isn't going to show, is she? He's looking sadder by the minute, and I've almost hit the point where I'll have to come out from the other side of the bar and buy him a drink and tell him to forget her. But then, the unexpected happens. Ella walks in the door. I'd been hoping to see her again somewhere, anywhere, and the timing isn't great, but—

Ella goes up to James. He stands, hugs her, and he's turned to the side enough that I can see his face has lit up in a smile, like how he smiled at his bicycle Christmas present when he was ten. I'm confused. I don't understand what is happening. She sits down with him and now they're holding hands.

I gasp when it all slides into place.

This is who James was meeting. Lucky is Ella, or Ella is Lucky – which name is real? What the fuck is going on?

I'm watching her, her face animated when she tells him something. It's a gut punch to see her with James, to see her with anybody. After I'd left her in that bar, I thought I'd imagined how gorgeous she is. I didn't. If anything, the opposite. She is way out of his league, out of my league, too. She's not just pretty or even beautiful – she's beyond that, into fantasy territory: creamy pale skin, ash blonde hair. Curvy and thin but not too thin. Those blue eyes that even from here I can see the colour. And I want to keep looking at her and never stop, but she's with James.

I'm jealous. I hate to admit that. If I'd stayed with her that night, maybe she'd be here with me now. Instead, she's with James and I can't see why she'd bother with my awkward brother after how she was with me. He goes to the bar for drinks. Once he's left her, her smile fades and with it there is something almost chilling in her eyes, calculating, as she scans the room. Too late I realise I'm staring, and now her eyes have found mine. *Way to spy, Jess.* She tilts her head in recognition. What do we do now? Should I confront her – ask her what her name is, really? But how would James take that? I don't know.

He's back now with their drinks; she says something and now his eyes have found me, too.

He leaves her where she is, comes over to me.

'What the hell, Jess? Have you been following me?'

'No. Of course not. I just wanted to get out—'

'Yeah, sure. *Don't* do that again.'

'Did she tell you we've met?' But he's not listening. He goes back to her and leaves me behind.

I've got to tell him. Whatever is going on, it's not what he thinks. There is no way she randomly hit on me one night, and then, when it didn't pan out, randomly happened to meet my twin. That's not just a little bit of weird, it's a whole lot of weird. But he's not going to listen to anything I say tonight. Not while she's smiling at him the way she is now. It shouldn't but it aches, inside, to see her looking at my brother like that instead of me. I head for the door. Whatever I do will have to be another time.

But what *can* I do? Try to tell him all this, make him see reason? It won't work. He's bewitched. Maybe all I can do is wait until it implodes, his heart along with it. That's what he wants me to do, but I remember when that witch Amy from school strung him along and cheated on him, how long it took him to recover. It wasn't just a broken heart. It was like it destroyed his sense of who he was, and sent him to a very dark place. I was so worried; everyone was.

Maybe he won't listen, but I'll still have to try.

For a moment I think about calling Mum, see what she thinks, but soon dismiss it. She has her own problems at the moment, and anyhow, it would totally break the twin-code. I couldn't do that unless something went far wrong.

James, please. *Be careful.* And despite telling myself that this is all about him, keeping him safe – I can't help it. I'm picturing them kissing, going to bed. I'm burning with jealousy.

I can't tell if this conviction that she is wrong for James, that something else is going on, is just because I want her for myself. Can I trust my instincts when I'm so twisted up inside?

I don't know.

56

FREJA

I am forty minutes late and didn't answer the messages James sent asking where I was, but he still smiles to see me – a grin that takes over his face. The unconditional love in his eyes is very like a puppy – it may be cute, but all that jumping up and slobbering would get annoying after a while.

He goes to get me a drink. I scan the room. With a jolt of recognition, I spot Jess on the other side of the bar. Her eyes are locked on mine, completely different to James' puppy eyes, and harder to look away. Yet there is enough of each of them in each other that if I didn't already know they were twins, I would have known they were brother and sister.

By the time he is back with our drinks, I've decided how to deal with this.

'There's someone who has been staring at me. Do you know who she is?' I gesture across the room.

He rolls his eyes. 'That is my twin sister, Jessie.'

'Seriously? Your parents named you Jessie and James?'

'Afraid so.'

'What's she doing here?'

'I could be wrong, but she might be keeping an eye on me.'

'Why? Aren't you an adult?'

'Of course I am,' he says, but winces at the question. They may be twins, but he's treated as the baby of his family, isn't he? And he doesn't like it.

'There is something you should know about your sister.'

'What's that?'

I look all uncertain, uneasy and have his complete attention.

'Is something wrong?'

'It's just – I met her. Last week. She was hitting on me pretty hard. I had trouble convincing her I wasn't interested.'

'Seriously?' He's surprised and I'm not sure at which part of the story. Maybe he knows Jess well enough to know that she wouldn't pursue anyone like that – it's not her style. Or maybe it's just the thought that she may have met me before he did.

'Completely. I don't think she took it very well. Anyhow, I think you should call her off. It's weird thinking someone is watching us – especially your sister, after what happened the other night.'

He gets up, walks across to her. Jess looks upset at whatever he says. She gets up a moment later, heads for the door. He comes back to me, a troubled look on his face.

'That's better. Now I can do this.' I kiss him, and whatever was troubling him about his sister is gone, forgotten. My puppy is back.

We have this drink, another. I cover myself and tell him that Lucky is a nickname – I'm really Ella.

I can see through him: he's agonising over whether the other night was a one-off. Will we, won't we? I alternate between flirting and cool, keep him off balance. Pretend I can't decide. But finally take him back to his narrow single bed. More enthusiasm without technique follows. This time I'm a little bored and don't hide it. Can't help but think his sister would have been more fun.

He's anxious afterwards, confused. Wants to hold me and talk. Ask endless questions about me, what I think, how I feel, that I mostly deflect.

I fall asleep and I'm annoyed when I wake up and the sun is streaming through the window. I meant to get home last night. His eyes are open, staring at me as if I'm precious, a work of art that he can't believe he can touch. He reaches for me, but I pull away. Get dressed and go.

57

LOU

After another night of poor sleep leaves me exhausted, Philip has no trouble believing I'm ill when he comes to check on me before heading to work. I try to get back to sleep, but whenever I close my eyes I see Freja, the horror movie child of my nightmare.

I give up. Get dressed to face the day. I need to leave the fantastical behind and focus on the facts. It all started with notes – all but one left on my car. And not just the car I had, but the new one, too.

When I found a note on the Mini after having lunch with Janice, not many people would even have known I had a new car, or what it looked like. The thought that I'm being followed – that no matter where I go, someone knows where I am – is horrifying. But how could anyone do this without being spotted? I'm always checking who is behind me, around me.

Unless they are somehow following me without being in sight.

How?

I do some internet searches. There are tracking apps that use location sharing on iPhones. As far as I know the only one enabled on my phone is to find it if it is lost or stolen. Just in case another app is enabled that I don't know about, I go to the security and privacy settings on my phone; turn location sharing off completely. Done.

Another way people can be found is if they check in places on social media. But I never do that.

There are tracking devices people use for their pets, kids, in case they get lost. Simple ones can be bought online – small discs that could be hidden easily. Could there be something like that on me that I'm not aware of? It'd have to be something I always have with me. I find my usual handbag, search through every inch of it. I even cut the lining to make sure nothing has been hidden and then stitched up. Nothing.

I can't think of anything else I've worn or always had with me besides my bag. Even my car has changed. Though… what if someone put a tracker on my Jeep, and then on the Mini, too? They'd have needed access to both vehicles, though that's not hard. They're parked on the drive at night. While it's possible the Jeep has been left unlocked long enough at some point in the past for something to be hidden inside of it, I'm certain the Mini hasn't been. So, it'd have to be somewhere that can be accessed on the outside of the car.

Some more searching online – trackers can be magnetic. So, someone could have placed one on any metal part of the car that can be reached from the outside.

I go out and survey my car from all angles, thinking where it could be that it wouldn't be easily seen or dislodged, then fetch a torch. First on my hands and knees, then lying on my back, I move slowly around the car. Shining the torch and looking everywhere my eyes can reach, feeling with my hands where they can't. I'm about to give up – maybe take it to a garage where they can put it on a ramp and search properly – when I feel something with the tips of my fingers. It's round, stuck on a part of the undercarriage not easily seen or reached. I move as close as I can to it to get a better grip, and tug; nothing happens. If it is a magnet, it's a strong one. I try again, this time pulling it to one side. It slides a little and I put some more force into sliding it towards me. It comes off in my hand.

I sit next to the car and look at my prize. A round, metal disc with a number imprinted on it but no other markings. If this is what I think it is, it's proof that somebody has been tracking my whereabouts. I'm furious, almost throw it as far as I can, but no. If it goes astray and they notice, they could put another on my car. I can't search it like this every time I go anywhere.

So, what do I do now? No one could call this a figment of my imagination: it's a real, physical thing. The police will have to believe me if I call them in officially. But maybe, instead, I can use it to my advantage. Whoever put it there doesn't know I've found it. They'll think they can still track me, and I can leave it wherever I want. Like here, for example. I can go out and they'll think I'm at home.

I take some photos of it on my phone, then push it down deep into the dirt of the flower bed next to our drive, noting where in case I want to extract it another time. I brush dirt from my hands, clothes, then head back inside.

What next?

There is a chance that Iona was right – that Freja is just a woman who has fallen for Philip, and that is all there is to her. But ever since I first saw her in bed with Philip, she is all I can think about. And I recognised her – I know I did. If I can work out why, maybe I can find some answers.

She's such a striking woman that I can't believe I can't place her. Unless... seeing her as a child in my dream was a clue from my subconscious, and I remember her from years ago?

That *feels* right, as if I'm onto something. When Freja was a child is likely around the same times Jessie and James made an appearance. Once they were born, taking care of the twins and Flick was my entire world. I often couldn't remember what day of the week it was, let alone much else.

But I try. I cast my mind back, to the nursery run, school gates with Flick; birthday parties and neighbourhood events. But I just can't remember a little girl that could be Freja.

Another dead end.

Could she have been involved somehow in one of Philip's cases – perhaps the daughter of a client? Or further back, when Philip was still in the Met. She could have been involved somehow in a crime or be the daughter of a criminal. But he didn't tell me much about his work in the police, and minors aren't named or shown in news reports, unless they have died or are missing. Either way, there'd be no reason for me to recognise her.

Yet I'd felt so sure that going back to the beginning was the right approach. Maybe it's my past instead of Freja's that I need to interrogate.

58

LUCY

My kit bag needs to be bigger, or I need to be more organised. Spare rackets, shirts, energy gel, shoes, laces. My questing hand finally feels the roll of tennis grip and I pull it out. As I do so, something flutters to the ground. I stare at it, forgetting the grip. Forgetting my racket, today's singles match and all that is dependent on a win.

I reach for the note. Unfold it. Read words that blur in and out of focus with fear.

I'm watching you now. I'll find you later.

'Time,' the umpire says, and I hear it as if through water. Look up when she repeats. I get up, resume the match, but my focus is gone. I keep looking around at the stands, the people watching us – is he the one? Or him? From winning the first set I quickly lose the next two and I almost don't care; at last, I can escape all the eyes, and those of my exasperated coach, too.

A hot shower soon soothes my muscles, but I stand there, feeling cold inside. *How* did he get a note in my kit bag?

I'm out of the shower, a towel wrapped around me when I see the blurry letters, written in steam on the mirror:

I've found you.

59

LOU

I pretend to be asleep until Philip leaves for Saturday morning golf. All the while, my mind is turning over everything I know about this woman. Her first name: Freja. Likely surname initial: L. The various notes that have been left for me to find. Lachlan going missing briefly – that was at Westfield London. Then I'm remembering what Steve said about the CCTV he checked: that he couldn't say for sure if Lachlan was taken or not because of a gap in the camera coverage. Then the same thing happened where the keys were found. This suggests to me that unless whoever did these things is very lucky, they know exactly where the cameras are at Westfield.

How would they know? Someone who worked there in security would do so. Stereotyping here, but Freja didn't look like any security guard I've ever seen. Would someone who worked at Westfield in some other capacity know where all the cameras were? If they are there all the time, maybe they'd scoped them out.

I make myself look at the photos that were left under our doormat again. In the first one, Philip is on his own, walking into what looks like a pub or bar. There isn't a sign or anything I can see to identify where he is, but it looks a little familiar, as if I'd walked past it before, but not so familiar as if I'd been there myself. If Freja works somewhere in or around Westfield, maybe the place in the photo is there? He's outside, so it might be on the southern terrace. There are many restaurants along there and a few pubs.

Philip knows I hate shopping, and malls in particular. I'd never have gone to Westfield the other day if Flick hadn't picked it. Maybe that made him feel secure, meeting her in public there. That I'd be unlikely to chance across them.

I'll go in person, have a look. Whoever put the tracker on my car won't know I'm on the move, buried in the dirt by our drive as it is.

I head out, and, as usual, wince as I look at the windscreen, but there is nothing there. The note writer must have other plans today.

I'm so tired, I drive with exaggerated care. Windows open and music on, I'm glad when I finally arrive and park my car. Iona is right – my car *is* like a bumble bee. It doesn't exactly scream discreet surveillance, but if anyone spots me, tough. It might be out of character, but I have every right to be here.

I walk around the southern terrace, the restaurants and pubs that line the walkway. It doesn't take long to find what I'm looking for: a place called The Bull. How apt. The photos are in my bag. I take the relevant one out, compare. Yes. This is definitely the place where he met her the other night. It's not far at all from where I had lunch with Flick and Jessie, and there is something obscene about their father meeting this bitch so close to where two of his children and his grandson were, just days ago.

I go in and to the bar, wondering how many times he's met

her here. Order a soft drink, have a seat at a table and look around. It's quiet. Only two staff I can see. I think for a moment and then go back to the bar.

'Excuse me. I met someone here the other day – she left her phone behind. I've got it but can't call her – since I have her phone! She comes here all the time, so maybe you know her? Her name is Freja.' I describe her, trying to keep spite out of my voice as I do so.

'Sorry, I don't know. But I'm daytimes only. Alice?' A waitress comes over, and I repeat my story.

'I know her. She's here fairly often after work. She works in a shop – can't remember which one. I think it sells, like, make-up and stuff like that?'

'Thanks.'

'Do you want to leave it here – she might come back for it if this is where she left it?'

I shake my head; say I'll see if I can find her in the mall first. Then I wonder if they'll ask if she got her phone back the next time she is in. Doesn't matter. It's about time someone besides me is worried about being stalked.

I finish my drink and check the store directory on my phone. There are a few possibilities. I make a list and head across into the mall and follow the directory to the first one. Walk up to the desk.

'Hi, is Freja working today?'

'Who?'

'Freja.'

'No one with that name works here.'

'OK, sorry, got the wrong place.'

I find the second place – same result.

I head for the third shop on my list. As I get closer, I recognise the brand on display. Philip bought me a load of stuff from the same company for my last birthday.

I'm about to walk in with the same question when I see her through the glass, smiling at a man who is making a purchase. It's her. She's there.

My birthday was four months ago. They were already seeing each other then. Did he ask her advice on what to buy his wife? Maybe she made jokes about the needs of more mature skin.

The rush of anger through me makes me want to march straight in and confront her, here and now. Demand to know what she is up to. But if she refuses to say anything, what will that accomplish? Nothing. It'll put her on her guard, that's all. And what if she tells Philip I'm on to him? No. Instead I'll do what has been done to me.

I don't know what time she finishes work, so hurry to a clothing shop nearby – buy a ridiculously expensive scarf. Use the mirror there to wrap it around my hair. Done. If she happens to glance back she shouldn't be able to recognise me, not if I don't get too close.

And now, I wait. There's a coffee shop near enough to watch the front of the shop where she works. I watch as she sells things to one person, another. Such a boring, dead-end job. No wonder she's after Philip – looking for a way out. She says something to the other woman she works with – they both laugh. Maybe they're talking about me, how I've been duped.

I hope she's not working all evening until closing time; there are only so many cups of coffee I can drink in one place. It's just after six when she disappears out back, reappears a few minutes later. Handbag on her arm and a light jacket on. She waves at the other woman and exits the shop.

I leave money on my table. Wait a moment, then get up and follow her. She's easy to spot in the midst of shoppers – she's tall and her fair hair is a beacon. She stops in one shop, emerges in ten minutes or so with a bag, something she's bought.

I follow her to Shepherd's Bush Tube station. I've stayed too far back and lose sight of her. I start to panic, looking all around and just catch a glimpse of her hair, disappearing down some stairs to a platform. A train is there. She's going through the doors; I'll miss it – I run and push through people and get on the other end of the same car.

She makes a few quick changes, and I follow as close as I dare, not wanting to lose her in the rush-hour crowd. When we get on the Metropolitan line to Uxbridge, she gets a book out of her bag, settles on a seat to read. Her eyes on the page, I risk studying her more closely. She is absorbed, intent, and I'm curious what she is reading. Stop after stop, we're nearly at the end of the line when she gets out of her seat, makes her way to the exit – we're at Hillingdon.

I follow her from the station, down one street, another. There is rubbish on the pavement, some boarded-up windows. Graffiti on walls and a rundown, unloved feel to the area. She walks up to a small block of flats, pushes the door open. Disappears inside. It's the worst-looking building on a not-great street.

OK, Freja. I know where you work. I know where you live. I've become what, until recently, I was most afraid of: a stalker. Of course, now I know there are other things to fear.

I consider waiting, seeing if she goes out and following her again, but I don't want to hang around here when the light starts to go. I head back to the station, retrace the journey to Westfield. To my car.

I drive home. I'm so tired that random thoughts and images are flitting through my brain, much the way they do just before I fall asleep. I open the windows, turn the radio up.

Stay awake. Think. Put things together.

Jess asked why I'd thought my stalker years ago was a man. I'd assumed he was a man with some kind of sexual obsession with me: a rapist or murderer looking for his chance. At the time, I thought Jess meant that a woman could have that kind of obsessive attraction to another woman, and of course, she's right. But that's not why I've been following Freja.

What if I had things completely wrong back then? What if my stalker, male or female, had some other reason for disrupting my life? If I was looking at things the wrong way – and the police were, too – that may be why they were never identified, caught. They didn't fit what was being sought. If it is possible that the current writer of notes is the same person, then if I can work out who it was back then, I'll get answers for today.

I need to go back again, look at things in a different way. I never understood the degree of access they seemed to have to me, my schedule – seeming to know where I was going to be almost before I did. I heard the rumours, that I'd made it all up. I was never sure if the police took what I told them seriously, and maybe the reason was that they, too, couldn't understand how an archetypal stalker did the things he – or she – did.

Maybe, that is where the answer lies.

60

James won't answer his phone. Is he still upset that I was there last night? What did she tell him? He doesn't answer a message either, but I can't leave things like this. I try a few of the places he's most likely to be on a Saturday and finally spot him in a café he likes, laptop open.

'Hey,' I say. He looks up, raises an eyebrow. Doesn't say anything when I sit down.

'Not answering your phone, or returning messages? Don't break the twin-code, James. Talk to me.'

He sits back, closes his laptop. 'About what?'

'What do you think?'

'I'm expecting the third degree about my date last night.'

Despite him looking annoyed at me, I can see it in the lightness in his eyes, the tiredness, too.

'You got lucky with Lucky again last night, didn't you? Congratulations.' I try to keep my tone light, as it was before I knew Lucky was Ella. I'm not sure I succeeded.

'You don't need to pretend, Jess. She told me.'

'Told you what?'

'That you'd met her. That you were hitting on her, couldn't take no for an answer.'

I'm gaping at James. That isn't just a small reframe or slant on things; she lied. 'That's just not true.'

'Really? Are you sure? Because you're not the only one with twin-dar, you know. I saw how you looked at her.'

'It's true that we met, but she was hitting on me, not the other way around.'

'Sure she was.' He doesn't believe me, and why would he? He's no reason to think the girl who kisses him and all the rest is even into girls. But that he believes her over me? I'm shocked, hurt. And even more worried for him than I was before. If she's already lied to him at least once, what else might she do?

I have to make him understand.

'That's not the only thing. It's her name, too. She told me it was Ella. That's why I was so surprised to see you with her. She's been using different names.'

He's shaking his head. 'Lucky is her nickname, that's all. Nothing suspicious there.' She knew I'd mention this, didn't she? And so explained it away before I had a chance.

'Listen to me, James. Think with your brain, not your hormones. We don't lie to each other. Never have and I'm not lying now. Have you thought for a minute just how completely unlikely it is for both of us to have met the same girl within a few days of each other? There's something going on – something about her that just isn't right. I'm really worried about you.'

He's gone from annoyed to angry. 'I can look after myself, Jess.'

'But—'

'We're done talking about this. You're jealous – that's it, isn't it? That I found somebody I could be happy with, and you haven't, and even worse, that it happens to be someone you think you fancy.'

'That's not true,' I say, objecting, but part of it is true. I do – I mean, *did* – fancy her. How could I now, knowing she's been lying to James? It's like she's trying to come between us. Just for some sort of twisted fun, or is there another reason?

He's shaking his head, getting up now, leaving his coffee behind and going through the door.

I'm stunned. If someone had told me a week ago that we'd fall out over a girl, I'd have laughed. For a start, the girls I like don't tend to like James and vice versa. But apart from that, we just never argue like this. We certainly would never believe someone else over each other.

Everything is just such a complete, colossal mess.

61

LOU

It's only when Flick calls the next morning to ask if I'm coming to collect her as usual that I remember. Roast dinner with Flick and Lachlan in attendance is the tradition on Sundays and we missed last week. I want to see them – especially my grandson – but can I pull off a happy families performance? I guess I'm going to find out. I enlist Philip to collect them while I go on a quick shop. Everything is in the oven by the time they come in.

'Hi, Mum.'

'There's my beautiful boy,' I say, take Lachlan from Flick's arms. He's awake, gurgling. Grinning. A smile for Nanna. Or gas. Either way.

'Dad said you haven't been feeling well. You look a little pale.'

'Just worn out, I think.' I know if I don't say any more, she'll ask. I have to say something, and it must feel real; I don't want to lie to her again. 'Life has been a bit stressful lately.' Understatement.

She insists I sit with Lachlan, finishes up dinner preparations while Philip sets the table. Lachlan's blue eyes are on mine and the rush of love for this small one we didn't know we needed until he arrived is overwhelming. I'd do anything to keep him safe.

He falls asleep, and we transfer him to a cot we keep for him in a spare room. We eat and manage to carry on a conversation. Philip mentions he'll be going to Edinburgh for work – a flying visit, there on Tuesday and back late Wednesday. Would I like to come, have a day there? If I'm feeling better, he adds. I've got things to do here, I say, without elaborating. I can feel Flick's eyes going between her dad and me, the questions she isn't asking. Things don't feel anything like normal even though we are trying to pretend that they are. I know if she gets me on my own, she'll have questions. But what can I tell her that isn't a lie?

After dinner, I feign a headache, and Philip takes them home.

When he returns, I'm on the sofa. The TV is on. Philip finds the remote, mutes it. Sits on a chair across from me.

'Flick was asking me if things were OK between us and I didn't know what to tell her. So perhaps you could tell me, Lou. What, exactly, is going on?' He's concerned, exasperated, maybe both. But how dare he ask me for explanations?

'With me? Nothing much. How about with you?'

'What is that supposed to mean?'

I'm on a knife edge: scream at him and show him the photos or try to convince him everything is OK.

No. I won't do that. Things aren't OK and I don't think I could pull it off, and, if I did, he'd expect me in his bed. That isn't going to happen.

Maintain the charade.

'Nothing. I'm fine. Still not feeling well, so I'm going to sleep early.'

I head up the guest room and close the door.

* * *

I dream about Freja again that night, back as a horror movie child in *Village of the Damned*. Every time I turn she is there, smiling. Closer. Then I merge that and *Doctor Who*; statues that look like her come closer whenever I blink. Grab me and take me back, back, through time. Deposit me in change room showers, to see the letters written in condensation on the mirror:

I've found you.

I wake up, covered in sweat, a scream just choked off.

I don't care what is logical or sensible any more. I'm going there tomorrow – where Freja works. I'll confront her, tell her to keep away from my family. Or else... or else what?

Never underestimate a mother lioness protecting her cubs, her pride. I'll find a way to stop her.

62

LOU

It's afternoon before I head to Westfield, slowed down by second thoughts. I'm a coward. Always have been. I didn't have the killer instinct to win all those years ago, but I can't let that stop me now.

When I go to Freja's shop, I can't see her on the shop floor. I go in. Pretend to browse, waiting to see if she'll appear from the room at the back. What will she do when she sees me – hide? Pretend she doesn't know who I am?

'Can I help you?' It's the woman Freja was working with the other day. A name badge that says *Yasmin, assistant manager*, and inspiration hits.

'Is Freja in today?'

'Sorry, no. She's called in sick. Can I help you?'

'I came in the other day. You weren't here, Freja was. She was so incredibly rude. I decided to come back today to ask her for an apology.'

'I'm so sorry to hear that.'

Sorry, she may be; surprised, she isn't. Freja must have form.

'She was helping me, and this man came in – good-looking, I suppose. She dumped me to help him. So, I left.'

'Please, accept my apology. I will certainly speak to her about this. Is there anything I can help you with today?'

I shake my head. 'I'm sorry, but I won't shop here again.' I march out.

That was incredibly bitchy – I didn't know I had it in me. But it felt so good. And it was so very well deserved.

Could she actually be sick, or is she in bed with my – or somebody else's – husband? I go back to my car, decide to drive over and watch her block of flats. See if she – or Philip – come in or out. I park close enough to watch the entrance, not that worried whether my car is spotted. In this neighbourhood I'd rather be inside a locked car than standing on a street corner. While I wait, I make a new profile on Tripadvisor with a little-used email address. Then I leave a scathing review of Freja's shop, making it sound very like what I said to her assistant manager earlier.

It's early evening when I see Freja come out of her building. My scarf in place in readiness, I decide to follow her on foot. The way she is dressed – a beautiful red dress. Low cut. Stockings and heels. She really is stunning, and I hate her even more.

So, she called in sick, and she's going out dressed like that? She stops to wait for a light to change and I get close enough to take a few photos, then head back to my car. Glad it is still intact when I get there and I get inside, lock the doors.

I find the company she works for on social media. I tag them with her photo: *your employee called in sick, but she looks well enough as she heads out for the night.* Ping.

Round whatever number it is: 1 for the wife, 0 for the mistress.

I head for home, thinking I've done rather well for a first-time stalker. I'm starting to feel uneasy about it all, but even if she loses her job, it doesn't come close to the damage she's inflicted on me and my family. I'm nearly home, catch a movement out of the corner of my eye. Slam on the brakes. Look back and see a cat scampering off, unhurt as far as I can tell. I missed it, but my nerves are shot. Maybe I should have seen it sooner; it was too close to being a tragedy. I drive slowly, carefully, the rest of the way home.

63

LUCY

Madrid. Clay court season is under way. Difficult for me in the past, I'm starting to love it – balancing with my centre of gravity over the leg that is sliding – keeping a wide base – slide to position first, then hit the shot for strength. After a practice session I'm back in my hotel before a singles match tomorrow, changing for dinner. I'm ready and go to the door. That's when I see it: a folded piece of white paper on the floor next to my hotel door. Hands shaking, I pick it up. Unfold it.

Five words:

I'm sorry about your cat.

My cat? What the fuck?

If something happened to him, my parents might not tell me, not at the start of a tournament, but I have to know.

I call home. It rings, rings – finally Dad answers. 'Ah, Lucy.' His voice, it doesn't sound right. Any hope I had that the note meant nothing is gone.

'What's happened?'

'Nothing at all.'

'What's happened to Mr Mittens?' A white kitten with black paws: I chose his name when I was eight years old.

A pause. 'How did you know?'

'Tell me.'

'I'm so sorry, Lucy. He got hit by a car – last night.' And I'm dropping the phone, staring at the note.

I didn't even know, so how did my stalker? Was it because he was the one driving? He could have done that last night and made it to Madrid by now.

I hang up and call Steve; tell him about the note. He promises me he'll find out what happened and call me back as soon as he can.

And he does. He's sure that it really was just a sad accident – he ran right in front of a car, they braked. It wasn't their fault. They stopped, took him to the vet to be identified by his microchip. They had nothing to do with the note.

But somebody here, in Spain, knew.

How?

64

FREJA

I'm on the train to Brighton. We're nearly there and I check my face using my phone. I was tired and had to wear more make-up than James has seen me in before. Dark circles under eyes on pale skin like mine stand out too much. Then I decided to go for it – smoky eyes, lashes. The works. Something to hide behind? Maybe. And instead of dressing simply in jeans and so on like I have when I've been with him before, this time I'm in a low-cut red dress; long, but with a slit right up one leg. Looking the part.

James has been messaging frequently, last night, today. I've answered just a few of them. One as I left, telling him I'd see him soon.

We pull into Brighton. I walk down from the station to meet him in the same pub, but I'm almost an hour late.

His smile is as wide as the last time he saw me, but hidden behind it is worry, uncertainty. His eyes, on what I'm wearing – does he like it? He's unsure even as he can't stop looking. I let him kiss me, but only kiss him back briefly. He holds my hand tight as if he is afraid to let go. We have a drink, another.

Then I tell him I want to go dancing. We go to a club.

We dance, but not really together on the packed floor. I pretend I like the music, love it; dance as if I'm by myself. Catching eyes here and there.

I choose one. Older than James, more muscular. I hold his eyes while I sway to the music. He comes over and James steps between us. I tell James to grow up. One shove from the other man has him sprawling. A bouncer comes over, but we leave the dance floor together before James can get up from the floor.

A glance back from the door. A wounded puppy.

Collateral damage.

Once we're out of sight, I disentangle myself and head for the station alone.

65

LOU

Philip is there when I get home. I'm surprised; it's early for him. But I suppose his girlfriend was busy tonight.

'Hello, Lulu,' he says. I avoid his arms, go into the kitchen.

He follows. 'Are you still feeling unwell?' I nod. 'I was surprised you were out. If you're not well.' I shrug, unwilling to bother coming up with a credible excuse.

We make dinner – he is trying to help but more getting in the way. He reminds me he is going to Edinburgh tomorrow, asks again if I'd like to come. I say no. I'm withdrawn and he is worried, I can see it in his eyes when he thinks I'm not looking his way. Let him worry; let him wonder if I'm on to his lies. Soon after we eat I say goodnight, go back to the guest room.

But I can't sleep. I'm on my phone, looking at the photos I took of Freja over and over again. Eaten up by jealousy and wishing that instead of on foot, I'd followed her in my car. Slammed her into the side of a building or just run over her, felt the thump-thump of her body under my wheels.

As I look at her, one question comes to mind more and more: *why* does she seem to want Philip? I mean, we're well off but not rich. Plus, with wife – together or not – three children and one grandchild, his money has other calls on it. The way she looks, she'd have options – she could find someone younger and richer than him, even, say, one who isn't married. Why bother with Philip?

She must have some other motive. I know Iona said that maybe she just fell for the wrong man, but I don't buy it. I could send her photos to Steve; see if there is a criminal record for a Freja L that fits her description. But I'm not sure he'd want to help me if he knew the things I've been up to. And he'd probably assume I'm being jealous and vindictive – OK, he might be right, there – trying to find dirt on her. And that any fears I have about her are unfounded and more to do with my history than anything else.

There is the possibility I'd thought of the other day, that maybe there is a connection between Freja and Philip beyond the current situation, perhaps when she was a child – one that could explain both why she has targeted him and why I recognise her.

I didn't know very much about Philip's work in the Met until it ended. A protestor died at a climate protest and there was a witch hunt to blame somebody. They tried to pin it on Philip. It was eventually proven that he wasn't responsible, but it was that experience – being accused of something he didn't do – that led him to the decision to leave the Met and become a barrister. To defend people who were wrongly accused. Not that the reality of being a barrister was much about that. Anyhow, he soon changed his aspirations to earning more, and specialised in commercial law.

I sigh. He was so idealistic back then. We both were. What happened to the people we were, so in love, ready to change the world?

Freja, that's what. And as unreasonable as it may be to blame every problem we've ever had on her, I'm going with it.

66

Yesterday I convinced myself I should leave it for a while, thinking James will come to his senses eventually. I last an entire day. I don't bother messaging or calling this time, I'll track him down. But he isn't in any of the usual places. No one was around his halls earlier either, but, running out of ideas, I try there again. Still no James but this time Ringo is in – his room is opposite James'. Despite being told I'm completely uninterested in the male of the species, he's a pain. But he's the only one about.

'Hi.'

'Ah the beautiful Jessie.'

'I'm looking for James – any idea where he might be?'

'And I was hoping you were after me.' A tragic sigh and I roll my eyes.

'Have you seen him or haven't you?'

He hesitates and now I'm more worried. 'You didn't hear it from me, right? Because he forbade anyone telling you.'

'Telling me what?'

'Jimmy boy had a big night last night.'

'Oh?'

'As in, he was completely wasted, and crying in his beer. Then he passed out. We had to lug him to his room and tuck him in.'

Ah. Sounds like things with Lucky Ella have already imploded. Poor James.

'Any idea where he is now?'

'None. Sorry. I'm just impressed he got out of bed at all.'

'Thanks.'

I try calling him now, no answer. Message:

> Where are you? I'm worried.

I'm guessing he may have limped to another bar and I have a hunt around the usual places. No sign. He's probably hiding away because he doesn't want to hear me say I told you so, but as much satisfaction as I'd get from saying that, I'm getting more and more worried.

I wish I could call Mum. But two things – she's dealing with other stuff right now, and the twin-code. If he's angry with me now, that's nothing like he'd be if I call the parentals on him. I reserve that for emergencies and I'm not sure this qualifies yet. I just need to find him, make sure that he is OK. He's had problems with depression before. If this is a trigger, I need to be there.

Finally, I call Flick. And tell her the whole story – Ella, Lucky – everything. Ask her what I should do. What she suggests is naff, but I do it anyway.

I send a message to James:

> I love you and I'm here if you need me.

67

FREJA

I'm ten minutes late when I rush into work in the morning. Yasmin is giving me a look.

'I'm really sorry, the Tube stopped for ages between stops.'

'Did it? Did it, really?'

'Ah, yes?' I see then that the part-timer, Aza, is here – we don't usually work on the same days. Has there been a timetable change?

'Watch things for us, Aza,' Yasmin says, and beckons me to the stockroom.

'What's up?'

'Are you feeling better?'

'I'm fine now. I had a terrible migraine yesterday, though.'

'Perhaps you could explain this.' She has her phone in her hand and shows me a post – a photo of me. In last night's red dress. On the corner near where I live. And what is said along with it.

I shake my head. The timing isn't good for this. I've spent too much making myself look good for Philip, on train fares to

Brighton, too. Rent is due next week, and my bank account is already overdrawn.

'That photo isn't from last night.'

'Oh, really? That's not what the photo timestamp says. And that's not all. We've had several complaints from customers about you, Freja. This comes from above my head; I have no choice. I'm afraid we're letting you go.'

Letting me go sounds like I'm the one who wants to go, but I know how these things work. I've lost enough jobs over the years, most of the time not my fault – bosses who wouldn't take no for an answer. Sabotage from jealous co-workers. Somewhere along the way I decided that there was no actual point in trying or doing things by the rules; it never got me anywhere.

'Do you mean you're giving me notice?'

'No. No notice. This—' she taps on her phone with a long red fingernail '—is grounds for an instant dismissal.'

'Yasmin, please. I won't make rent this month—'

'You should have thought of that before you lied.'

She's enjoying this. She liked to pretend to be my friend, to hear about my life, which was so different to her own, with two kids and a mortgage. But she was just sightseeing and then straight back to her safe, smug family.

'You can't do this.'

'Get a lawyer if you want to, but I don't think you'll get far with that. Goodbye, Freja.'

I leave, see the pleased look Aza gives me as I go past. I keep my head high even though I'm crumbling inside.

A lawyer – Philip is a lawyer. I'll go to the pub. It's early but I don't care. I'll get a drink and then call him.

I walk the short distance, then up to the bar. Alice is there. 'Hi, Freja. Did you get your phone back?'

I frown. 'My phone?'

She exchanges a glance with a co-worker. 'A friend of yours said you'd lost it. They went looking for you at work?'

'Oh, yes. Of course. Yes,' I say, holding my phone up.

Who was that? Whoever it was, I'm guessing they somehow traced me to here, then to my work, then followed me to where I live, and took the photo of me in the red dress last night. Could it be Philip's wife? There's no one else I can think of who would have done this. I've underestimated her.

I ask for a large glass of red. Sit at a table by the window and have a sip, then call Philip. It rings and rings. No answer. I try a message, deliberating for a while what to say, but in the end go for simplicity.

> I need you xx.

He'll think it is one kind of need, when it is another. No matter. If he is next to me he won't be able to say no to anything, even a loan. The kind that won't get paid back.

The timing of losing my job couldn't be much worse. I'm angry. I've got no family to fall back on, no friends who would help. Since I was a kid I've never had anyone looking out for me. Lou, on the other hand? The big house. Children who love her. Relatives here and there, no doubt. And Philip loves her, too. I know he does, even though he can't resist me at the same time – I'm under no illusions there, not any more.

My original plan was for him to fall in love with me, dump his wife, and then, when his life was in tatters, for me to leave him – break his heart – and take as much of his money with me as I could manage to extort. But he hasn't played his part as he should. After Lou walked in on us, I was sure she would leave him – that I could get there via another route. She did, but only briefly. She's back and doesn't look like she's going to go anywhere. And where does that leave things? Philip is back to having it all – his wife and family, me on the side. Messing with his children has been fun but I doubt he has even noticed.

Lou has everything; I have nothing. And now she's taken away my crappy little job, too. She makes it easy to hate her, which is good. It'll make it easier to find another way to destroy Philip.

By the time my second glass of wine is mysteriously empty, Philip still hasn't responded. A new plan is taking shape in my mind, but I need time. I need money.

I don't want to do this – I was finished with him. But I'm in a corner and my options are limited.

I think what to say, how to say it, and call James. No answer – either he's busy or doesn't want to speak to me, or both. I can't blame him.

I leave a voicemail. 'Hi, James? I'm so very sorry. I think I panicked with how much I care for you – it scares me to feel this way. Please, please, give me another chance? I... I think I love you.'

It's only a few minutes later when my phone rings – it's him. I answer at the first ring.

'Hello? James?'

'Hi.'

'I'm so sorry. Please. Will you ever forgive me?'

'What about that other guy? Did you go home with him?'

'No. Of course not. As soon as we left, I knew it was a mistake. I went back to the club later and looked for you, but you'd already left. Please, please: give me another chance.'

There is a pause. 'I don't know. I need to see you, Lucky.'

'When?'

He starts going through times, days, and each time I make an excuse.

'You don't really want to see me, do you?'

'It's not that. I promise.' I start to cry – crying on demand is a useful skill.

'What's wrong?'

'I owe some money. I borrowed from someone I shouldn't have. He's threatening me now – I have to work it off. Dancing, in this horrible nightclub in London.' I embellish. Say how I can't go to my parents, that they'll disown me if they find out what I've been doing, and I don't know what to do.

He wants to help me. I insist I can't let him, no way, but finally give him my bank details – sort code, account number. And even remember to say that Ella is my middle name; my account is under my first name, so Freja Larsson – so a deposit won't come back as account details don't match. We arrange to meet tomorrow night.

I whisper 'I love you' when we say goodbye.

There is a chance that he'll think about this some more and not come through. But unlike his father, I'm sure of him. I have another glass of wine to celebrate.

68

LOU

I'd been glad Philip was going away. He emailed the flight details from the booking, so I know he won't be back until tomorrow night. But now the sun is low in the sky and I'm in the empty house, alone. And whoever has been following me and messing with our lives knows it – the disc is still buried in the garden next to my car.

I check all the windows and doors are locked, then search every nook and cranny of the house. Scared every time I look in a cupboard or under a bed that someone will jump out at me. Nothing is amiss, no one is hiding, but I can't shake this feeling of being watched.

I need something to keep my mind busy, to stop me from panicking.

I fetch my laptop, and sit in the chair that faces the window – if anyone approaches the house, I'll see them. I'll try to find out more about Freja, and where do people her age spend most of their lives these days? Social media. Someone who looks like her is bound to be all over it.

It takes absolutely ages and several glasses of wine, but I

finally find the correct Freja in London on socials – the profile photo is her. Unfortunately, there is no surname in her username for me to investigate, but there are other things I can do.

I set up a profile with username, @imhiswife23 – the number representing the years we've been married. I start by leaving sarcastic comments on images she's posted – things like, *did you wear that when you hunted down another family to destroy?* I find a few photos she's posted where she looks particularly up for anything, and repost them with tags like, #Ilikebadboys #messageme #willyoupaytoplay #eighteenplus #ratedR. They'll probably get taken down eventually, but in the meantime, that could keep her busy.

My phone pings with a message – Philip. All he says is:

Missing you xx

Who knew that ignoring him and sleeping in the other room was all it took to get his attention? I don't answer.

I have another glass of wine and then another.

It's time to do something I've wanted to do for a while. I write down the words so I don't get them wrong or forget; I practise a few times, trying not to slur my words. Then call Freja's number, with mine withheld. Relieved, I'll admit it, when it goes to voicemail.

The beep sounds.

'Keep away from my family, or this is only the beginning.'

There. I've told her. I feel like I'm in more control even as I'm getting drunker.

Finally, I drag myself up the stairs to the guest room, get into PJs. Despite my fears earlier, the wine makes me fall asleep almost instantly.

I dream that Iona calls – that I'm telling her Freja is no match for me. Then I'm crying because nothing I can do will make things be the way they were before.

69

JESSIE

A message from James at last:

> Stop pestering me, I'm fine.

> Where are you? I won't believe you until I see you.

> You're worse than Mum. If you must know, I'm at halls, all right?

I head over. He's sprawled on his bed with his laptop open. He's pale, red eyes, but apart from an evident hangover and looking tired, he doesn't appear to be in an abject state of despair.

'You've seen me, now go. I've got an essay deadline.' He waves a hand at the door.

I sit on his desk chair. 'Are you going to tell me what's been going on? Don't shut me out.'

Cue a tragic sigh. 'If you must know, Lucky and I had... a bit of a falling-out. But we've sorted things now.'

A sinking feeling in my gut. 'So, you're still seeing her?'

'Yes, I am. Whether you like it or not. Now get lost.' He taps on his laptop. 'I need to finish this before I see her tonight, all right?' The smile is back, just to think of seeing her, and he may be more or less sober but I'm even more concerned. But crowding him won't help. And it's a good sign that he's doing his coursework.

'Fine. I'm going. Look after yourself. All right?' He rolls his eyes and gives a thumbs up, turns back to his screen.

70

LOU

An insistent ringing makes me open my eyes. It's daylight. I reach for my phone, knock it on the floor. It stops ringing but as I reach to pick it up, it starts again. It's Iona.

'Good morning,' she says. 'How's your head?'

'Ah... not brilliant?' I squint at the clock: 10 a.m. Despite how late it is I feel as if I haven't slept at all.

'I'm not surprised. You sounded in good form last night.' So that wasn't a dream; we did talk.

'Sorry. Was I a pain?'

'Not at all, though I couldn't figure out half of what you were saying.'

I'm embarrassed, worried what else I might have said or done. 'I'm really sorry.'

'Don't be. If anyone is entitled to let loose just now, it's you. But preferably not alone, OK?'

'You're right.'

'So, let's plan a night out.'

'Ugh. I don't want to drink anything ever again.'

She laughs. 'Well, once you've got over that, we'll plan something. OK?'

'Maybe. Now if you'll excuse me, I think I might be sick.'

'Go, go! Check in later so I know you survived.'

I'm not actually sick in the end, just keep feeling like I'm about to be. I call Ana, our cleaner. It's her afternoon today and I ask her not to come – I couldn't face her this way. Say we'll pay her as usual, of course. I can hear the curiosity in her voice, but she'd never ask. She must see all sorts in her job, maybe imagines I've got a boyfriend scheduled or some other skeleton rattling away in my closet.

She'd never ask.

She's always efficient, polite. Kind, too. We've chatted now and then, and she's not even once said anything about other people she cleans for. Now I think of it, it's odd that she'd said anything to Steve's aunt, about our place being a mess when I left. I shrug. She was his aunt's cleaner before she was mine. Maybe she's known her for a long time and shares more readily than she does with me.

I manage some tea, toast. As I revive, more of last night is coming back. I go online, see the posts and comments I made. Not sure whether to laugh or cry; not sure whether to delete or leave them as they are.

I'm pathetic. Getting drunk on my own like that? Imagine how I'd have felt if one of the kids saw me that way.

I need to get a grip. When I get upset and angry, bad things happen.

71

LUCY

Paris. It's the lead-up to the French Open at Roland Garros. Iona insisted that we come a few days early, rent a car. Do some sight-seeing out of the city. I've not long had my licence and the wrong side of the road thing kind of freaks me out. But she's failed her test twice: I have to drive.

She convinces me it'll be fun, and has a plan. We head for Epernay, the champagne capital of France. Our goal? To find the very best champagne to celebrate, because between us we are, of course, going to win both the French Open doubles and singles. She doesn't specify which of us will win the latter.

Vineyards, tours. Tastings, too. As I'm driving, I taste the way you are supposed to: take a sip, swirl it around, spit it out. Iona makes up for what I miss, despite me reminding her about training tomorrow. We pick a favourite and buy a few bottles, then head to a fancy place she's booked for our lunch.

Iona did French A levels and more or less manages to translate the menu, to order. The food is *amazing*. I'm relaxing, having fun, not thinking about the competition or he-who-has-yet-to-be-thrown-in-jail-for-being-a-serial-pest – a label Iona came up with after hearing him called *my stalker*, because that made him connected to me, as if he was mine. She said that was all wrong, and she definitely had a point.

'Lunch is on me,' Iona says.

'You don't have to—'

'I do! I made you drive – which you've been doing excellently, by the way. It's only fair.'

Iona gestures and they bring the bill, put it in front of her.

'What the fuck?' she says, and the note of shock in her voice isn't from the total. Before I even see it, my stomach twists. An envelope, with *Lulu* written on the front, came with the bill.

'How did he find me here?'

I'm shaking, looking all around. Iona calls the waiter back, speaks in French then gives up and goes to English.

'Where did this come from?' she says, pointing at the envelope.

'It was left at the front, a note to take it to your table. Something is wrong?'

'Don't open it,' Iona says to me. 'Let's take it to the police.'

I can't not look; I have to see what it says. I open it. A folded piece of white paper, and five words:

You can't hide from me.

Iona pays and asks if anyone saw who left the envelope. No one did.

She wants to call the police, but I refuse to stay any longer. He must be here, somewhere, watching us now, and all I want to do is leave. She takes the note to give to the police in Paris – I won't touch it again.

I start the car, rev the engine too much. Pull out, tyres squealing.

'Take it easy, Lulu. I'm with you. Nothing can happen when we are together, right?'

But she was wrong.

A fast corner. A tractor on the road.

Our brakes, squealing.

An impact.

A scream – Iona's.

72

FREJA

I listen again to the message left on my voicemail: 'Keep away from my family, or this is only the beginning.'

Lou has a posh accent – of course she does – but I know she didn't start out that way. Her early life is online because of her tennis, so I know that her dad was a builder and her mum, a sales rep. Lou must have worked at it over the years to get the posh accent to go with her perfect life.

At first I thought that her message referred to me losing my job, but then all the notifications on socials started beeping on my phone. It took me a while to weed them down, to work out what was going on. I've been trolled – by someone called @imhiswife23. Twenty-three years of marriage, I'm guessing. She's not exactly trying to be subtle, is she?

I've gone past upset and worried about paying the rent, to angry. I wonder how Philip would react if he knew she was onto us, that she has been targeting me? I like to think he'd come over all protective at her being a bully, but somehow I doubt it. More the opposite. Girls like me are always expendable.

I do feel uneasy about James, though. I can still see the

wounded puppy in his eyes the other night when I left him on the dance floor, went off with someone else.

I check my online banking; he was as good as his word. What he's transferred would be enough to take care of rent for a few months, and that's what I thought I wanted it for. But not any more.

Philip won't leave Lou; Lou won't leave Philip. It's time for another plan.

There really is only one way to rip the heart out of Philip. I wasn't sure I could do it. But she's making it easy to hate her.

The messages from James have started. I ignore them for a few hours, then send one back:

> I found something better to do. Don't be so needy.

Instead of rent, what James sent will be fuck-off money. I'll use it to get the hell away.

73

JESSIE

A message pings to my phone. It's late. I was just going to change for bed, and it's from Ringo. He's sent nonsense before and I almost delete it without looking, then think again. Open it. He's sent a photo – of James. He appears to be standing on the *roof* of their building. Four words to the message underneath:

Can you come – now?

I'm flying down the hall and the stairs, messaging *yes* as I go. Fear has me run faster than I ever have before.

There is a cluster of worried people on the pavement below James. Fuck. He's walking along the peak of the roof, unsteadily. Three floors up.

Ringo is in the window above. 'Jessie! Come up,' he says, and I run up the stairs, breathing hard.

'Has he been drinking?'

'Yeah, but I don't know how much.'

'Might he have taken something?'

'I don't know. We've tried to get him to come down – he won't. Just keeps walking back and forth.'

'I'm going out there.'

'Should we call the police or fire department or something?'

'Let me try, first.' I climb out the window. There is a flat part of the roof here, where students often sit outside on sunny days. But James has walked on from the flat part of the roof – to where it is peaked, and steep.

'Hey, James. Hello there.'

He turns towards me, wobbles, and my gut turns to liquid. He regains his balance. 'Ah, there she is. Jessie has come to save the day.'

'That's my job, looking after you. And your job is to look after me. Right?'

'I know why you're here.'

'To get you to come down?'

A moment of confusion. 'No, that's not it. You're here to tell me I told you so.'

'Whatever has happened, James, I won't say that. I promise.'

'You will!'

'OK. I told you so. There, I've said it – it wasn't that bad, was it?'

He laughs, loudly, tinged with hysteria. 'I was right about something! At last!'

'Yes, you were. Now come down from there. Please, James. I'm scared.'

He looks at me – really looks at me now. Takes a step towards me – another. Wobbles again.

I go on my hands and knees. 'Do it like this, James. Hold on with your hands. OK?'

I start to edge towards him, onto the pitched roof. A loose stone bounces past me and off the side of the roof and fear lurches in my gut. He's trying to do as I said, leans over and holds on with his hands and bends his knees, but can't seem to get his feet to do what he wants. He takes a shuffling step towards me. Another. His foot slips; he's losing balance. I'm too far away to reach him.

Time slows down, each fraction of a second a slow-motion nightmare. He scrabbles with his hands against the tiles, and he's slipping, falling, to the edge of the peak roof, and over. His hands – he's hanging on to the gutter with his hands. Then the gutter gives way. He falls.

74

LOU

Lack of sleep and a hangover are a strangely focusing combination, as if they take away the raw emotion and leave a spotlight behind, one I can shine where I will.

I settle at our breakfast bar with a cup of tea. I go back to socials, the place I spent so much time last night. But this time I just focus on Freja's updates, her photos. Study them, one after the other. Now that the heat of jealousy has cooled, the sense of déjà vu is so strong. Her features, something about her slightly wide-set eyes. Think, think: what is it about her that I recognise?

It feels like I haven't got something quite right. Maybe it isn't her that I remember – could it be someone else who looks like her? A parent, a sibling, or—

A mother. Her mother. I've got it now. It is her mother I recognise in her – a face that had haunted me, so many years ago. It was in the news when she died – it was suicide. She was the girlfriend of the man who died in custody after the demonstration. Philip was accused of causing his death. It was proven that he wasn't responsible, but it is why he left the Met.

Now that I've localised the memory, I can find the news from the time. Her name – Agnetha Larsson. I find her photo and compare with those of Freja on her socials: there is much of her in Freja. And she was FL on Philip's phone. Is she Freja Larsson? I'm almost certain.

If I'm right about her identity, I don't think it's possible that Philip would have taken up with her if he knew who she was. Freja's mother had a different surname to her father, but wouldn't Philip have recognised her if I do? It may be that either he didn't see the resemblance so many years later, or that he didn't see the news report with Agnetha's photo at all. I didn't point it out to Philip when I did; I knew it would upset him, even though he was exonerated in her boyfriend's death.

Agnetha killed herself two years after her boyfriend died. She never recovered from his death, reports said. And she was found by her daughter – a child. The daughter isn't named, of course – minors' names are not generally published. Was it Freja?

I go back to reports of the original climate protest – it states that his daughter was with him. It was when she was taken from his arms that he reacted, struck Philip who in turn hit him with the truncheon.

If I'm right, it was Freja's father who died in custody. Her mother killed herself, two years later – Freja found her. The person she may well blame for both deaths – wrongly as it happens, but it's not hard to see why she might do so – is Philip.

She must hate him. She tracked him down, seduced him, with what goal? Revenge. To cause pain, to him, his family?

I've got to call Philip. Tell him what he's done – let a dangerous woman into our lives.

I take my phone out of my pocket, unlock it. He's flying back from meetings in Edinburgh today. I check his flight times – he's in the air now. I'll have to call him later.

I've been concentrating so hard on the puzzle I've been

solving that small sounds, light footsteps, don't penetrate at first. When I notice them now it is like an echo of something I should have heeded. I get up, go through to the lounge. It's Freja. Her eyes are wild, her face twisted with anger. But it's hard to focus on anything but what is in her other hand – a gun.

'Hello, Lou.'

75

JESSIE

I can't breathe and I'm running, running, down the stairs. Outside now, and there are too many people. I push them away to get to James. There are sirens in the distance, coming closer, by the time I reach him. His legs – muscle, bones – shouldn't bend like that. He's not moving; his eyes are shut. I'm there and holding his hand. A medical student has appeared, said not to move him. I tell him he's going to be OK and that I love him over and over again. I hope he can hear me. If he does he shows no sign.

Paramedics arrive. Someone pulls me away. They put a collar on his neck, immobilise him, put him carefully onto a stretcher and take him. I scream that I'm his sister until they let me go with him, but make me sit in the front.

I call Mum's mobile – no answer. Then the home number, but it rings and rings; she doesn't answer. Dad's mobile next and it goes to voicemail. I don't know what to say, if I should leave a message about something as terrifying as this. In the end I say that it is urgent, call me.

We arrive at the hospital. James is still unconscious, and he's rushed off and I'm told to wait. Still no answer from Mum, Dad. I call Flick.

'Hello?'

I'm crying. I try to tell her that James fell and he is hurt, I don't know how badly, and I can't get Mum and Dad on the phone. She says she'll find them and to let her know anything and everything as soon as I can.

I know Flick loves both of us. Our parents do, too. But no one who hasn't experienced it themselves can understand what it is to be a twin. It's like half of me has been cut off, and I don't know if I can get it back.

'I'll have that.' Freja gestures at my phone in my hand. 'Put it on the table and then step back.' I do so and she takes it, pockets it.

'What do you want?'

'Your life. But you can hang on to it for a big longer. Sit.' She gestures at a chair, and I do so, trembling. My... life? Does she mean she wants me to disappear so she can live here with Philip, or does she mean she plans to kill me? She's looking around the room – sees the landline. Pulls the cord out of the wall.

I have to keep her talking. Convince her that she's got things wrong.

'You are Freja Larsson, aren't you? And you think Philip caused the death of your father.'

'You've worked it all out, have you? Aren't you clever. Not just my dad. Mum, too. And he's going to pay. You were just collateral damage, but you've been a naughty girl, too, haven't you?'

'You're wrong – Philip didn't kill your father. They found he wasn't responsible—'

'People like you, like him, get away with things all the time.

Unlike me. I always get the blame, so I might as well deserve it for a change.'

'I was there, in court. I heard all the evidence. He didn't do it.'

'He *hit* him. With a truncheon.'

'There were expert reports – the angle of the blow was wrong. It wasn't the blow that killed him.'

'Were you there when it happened? No? I was. I saw it. I know why my father died.'

77

FREJA

I need to remember, to remind myself *why*, so I can do what must be done. I need to go back to the day that started it all.

I'd listened in from the top of the stairs the night before – Mummy, Daddy, friends. Talking about saving the world. At least that's what Daddy said he and their friends wanted to do.

Sometimes Mummy was there but not there, something I didn't understand yet then. She stayed quiet and to the side of their plans. She didn't want me to go – she said I was too little, that she and I should stay behind. Maybe I was just an excuse, so she didn't have to go. I protested, wanting to go and see what I kept hearing about. Later, I wondered if things would have been different if she and I had stayed home; if instead of saying I wanted to go, I had said the opposite. But Daddy promised Mummy that he'd look after me. And he said it was me they were really doing this for, and somehow convinced her.

I was on Daddy's shoulders, Mummy alongside. The last time the three of us were together. In my memory, we were in our own little bubble even though there were people all around us, walking up the road, carrying signs, noise and bustle, so the way I remember things probably isn't quite true. I got Daddy to read the signs to me even though I was a good reader, years above my age group, and most of them I could read myself. Climate justice now. Save the planet. There is no planet B – he had to explain what that one meant.

There were chants and noise – cars honking their horns, whether because they agreed with us or they wanted us to get off the road so they could get on their way. We were blocking entire wide roads and bridges in London. There were sirens, police. They moved in with shields held in front of them, taking people on the edges, dragging them away, and the mood suddenly changed – from an exciting day out to something *else*. Pushing, shoving, yells. Screams. I was scared.

Most of what happened next is a blur. It is more the sounds I remember, as if my eyes were shut or my face against Daddy's chest where he held me against him now. Then I was torn away from him. Mum was behind us somewhere, screaming. And I saw him – that policeman. The stick in his hand that hit Daddy. Daddy fell to the ground, and I never saw him again.

Not until the funeral.

I didn't really understand what was happening at the time; it was more later that I understood. That the police grabbed me away from Daddy and he tried to fight back, but they hit him. He died in custody that night. There was an inquiry, but the police involved weren't found responsible even though they killed him. They said he tripped, fell. Hit his head. A likely story, Mummy said.

Daddy's friends tracked down the policeman they say killed him. I saw his photo online – I remembered it from when Daddy was hit. It was quickly taken down, but I never forgot. Every time I saw police in uniform I checked their faces, but never saw him anywhere. Years later I thought I never would, and I moved away from London. Tried to put it all behind me.

But last year, I finally saw him. He wasn't in the police any more; he hadn't been for a long time. That's why I could never find him.

He was a lawyer now – a barrister. There was a big case he'd won, and he was on the news. I paused it, studied his face. I was sure. I'd finally found him. He was going to pay. But it wasn't enough to hurt just him, oh no. Not after what he did to my family. His must suffer, too.

To this point in my life, the way I looked was a curse. In care and afterwards – it led to pain, to being used – whether I said yes or no the result was the same, until I learned to arm myself, to fight back. First with a knife, then upgraded to what I hold now – acquired from an old boyfriend, one who died in a fight not long after. Once I found Philip, instead of trying to hide my looks away, I used them to get into his life. It was a weapon, like the cold weight of the gun in my hand now. This time, I'll be the one who wins.

We'll wait until Philip gets home. Then, Lou will kill him and herself – a murder-suicide, by a jilted wife. Perfect.

78

JESSIE

I'm in a waiting room. A few of James' friends have made their way here now as well. They press coffee into my hands but I don't want it, don't want them. I just want James. I try Mum's and Dad's numbers again – no answer, calls go to voicemail. Where the hell is everyone? Another try of the home number; this time I get a message that the phone is disconnected. What the hell? I message Flick, tell her.

When a doctor finally comes to talk to me, I can't read it on his face. Can't tell what he is going to say.

'You are James' sister, Jessie – is that right?'

'Twin. We're twins.' It seems important to say that somehow.

'And your parents?'

'I've called but no answer. Our other sister is trying to find them, but please. Just tell me.'

'He's got multiple fractures in both legs. His spine and neck are thankfully intact. But the real problem is a head injury, and that he is still unconscious. It's a waiting game now. We've done all we can. We hope he'll regain consciousness soon. The longer it takes, the more likely that there may be permanent brain damage. And there is a chance that he might not wake up at all.'

'Can I be with him?'

I get led to a bed in ICU. His face is so pale. He's hooked up to many machines. I can both see and hear his heartbeat on one of them, *b-beep*, *b-beep*, traced across a screen. I sit. I hold his hand, and I pray.

Then I call Flick.

79

LOU

Freja is so young, so desperate. Dangerous, too, but not many years older than Flick. First her father died, then her mother – such tragic circumstances. Is what I've done part of what has driven her to this? I don't know.

But I do want to know how it all started.

'How did you find Philip?'

She tilts her head to one side, as if deciding if she will answer, then does so. 'Smiling on TV after he won a case,' she finally says. 'I was only six when he killed my father, but I never forgot his face. I knew who he was.'

'And then?'

'I tracked him down. Went places he went to. It was easy enough to catch his eye.' It hurts to hear her say that. I never thought Philip would be one to stray so easily.

'What was the plan? Was it always going to lead to this?'

'No. I hoped he'd leave you. Destroy your happy family. Then I'd make him as miserable as possible before dumping him.' She shrugs. 'I had to replan after a while.'

'Is that why you left the note – so that I'd find the two of you together and leave him?'

She frowns. 'A note? What note?'

80

FREJA

Before she can answer I hear what I was waiting for: a car is pulling in out front, lights on the window. He's home!

'If you make a sound, anything at all, I'll pull the trigger.' I get up, come around the chair she is sitting on, so she is between me and the door – the gun, in my hand, pointing at her head.

She's scared, round eyes, trembling. Will she or won't she try to alert him that something is wrong? Either way I win, because if she does and I shoot her and he comes in and watches her die, he'll suffer before he joins her.

She stays silent.

A key scrapes as it turns in the lock, the door opens and – oh. It's not Philip. Lou gasps when she sees that it is Flick, daughter number one.

'Please, do come in,' I say. 'Join us. Have a seat.'

'Mum? What's going on?' Then she sees what I'm pointing at her mother's head. 'Fuck.'

'Sit,' I say, pointing at the sofa. She does so.

'She has nothing to do with this,' Lou says. 'Let her go. Please.'

'I had nothing to do with my father's death, or my mother's. But I still suffered.'

'What is she talking about?' Flick says, looking between me and her mother.

'Let me introduce myself. Your father killed my parents, and I'm your father's mistress. Well, I was. Because I've had enough of both him and his wife.'

She's shocked, silent. She didn't know any of it, did she?

'By the way, thanks for the key.' I hold it up in my hand. 'It came in useful today.'

'It was you who took Lachlan, and Flick's keys,' Lou says.

'That really happened?' Flick says, first shocked and then horrified. 'I had an extra front door key made – it was on my keys. I should have told you. I'm so sorry.'

'Doesn't matter,' Lou says. 'Please, don't hurt her. Please.' She is pleading for her daughter's life.

This is getting complicated, and there has been way too much talking. I need to think. 'Be quiet! Not. Another. Word.'

Flick is a mum. She has a baby. A baby who doesn't seem to have a dad in his life either, and I can't do that to someone else – make them grow up without anyone, like I did.

I can't see how I can let her live, though. Not with what she will see. But maybe I was fooling myself to think that I could stage a murder-suicide and just walk away. This is the end, for me, too. Isn't it?

It doesn't matter. I won't go to prison. I'm dead inside, much like my mother was before she killed herself.

81

LOU

Freja looks more and more rattled, since Flick's arrival – why is Flick here? If I'd known it was her at the door I'd have screamed for her to get away, no matter what might have happened to me.

'Where is Lachlan?' I say, quietly.

'With a neighbour.'

'Why did you—'

'Be quiet!' Freja snaps.

But why do what I'm told when I've already been told I'm going to die? And there are things I want to know.

'I have a question.' She glares at me, eyes wild. She's losing it. Isn't she? I'll keep it calm but persist. 'When I mentioned the note that brought me home the day I found you and Philip in bed, you didn't know anything about it.' I hear the sharp intake of breath – Flick's. But Freja is focused on me now and she has to have my full attention.

'I thought it was from you,' I say. 'There was a note left on my car. It said, "If I were you, I'd go home. Now." If you didn't write it, then who did?'

'I have no idea.' She frowns. 'The timing was wrong; it was too soon and messed things up.'

'And the other notes? The one that asked if I knew where my children were. And saying I'd regret it if I went back to Philip.' I have her attention now. She's calmer, thinking. 'The note writer knew about you and Philip. They were tracking where I was with a tracker disc, hidden on my car. If it wasn't you, who could it be?'

She shrugs, but then she tilts her head to one side – something has occurred to her.

'There was a friend of Philip's who saw us out together. It was a few weeks ago. But why would a friend of his do that? And how'd they know where we were that day anyhow?'

She's right. Why would a friend of Philip's do that? They wouldn't. Therefore, it wasn't a friend, just someone he knew. Someone who had a grudge against him, maybe, or—

Oh. Something that bothered me the other day slips into place. Steve said he knew Philip and I had split because our cleaner told his aunt. I know we have the same cleaner so didn't question it. But once I thought about it, it seemed unlikely – Ana never gossips. It kept niggling at me, and all at once I see why. It was a Thursday I caught Philip and Freja in bed. Ana cleans on Wednesdays, and I was back by the next Wednesday. There's no way she could have known anything about it. Unless Philip asked her to come an extra day, which is possible, I suppose. Though not likely, given what a mess the place was in when I came to pack some things on the Saturday.

If our cleaner didn't tell him, Steve lied about how he found out, and I can't think how he could possibly have known. I suppose it could have been Steve who saw Philip with Freja, but that alone wouldn't tell him that I left Philip.

First things first: was it Steve who saw them?

'Can I show you a photo on my phone?' I ask. 'I think I might know who it was that saw you with Philip.'

'What does it matter?'

'Someone has been messing with both of our lives. Don't you want to know who it is?'

She pauses, finally nods. Puts my phone on the table, steps back and gestures for me to get it. I go to messages – profile shot – put the phone down.

She comes forward to look, then nods. 'Yes, that's him. Who is he?'

'Steve. Steve Fitzpatrick. Philip used to work with him.' My mind is racing, trying to figure out what all of this means.

If Freja is right and Steve saw Philip with her, how would he have reacted? He disliked Philip, intensely. He might have wanted to tell me. Given our history, I'm not entirely sure I would have believed him. I'm feeling sick to even think it, but was it Steve who left me the note so I'd catch them in bed? How could he do that, knowing how upset I'd be to find an anonymous note, given my history?

Maybe he was angry with me, too. For dumping him for Philip all those years ago. This way he could get back at both of us. And the tracker in my car – was it police issue? Maybe there was one on Philip's car, too, and that's how Steve knew where we both were when he left the note. Philip being parked around the corner from our house was suspicious enough that he probably guessed what was going on that morning.

I glance at Freja – she's still got my phone in her hands, staring at the image of Steve. She's naturally pale but even whiter now.

'Tell me about Steve,' she says.

'He was my boyfriend years ago. I left him for Philip. They were both in the Met back then.'

'I think I recognise him. Maybe he was there – at the protest. When Philip hit my father and he died that night.'

'Steve may have been, I don't know. But Philip didn't cause your father's death. The experts said your father had a blow to his head that eventually killed him, but it was on the other side from that struck by Philip, and they didn't know who struck that blow.'

She stares back at me. 'I don't believe you. They were covering for Philip, the police that investigated what happened – protecting their own.'

'What if you're wrong, Freja?'

82

JESSIE

I'm holding James' hand. Willing him to wake up, to open his eyes. Watching the time, knowing that each minute that ticks past lessens the chances of him doing so. Wanting so much for Mum, Dad and Flick to be here with me now. To call his name, help him come back from wherever he is hiding. A different kind of hide-and-seek.

Hasn't Flick reached any of them yet? I'm not sure I'm supposed to use my phone in here but try and stop me. I call Flick again. It rings, rings, goes to message. Now she's not answering, either.

Another slow hour has ticked by when my phone vibrates in my pocket. I take it out – it's Dad. At last.

'Daddy?'

'Hey, monkey, I was in the air. What is so urgent?'

'It's James.'

83

FREJA

I can't believe I've agreed to this. Lou is just trying to deflect attention away from Philip, what he's done. But she's right: what if I'm wrong? Then it'd all be for nothing. She has called Steve, asked him to come over so I can ask him what he saw at the protest. I have Flick with me, in the kitchen, ready to listen in. Lou doesn't know that I wouldn't kill Flick; she thinks Flick is my hostage, so she won't try anything stupid. I've tied Flick to a chair, so I don't have to keep an eye on both of them in different places at the same time.

The doorbell rings. I hear footsteps – Lou heading for the door. The lock turning and door opening.

'Steve. Thanks for coming.'

'You said it was urgent. Has something happened?'

'Well, yes. I've worked some things out.' Lou sounds calm, not like someone has a gun on her daughter in the kitchen. Well done.

'Oh?'

'I know that you saw Philip with his girlfriend. That you left the note, so I'd come home, find them together. Why did you do it, Steve?'

A slight pause. 'Whatever made you think that?'

'You slipped up. You said you'd heard via our cleaner that we'd split. But she only comes once a week – on Wednesdays. There was no way she knew when you called me. We never told anyone, apart from Iona, so the only way you could know is that you engineered it. And then there is the police-issue tracker I found on my car.' She doesn't know that it was police issue; she's bluffing.

There is silence, as if Steve is thinking what to say.

'Don't you see, Lucy – I couldn't let him hurt you like that,' he says finally. 'I did it for you.'

So, she was right. What about the rest?

'Come on. You must have known how scared I'd be to get an anonymous note. *Don't* say you did it for me. And the other notes – were they so I'd keep asking you for help? Was that it?'

'You know how I feel about you, Lucy. I'd do anything for you—'

'Start by telling me the truth. I've got the tracker disc you put on my car, Steve. You can't explain it away. And I bet it can be traced to you.'

There's a pause, as if he can't decide what to say, how to deal with her accusations – because it's all untrue or the opposite?

'Philip was a snake – you could never see it. But he's proved it now.'

I can't listen any more – I have to see him, see if I'm right that he was there, at the protest. I take off my cardigan – put it over my arm, hold the gun underneath. And step out of the kitchen. Lou's eyes skip over me. She looks at the cardigan – she's worked it out.

'Steve, meet Freja. Freja, meet Steve.' His eyes are wide with surprise to see me here, in this house, in the same room as Lou.

But not with alarm. Not yet. 'You didn't even realise who Philip's girlfriend was, did you?' Lou says. 'The man who died in cells that night after the protest was her father.'

There is shock on Steve's face. But I don't say anything. I'm going back. Remembering. The sound – sirens nearby; people shouting, pushing, shoving. I'm being jostled in Daddy's arms. He's asking for help.

A policeman says, *take her*! It's him, the one who is standing here now. I'm sure of it. Another policeman dragged me from Daddy's arms while Philip held him back. Daddy twisted, punched at Philip to get free – Philip then hit him with a stick, and Daddy sunk to the ground, people surging all around. This man – Steve – he leaned down, out of sight a moment, then pulled Daddy up from the ground. Daddy was bleeding, but on the other side of his head from where Philip hit him.

My head is spinning. I'm confused, disorientated. Something I've always known to be true has been turned upside down and I don't know what to think.

'You did it, didn't you?' I say. 'Kicked him or punched him on the ground. All the videos made it look like it was Philip, but it was *you*.'

Lou makes a sound, an involuntary gasp of distress. 'Did you do that, Steve? Did you set things up so Philip would take the fall?'

He's holding up his hands, looking between us. 'Now, calm down. You're mistaken. That's not what happened at all.'

'Stop lying,' I say. 'I was there! I saw what you did.'

I drop my cardigan. He sees the gun. Time slows down. He faces me, sees his death in my eyes – rushes me and grabs for the gun. His hand is over mine, pulling at the gun and we're struggling – there is an explosion of sound, a recoil.

For a moment I'm not sure if I'm hurt or he is or neither of us. But then he slumps forwards, to the floor.

Now Lou is here, pressing her hands against his chest as if to stop the bleeding but there is so much blood, too much, and the sight of it threatens to take me back to the horror of my mum's death. I fight to stay here, now.

What will happen to me? I was going to turn the gun on myself. I don't have it. Steve – he wrested it from my hand, then it went off.

I didn't do this.

Flick, in the kitchen, is screaming to know what has happened.

Steve is struggling to say something to Lou, choking on blood, his words. Then his eyes roll back. His head lolls.

It's over.

84

LOU

I'm kneeling on the floor next to Steve. His eyes are open, staring but not seeing me, not seeing anything. He... he's... dead? Warm, red blood, all over his chest, metallic and sticky, seeping through his clothes, into the carpet, and covering my hands and arms from when I was trying to stop the flow. Part of me is screaming inside, in shock, horror, but more of me is numb. I rock back on my heels, arms around my knees.

Then the front door opens – it's Philip.

He rushes to my side. 'Are you hurt?' I shake my head. I'm trembling, my teeth chattering now. He turns to Steve. Feels for a pulse but it's obvious, isn't it? And I can't take it in, I can't. I trusted Steve. I shouldn't have. But for this to happen?

I notice the gun – it is in Steve's hand. He had it when it went off?

Philip's arms wrap around me. He looks from Freja, to me, not understanding why we are in the same place. She's sitting on the sofa now, face white. Blank. Philip asks me what happened but I can't answer, still trying to make sense of it all.

'What's happened?' Philip asks, again.

'Steve k-k-killed him.'

'Steve killed who?'

'The man who died in custody, after the climate protest. Freja was his daughter.' He's shocked, struggling to process that this girl he knew has this connection to his past.

'Steve said he did it?'

I nod. 'He told me just before he died – he punched him under cover of the crowd. Didn't mean for him to die but never told anyone what he'd done. Wanted you to take the fall.' He also told me he loves me, but I keep that to myself. What kind of love does the things he has done?

Flick yells out again from the kitchen. Philip goes to cut her free.

Police arrive, then ambulance. Philip says he called the police before he came in, that he'd heard the shot but ran into he didn't know what.

Flick asks Philip something, then she starts crying.

'What is it?' I say.

'James has been hurt,' Philip says. 'But I heard from Jessie again just before I arrived. It looks like he's going to be OK.'

85

FREJA

I'm numb. The man who killed my father and caused my mother's death is dead, but it wasn't who I thought it was. Lou said Steve confessed to her – the words he whispered as he was dying. Or maybe she's lying, covering for Philip, but I don't think so. Seeing Steve triggered my own memory – what I saw backs up that it was his fault.

Philip is talking to the police now and I turn to Lou. 'I'm sorry. For everything.' I hesitate. 'Nothing I'd planned was working the way I wanted it to – and the reason? Philip really loves you.' She's listening but I don't know if she believes me.

The police want to talk to me now.

'Wait,' Lou says. 'She needs to talk to her lawyer, first. Philip?'

He's surprised – eyes widened as he looks between Lou and me.

'Conflict of interest. But I'll see you have the best.'

I can't believe she's trying to help me like this. But she doesn't know about James. If she did, everything would change.

I lock eyes with Lou. 'If you ever need help with anything, anything at all, call me.'

86

JESSIE

Mum and Dad are finally here by James' bed. He's lying back, legs up, hanging on some sort of pulley system. They've just spoken to the doctor.

'So, we're told two legs broken in multiple places, and concussion,' Dad says. 'A lucky escape, according to the doctors.'

James glances at me. 'Don't call it lucky. Please.'

'Well, you wouldn't need luck if you weren't larking about on a roof in the first place,' Mum says. 'What were you thinking?'

James has already made me promise not to tell them what an idiot he'd been over that girl. It seems a near-death experience made him realise that she wasn't the centre of his world after all. He's going to be OK. And we're OK – back to twin-dom: the two of us against the world. I've managed to only say I told you so a few more times, and he's asked me for a loan, so the parentals won't realise what he's done with his money.

When I think how much worse things could have been? I am feeling pretty lucky, despite the word. My family is whole.

Well, sort of. Mum is back to having left Dad.

87

LOU

It takes a while for me to come to terms with everything. That the people I trusted most in this world didn't deserve it. Philip lied to me, repeatedly. I know Freja was telling the truth when she said he really loves me, in his way. And he seemed to think that once I knew that she sought him out and targeted him deliberately, that somehow made it all not his fault. He was wrong. How can he say he loves me and then betray me like that? He cried when he finally accepted there was no way back to what we were.

And Steve, too. I never understood the depth of his feelings for me, but the things that it led to? As far as Freja's father goes, he may not have meant for him to die, but if he'd told the truth it would have exonerated Philip. He wanted Philip to take the fall. And then, when he chanced to see Philip and Freja together, he left me the first note that set everything in motion. I'm not sure if part of that was to terrify me, to get back at me for leaving him, or if he was trying to get Philip out of the picture and him back into it. Maybe, both.

Regardless, both Philip and Steve had me completely duped. I don't trust my own judgement any more.

And I can't forgive myself for not paying more attention to my children – not being there for them when I was most needed. And OK, being held at gunpoint is a pretty good reason for not answering the phone, but still. I was so fixated on Freja, on jealousy, anger, that there wasn't room for anything else.

But that's not all.

Another impact of Steve's notes was me going back and thinking through the past – looking at things in a different way. I'd thought I played so much better in doubles than singles matches because I had Iona with me – which is certainly true, to an extent. But I also realised something I hadn't, before: every time a note or delivery scared me, it was before a singles match – never doubles.

That could be random, or perhaps my stalker wanted to target me when I would be playing alone, for maximum reaction.

Yet something about this is niggling like a sore tooth, one you ignore for ages, but it won't go away, and you know that you better get it taken care of, or things will only get worse.

If there is any chance that I got things so wrong back then, I can't leave it alone.

88

LUCY

Iona's name lights up on my phone. I don't know if she is about to call me every name under the sun for ruining her career. I don't care – I just want to hear her voice. She's refused to see me or speak to me for so long.

'Iona?'

'Hi.'

'I'm so—'

'Shut up and listen. It wasn't your fault. It was an accident. I just needed some time to process that. I'm sorry I've blanked you.'

'I'm so sorry—'

'Stop apologising and come visit me. Bring chocolate – the expensive kind. From Belgium.'

'Where are you?'

'My flat in London. Islington. Had just enough prize money socked away to buy it and it's all mine.' She gives me the address and I'm straight onto the Tube, first to a chocolatier and then to her door.

She opens it before I have a chance to knock – she must have been watching. She holds her right arm awkwardly against her. I know what was in the news – that her arm and hand are too damaged. She'll never be able to play again. Seeing her like this makes tears come into my eyes. We stare at each other a moment, awkward, and then both start talking at once.

'Wow. This place is yours?'

'Yep – it's all mine. Come in,' she says, and I follow her into a hall, through a door to a lounge room.

'I'm so sorry—'

'If you don't stop saying sorry, you can't play with my kitten.'

'Kitten?'

I see her now, curled up on the sofa. Waking up now with a yawn and stretch.

'This is Laraine. Or Laurie for short.'

'Oh my God. She's so cute.' Not more than a few months old, black, with white paws. 'Almost the opposite of Mittens.' My eyes are welling up again.

'She was a house-warming gift from my uncle. A litter of kittens were abandoned outside the vet's where he works. He said this one was the most stubborn and wilful and would suit me perfectly.'

I'm scooping up the kitten, who then climbs up to my shoulder and starts playing with my hair.

'Now that I've got the kitten, there is something I need to say, and you have to listen. I'm sorry.'

'It was an accident, Lulu.'

'But I was driving when I was scared and upset. I shouldn't have got behind the wheel.'

She comes close, puts her left hand on my shoulder. A serious moment made less so by the kitten clambering across to her.

'Now listen to me. You wouldn't even have been there if it

wasn't for me, insisting that you drive. It was an accident, and that's it.'

I nod, tears in my eyes, unable to speak.

'That's it. End of. We will never speak of this again,' Iona says. 'Now shut up and hand over the chocolate.'

We catch up on so much. I tell her that I'm dating Steve – the policeman I met when I got sent that box of nettles.

'Ooh... a man in uniform! Has he got a friend?'

'He's asked me to some pub meet-up with workmates. Come and you can find out.'

I ask about her mum, how she is handling things. She was always so invested in Iona's tennis – Iona had support like I always wished I did.

'I don't care. I've cut her off.'

I'm shocked. OK, her mum could be over the top. But she's still her mum. Iona won't be drawn as to why, no matter how many times I ask her.

'Are you going to the US open?' she asks.

'No.'

'Why not?'

I shake my head. 'I don't want to play any more.'

'What? Are you crazy? You can't throw it all away. Listen to me, Lulu. I can't do this any more. You have to do it – for both of us.'

And because she wants me to, I try. For a while. But I just can't.

89

LOU

I'm on my way to Iona's. Thinking things through as I drive.

Despite everything that happened because of Freja, there is part of me that admired her. She was dealt a shocking hand, and she didn't just take it. She fought back. And yes, her plans were misguided – especially when she pulled a gun on me – but I couldn't let her take the fall for Steve's death. Not after all the things he'd done. So, I may have stretched the truth a little to the police. I didn't tell them she said she was going to kill me, or that she tried to kill Steve. I said she was just trying to get him to confess but he rushed her, pulled the gun away and it went off. Her lawyer is one of the best, found and paid for by Philip when I asked him to. I hope she can move on from all of this. But at the same time, I'm still so angry, hurt, by Philip straying so readily when she tapped on his shoulder. I hope even more to never see her again.

The notes that Steve wrote had me going back, reviewing everything that happened years ago, in case the same person was involved. They weren't.

But I did work out a few things I hadn't before, starting with that all the notes, broken roses, nettles and so on, only ever appeared before singles matches. It was against different players, and I wasn't threatening anyone in the top rankings at that point, but British rankings? That could have been different. There'd been a few of our top players retiring or injured. There'd been much made in the press about it before Iona and I played each other at Wimbledon – which up-and-coming player would reach UK number one? If either of us had got through a few more rounds, we'd have been there. Of course, after beating Iona I lost the next one, so it didn't happen. But every indication was that it would, one day.

It was between the two of us.

Me and Iona. The most competitive person I've ever known.

I recently told Iona that she was the only one in the world I could completely trust. Thinking about it after the fact, her reaction was odd. She didn't comment on my words – and she turned to the mirror to straighten her hair. Was that so I wouldn't see the unease in her eyes?

It's time to learn the truth.

90

LOU

'Hi, Lou. It's lovely to see you.' Iona reaches to hug me, but I don't reciprocate.

'Is something wrong?'

'Maybe.'

'Come in.'

I follow her from the hall to her front room. Ginger Biscuit is on the back of the sofa, tail swishing. I think he senses the atmosphere.

We sit down.

'Here goes,' I say. 'When Steve started leaving me notes and I was scared they might be from the same person who stalked me all those years ago, I made myself go back and think it all through, in case there was something I'd overlooked that could identify them. And I realised something I hadn't before. Every time I had a freaky note or something else happened to scare me, it was always before a singles match. Never doubles.'

She flinches as if my words have found a mark. Looks down, avoids my eyes. Part of me was hoping she'd deny it all, that I'd believe her. This is one time I don't want to be right.

'Then there was how my supposed stalker always knew where I was, what I was doing. Even knew when my cat died. I checked, Iona. The vet who scanned his microchip after he died was your uncle. Did he say something that got back to you? It's time for the truth. The notes, the dead flowers, the writing in steam on the mirror: was it you all along?'

Her eyebrows shoot up, eyes wide – is she shocked at my words because she didn't do it, or because she can't believe I've figured it out?

She shakes her head. 'Of course not,' she says. But there is something in the interplay of emotions on her face, hiding behind the denial.

'Come on. I can tell there is something you're not saying.'

'I didn't know. I swear it—'

'Know *what*?'

She stares back at me but says nothing. Her eyes are pleading, asking me to make this go away. There was I time when I would have done anything for her, but that time is over.

So, she's denying it was her, says she didn't know – she must be protecting someone.

'Tell me, Iona. If it wasn't you, then who was it?'

Then I gasp as another piece of the puzzle falls into place. 'When you called me, after the accident – and I came to see you – I'd asked about your mum. You said she was cut off, and you never mentioned her to me again. And you'd never tell me *why*. Was it her, Iona?'

She's shaking her head – not with denial. She doesn't want me to make her say it.

'Tell me!'

Her eyes fill with tears. Then she nods.

Her *mum*? She was always Iona's loudest cheerleader – and

fiercest critic when she didn't win. Travelled with her most of the time. It was almost like it was more her career than Iona's. She was always there, and the odd time she wasn't – like that day we had lunch near Paris before the accident – she'd have known just where Iona was going and that I'd be with her. Iona's mum was really into champagne; it was probably her idea that we even went where we did. She likely recommended the restaurant that Iona booked.

The shock as the pieces fall into place has taken the anger away. 'When did you find out?'

'After the accident. I'd been struggling to deal with it all. I knew it wasn't fair, but at least in part, I blamed you. But then, something Mum said made me wonder. I confronted her, and it all came out. She got the idea from that court invasion – you were playing brilliantly, then when that happened, you lost. She couldn't stand that you could be a better player than me, and so she sent you the notes and did all the rest. Which led to the accident that ended my career. And yours, when you couldn't continue playing afterwards.'

'So when you called me and I was begging for forgiveness, all along, you knew?'

She is still, arms tight against herself, eyes downcast. She swallows and looks up. Eyes glistening. 'I'm not proud of it. I never forgave her, but she was my mum. I couldn't let it get out. She might have been arrested, ended up in jail. And the longer I didn't tell you, the less I could.'

'I've spent my whole life being afraid of something that wasn't real. And it was the combination of that and the guilt I felt about the accident that made me quit tennis. If you'd told me, I might have been able to move on, to play.' My anger is back.

She blinks and a tear slides down her face. 'I'm sorry. If I could change what happened, I would. Please, forgive me. I love you, Lulu.' Sounds very like Philip's parting words. Steve's, too, just before he died.

I tell her that I need some time to get to grips with everything. Should I forgive her? I don't know.

I do know I need to live my life on my own terms for a while. In the past, whenever things were hard I've sought someone else to lean on, to make me feel safe. I need to stop doing that and rely on myself. Once I can do that, we'll see.

I leave. Walk past Iona's brand-new Mercedes, parked out front – her prize for being agent of the year. Was needing to win all the time innate in Iona, or something instilled by her mother? Either way, it is so much a part of who she is that I doubt she'll ever break free of it.

For me, tennis was all about playing the game – training, too. I loved both. Winning was essential to fund continuing to play. With Iona, all that mattered was winning. Once she couldn't win any more she turned her back on it. I did, too – out of guilt. How could I play when she couldn't? But I've been depriving myself. It's time to get back into the game. Not as a pro – I'm not kidding myself that is possible after so long – but for the joy of it. I'll rejoin my aunt's tennis club in Halton, where everything started for me.

I drive back to my new place in Tring, not far from both Flick and Halton. It's all mine – bought with part of the divorce settlement with Philip. Well, mine and two six-month-old Maine Coon kittens, William and Elsbeth. They're watching me from the window as I go in.

William jumps down, runs over and I scoop him up for a cuddle. Sit on the sofa with him and Elsbeth, while they meow and chirp about their day, then pounce on my hair.

A woman of a certain age with cats. I think we'll be all right, now.

* * *

MORE FROM TERI TERRY

Another book from Teri Terry, *The Birthday Party*, is available to order now here:

https://mybook.to/BirthdayPartyBackAd

ACKNOWLEDGEMENTS

The Stalker began in NaNoWriMo – half written in a month and then languishing on my hard drive. I always have too many ideas and was juggling projects, struggling to focus, and then along came agent Nicky Lovick! She convinced me to focus on this story and then found me and my story a new publishing home. I'm beyond delighted to be with Boldwood and editor Emma Beswetherick, and I'm very much looking forward to the books to come. Thank you, Nicky, Emma, and everyone at Boldwood!

After spending so much time at my husband Graham's tennis club, it seemed inevitable that tennis would form part of one of my stories one day. Thank you, tennis coach Hutch – aka Alan Hutcherson – for answering questions and putting up with me occasionally at pickle ball. Of course, *The Stalker* is a work of fiction and not based in whole or part on any happenings, past or present, at Halton Tennis Club or elsewhere. Safeguarding young players is taken very seriously.

Writing can be a lonely business, but I'm blessed to be part of motivational and supportive writing groups. Thank you to the Slushies, the Furies, the Harry Writers, CWA, the Nearlies, LSF, the Savvies and all the rest, for cheerleading, handholding and just generally being there. Thanks to Emma Beswetherick, Karen Minto, Annette Caseley Chapman and Tracy Darnton for insight into barristers in the UK. And thank you, Hannah Brennan and DF, for answering endless police-related questions – and

Hannah, for being the Harries social media guru. Of course, any errors or changes in furtherance of plot are my own.

I've never won the Broken Beaker Award like Jessie did, but it was a real thing in the Microbiology Department at the University of Alberta in Canada, where I studied a long time ago – complete with a highly coveted trophy, made of bits of broken lab equipment.

I'm sure cats featured in this book because of the woman of a certain age with a cat comment in US politics when I was writing. There were so many gorgeous moggies appearing on social media and cat accounts that I then followed, particularly on Threads, that, to this day, much of my feed is kittens and cats. (Don't tell Scooby!) And I must give a nod to Ginger Biscuit, Philip Ardagh's son's cat for his great name, to Melanie Power Antweiler for all the joy of Elsbeth and William, and kitten fosterer @joann.welsh for naming Iona's kitten Laraine, for the founder of Kitten Korner Rescue in NY.

And first, last and always, thank you, Graham and Scooby.

ABOUT THE AUTHOR

Teri Terry is the internationally bestselling, award-winning author of over a dozen young adult thrillers, including the Slated trilogy and *Contagion*. She has lived in France, Canada and Australia, but now lives in Buckinghamshire and writes full time, with a focus on psychological thrillers for adult readers.

Sign up to Teri Terry's mailing list for news, competitions and updates on future books.

Visit Teri's website: www.territerry.com

Follow Teri on social media here:

instagram.com/teriterrywrites

facebook.com/TeriTerryAuthor

bsky.app/profile/teriterrywrites.bsky.social

threads.com/@teriterrywrites

THE *Murder* LIST

**THE MURDER LIST IS A NEWSLETTER
DEDICATED TO SPINE-CHILLING
FICTION AND GRIPPING
PAGE-TURNERS!**

**SIGN UP TO MAKE SURE YOU'RE ON
OUR HIT LIST FOR EXCLUSIVE DEALS,
AUTHOR CONTENT, AND
COMPETITIONS.**

**SIGN UP TO OUR
NEWSLETTER**

BIT.LY/THEMURDERLISTNEWS

Boldwood

Boldwood Books is an award-winning fiction publishing company seeking out the best stories from around the world.

Find out more at www.boldwoodbooks.com

Join our reader community for brilliant books, competitions and offers!

Follow us
@BoldwoodBooks
@TheBoldBookClub

Sign up to our weekly
deals newsletter

https://bit.ly/BoldwoodBNewsletter

Printed in Dunstable, United Kingdom